Footloose in the Front Forty!

by
Colin Manuel

Illustrations by
Ben Crane

May all life's experiences leave you with a smile on your face!

Colin M.

🍁PPG

Footloose in the Front Forty!

E-Book ISBN: 978-0-9918604-1-8
Paperback ISBN: 978-0-9918604-0-1

Additional copies of this book may be ordered by visiting the
PPG Online Bookstore at:

❦ PolishedPublishingGroup

shop.polishedpublishinggroup.com

or by contacting author at phone 403-845-4914, by fax 403-844-8482
or e-mail at colinmanuel@hotmail.com

Due to the dynamic nature of the Internet, any website addresses mentioned within this book may have been changed or discontinued since publication.

I dedicate these scribblings
To Mark and Anne-Marie Bertagnolli
With whom so much laughter has been a shared experience.
To dad Brinkworth, the iniquitous saint.
To Leo and Marie Quinlan,
Who always made us smile when times were tough.
To Dan and Faith Hunter
Whose irreverence rescued many a day.
To Kevin, Andrew, and Neil–Manuels all–
And, of course, to Marty Umscheid,
Our family; they enrich our lives beyond measure.
To my wife, Felicity,
Who takes me as she finds me!
And, of course,
To Clayton Cole
And all of those farmers bold enough
To tell their stories to one such as me!

Contents

First vaguely conceived as a bucolic answer to Stuart McLean's *Stories from the Vinyl Café*, this rustic enterprise took on a life of its own. Knowing—as all farmers do—the long hours that so many of us spend in our tractors, it is hoped, among other things, that these stories might be adapted to the radio format, if only to stop an operator falling asleep in the longest of furrows. The stories are based mostly on true-life incidents that have been creatively massaged to fit the adventures of a retired policeman, Aubrey Hanlon, and his wife Sabine when they decide to try their hand at farming.

Chapter One
FROM MELAMINE TO MARBLE

*A*ubrey and Sabine Hanlon bought the farm near Rocky Mountain House, Alberta, way back in '76. Actually, Aubrey will insist to you that it was he who bought the farm; it was Sabine who bought the house. Sabine will tell you that the whole deal came about because her husband was tacking his clumsy way through menopause, although she herself would never have grumbled too much about living out in the country, least of all in the foothills of the Rocky Mountains.

On the other hand, the neighbours, long-standing farmers all, will tell you that they knew at once that the newcomers weren't farmers; you could tell that just by looking at their names, now couldn't you? "Aubrey" might pass at a pinch, but "Sabine"? "Merry Meg" or "Marauding Marie" yes, but what could you tack on to a name like "Sabine"? "Savage" maybe, but she wasn't. She was more like one of those exquisitely crafted porcelain dolls, much too delicate and ornate to be out in the rough on the farm. Of course, it soon became readily apparent that the Hanlons were not farmers when the locals saw how Aubrey went about his farming business, but being the hospitable neighbours they were, they were always quite ready to make allowances.

"That's quite okay," they said. "He's a retired cop with pots of pension money so he's perfectly entitled to make any and all the mistakes that he pleases. But one of us should at least tell him that he's swathing his barley ten days too early." One of them did tell him, and was agreeably surprised at how gracious Mister Hanlon turned out to be. Not only that, he actually took the advice that he was given. Maybe he was wiser than he looked.

To refine the story a mite further, in truth it was Sabine's falling in love with the house that clinched the deal. The old couple who had built it some years before had seen it as the culmination of their dreams, but Lady Luck had never been on their side. The old man had passed away six months after they had moved in. His widow, pining for the companionship of her mate, followed his trail soon after. For Sabine, after the ghastly view of the block of apartments facing their own fifth-floor condominium in the city, the vista of the Rocky Mountains from her new sitting room window was nothing short of glorious. The house itself was so spacious it seemed all that she could possibly ever want after the cramped confines of their little shoe box in south Edmonton. Beyond this though, with its heated hardwood flooring, it seemed luxurious, even decadent. Its beautifully appointed cabinetry in kitchen and bathroom, its glassed-in deck ready to trap the warmth of the morning sun while denying the attentions of the bleating wind, all conspired to capture Sabine's heart.

Above all, being something of a "primper", Sabine adored her bathroom with its stylized mirrors and the deep pile white carpet. Even the melamine vanity top in French provincial style was not a bad imitation of the marble that she would have preferred. The deep tub with its soothing jets was a newfound bliss that she had never envisaged. Now she could wallow in soapy luxury, soaking up the fragrances of jasmine and lavender, reveling in those mysterious silky oils that rejuvenate the skin. She could fuss about with her hair, her eyebrows, her complexion, all those things that a fashion-conscious, cosmopolitan city woman might play with, and uninterrupted at that.

At the same time, husband Aubrey was never happier fixing up tumbledown fences or slapping up new boards on the twisted livestock barn with its distinctive lean to starboard. As long as he could contain the first ten cows that he was to buy at Cole's Auction Mart, he would have achieved his first short-term goal. Ten cows would translate into ten calves, right? He would recoup most of his investment in the first year. Buying bred cows in a balmy fall makes you think like that. Yes, he would buy his girls marked to calve in March or April, by which time the weather would have shrugged off the extremes of winter. The calves would hit the ground running and warm. What a simple way to make a buck or two: "money for old rope" as the English might say.

Buying the cows was a story all of its own. So was getting them home. Because they had been consigned from different homes, none of the cows was familiar with any of the others. That meant a new pecking order had to be established, which in turn meant additional fence repairs for the first couple of days as they duked it out. The undisputed champion proved to be a little Red Angus-cross with a white patch around one eye and one stubby horn which she did not hesitate to use, mostly with devastating effect. Aubrey promptly named her Nellie, after Nellie McClung. He had bought her believing her to be due in April, as was most of his little herd, so even though she resembled something of a blimp already, Aubrey was not unduly concerned. After all, it was a practicing veterinarian who had checked her out, and he had been doing the job for a hundred years judging by his haggard looks.

For Aubrey, his little mob of cows became his pride and joy, an indulgence even. All through the winter, he fed them premium hay and bedded them generously with straw, making a point of walking among them and talking to them every day so that they got used to the sound of his voice. Being the kind of spontaneous character that he was, he would quite often burst forth with his own rendition of Elvis Presley's "Blue Suede Shoes" or Jerry Lewis'"Great Balls of Fire". Eventually, the cows got habituated to this, too, although on the first occasion that he tried it, Nellie led them all on a smash and dash raid through the plank fence and out to the road. Not so good! But within weeks, he found that he could let loose like a poor man's Tom Jones with no more of a violent reaction from his girls than an unhurried and sloppy defecation.

It was on a particularly cold day in February, minus 25 Celsius, that he came in with frozen feet, of course having just sung a hasty goodnight to the ladies. Aubrey was nothing if not stout and large-framed. His toes were right on the cusp of a serious frostbite. His dear wife, glued to the TV in the living room, barely acknowledged his presence. Celine Dion and friends were in too fine a form this night for her to be bothered with a lumbering husband whining about the cold.

He worked his boots off, the felt liners doing their best to make it both a protracted and aromatic affair. He removed his frigid socks and headed off to the bathroom like a mad thing. Damn, the tub was out, there was a bunch of sweaters lying in state in it. That left only the vanity sink. The intense pain allowed for no further thought or debate. He turned on the faucets, pulled up his pant legs, and plonked himself down on the vanity top, both feet immersed in the rising warm water. The pain was excruciating but the relief was blissful. He dismissed the first ominous creak as harmless; the blood beginning to thaw and circulate in his feet was just too pleasing. He had no time to react to the second, more urgent creak because it extended itself into a rumbling crash as the entire structure broke away from the wall beneath his two hundred and forty pound body.

Now the one saving grace for Aubrey was that when Sabine gets really angry, she also becomes totally speechless. In an instant she was at the door, her eyes widening in their incredulity as they registered the destruction. There was Aubrey, her dear husband of fifteen years, sprawled on the floor amid a pile of matchwood, her vanity top cracked into at least three major pieces around him. Two broken pipes were spewing hot and cold water merrily but indiscriminately from the wall.

Finally she managed a whispered, "What on earth were you doing?"

"Warming my feet. Quick. Go downstairs and turn off the water." This was the tried and tested strategy of all husbands in an emergency; send the emotionally affected spouse off on an important errand of her own.

She, on the other hand, was still having trouble finding her voice. "Where... where... do I.... do I.... shut off the water?" The question came out falteringly, like a skittish gopher unsure whether to leave the sanctuary of its warm burrow.

"Downstairs. Next to the pressure tank. Hurry!" The blank stare told him that she did not have the faintest idea what he was talking about. "Ugh, it's okay, I'll go do it." He knew well this would only give her time to position her cannons, but what else could he do? Like the phoenix arising from the ashes, he picked himself up with as much dignity as he could muster and shambled off to turn off the flood.

When he made it back upstairs, his wife was in tears. "Look at what you have done," she whispered hoarsely. "You have completely destroyed my bathroom."

He resorted to the time-worn tactic of refocusing her priorities. "I'm bleeding," he said.

"Quite badly," he added in hopes of diverting more of her attention.

"Never mind that!" Her voice was gathering steam. "Look at what you have done to my bathroom." The level of her anguish was evident in that she totally ignored what he was doing, dripping blood into the now soggy deep pile and increasingly off-white carpet. "What are we going to do?" she howled. "I mean, just look at this foul mess that you have made. How are we ever going to clean it up?"

Aubrey knew that he had to take charge or face up to a full frontal attack. "I'll fix up my leg first, and then we'll think about it." Only then did her more humanitarian instincts kick in. She took a closer look at his leg, and promptly passed out. Aubrey caught her in the nick of time, took her over to the living room couch and returned to the bathroom to ferret out the First Aid box.

It took him two weeks, an expensive plumber, and a genuine marble vanity top before he was able to redeem himself. But he managed to avoid having to buy a new carpet, largely by showing his wife the plumber's estimate for the sink job. Only when it was all over did his partner allow herself to laugh and tell the story, increasingly embellished at his expense with every telling. "You should have seen old Aub sitting there, his bum firmly stuck in a great big chunk of the sink....", that sort of thing. Her carpet remained somewhat blemished.

Misfortunes never happen singly: they tend to cluster in threes, according to Murphy's Law anyway. So two days later, as Aubrey braked too late on the ice, he was not surprised that his car slithered almost zestfully through the closed garage door. "You'd be amazed at how often this happens," said the amicable body shop manager in mitigation. "You hadn't been drinking by chance, had you, you being an ex-cop and all?" he asked with a knowing wink.

Aubrey could only wait in anticipation for misfortune number three.

It began innocently enough.

He had arrived home late, well after dark, having spent the day in Edmonton at a retired policeman's conference. It was bitterly cold: the kind of cold that February uses to test your mettle. His wife had given up on her husband and retired to bed. Something made him go up and see his beloved girls, maybe the surfeit of black coffee that he had been drinking all day and which would not allow him to settle. He was in a jovial mood as he unlatched the gate into the corral, belting out Johnny Cash's "Folsom Prison" to his bemused audience. He had taken about ten steps inside when his powerful flashlight picked up the fearsome Nellie in the far corner, apparently sizing him up for a coffin. His song continued, but now with a certain hesitancy, the volume toned down a notch or two. He took another five tentative steps. Nellie shook her head menacingly, daring him to come on. The other cows were all grouped together at the opposite end of the corral.

"Whoa! Now what's got into you my girl?" He paused to take stock.

She shook her head again, as if daring him to come closer. He hesitated only a moment, and then that macho policeman in him urged him to announce to her that there was no damn way he was going to be held at bay in his own corral by some unarmed cow. He approached to within twenty feet. Still she stood defiant. That's when he spotted the shiver of a movement behind her. There was a brown blob covered in hoar frost lying stretched out on the straw bedding. It was an ear attached to this brown blob that had twitched momentarily. Aubrey's brain struggled to make sense of what he was seeing. Nellie was not scheduled to calve before mid-April at the earliest; this was February, for heaven's sake! And that was definitely a calf. Ah-hah, so she had calved! So pregnancy testing had to be an inexact science like... like reading tea leaves. Well, the vet was sure out on this one, but now what? It was minus 28 Celsius and not an ideal time to be asking "What-do-I-do-now?" questions.

He kept on chatting to her as he approached for an even closer look. Surprisingly, she let him, albeit still shaking her head vigorously. "Oh man," he thought, "the poor little mite is just about frozen solid." He had to do something. He could not leave the poor thing lying there to freeze and die. That's when he recalled the last conversation with a neighbour in a local coffee shop. "Stick 'em in the bath tub if they're cold. That's what you gotta do to save 'em. Works a dandy."

"Okay, okay," sighed Aubrey, "here goes." His mind was still questioning why Nellie had not propelled him over the fence. He gritted his teeth, leaned over the calf, and heaved it up over his shoulders. The last drops of birthing fluid that had not yet frozen dripped down his neck, encouraging him to get this phase of business over more expeditiously. He made for the old barn, Nellie two urgent steps behind him, her heavy breathing urging him onward. He dared not stop now nor put the calf down to open the side door; Nellie would surely bunt him over the moon if he did so. Stoic to the end, he made it through the main sliding door, somehow managing to slide it shut in mama's face with not a second to spare. Her loud bellowing let him know that she did not much appreciate being left out of any further action.

Then he began the mad dash down to the house, the calf managing to lift its head just the once to let loose a pathetic groan to be answered by a fearsome roar up at the barn. Thank goodness Sabine was a heavy sleeper. He blundered into the house and made straight for the bathroom, not even bothering to remove his boots. He dumped the near comatose

calf into the bathtub and turned on the water, blending a warm mix of hot and cold that he had no doubt would be pleasing to the baby. Holding the head up, he began splashing water over the body, rubbing the frozen ears as he went. As the tub filled, the calf began to shiver uncontrollably. Finally, it let loose a full-throated bawl as if to announce to the world that it was back on track.

That was when Aubrey heard the whispered "Oh no!"

He turned. It is difficult to imagine who was confronted with the more amazing sight. Aubrey, with his wife standing there in a nightie so voluminous, it put him in mind of a two man hunting tent, her head loaded with all the machinery a woman might put in her hair to make it do something significant in the name of fashion. Or Sabine, her husband kneeling very reverently beside the tub, flecks of manure peeling off the soles of his boots, his prized leather jacket splotched with amniotic fluid and bits of straw. In the bath, a wide-eyed calf was staring at her as if he was fully entitled to all this pomp and circumstance in her throne-room.

It was the calf that saved the situation. He decided it was time to have a mighty flounder in the tub.

"Come and give me a hand," yelled Aubrey. With not the slightest hesitation, Sabine was there at his side, cradling the animal's head as Aubrey ladled more warm water over it with the soap dish, holding the body steady as he went.

"Do you have any old towels and an old blanket?" he wheezed, determined not to let her get enough of a respite that she could mount the offensive that he knew would be coming.

"Here, hold its head. I'll go and take a look." She was back in less than a minute.

"You let the water out while I hold him. Then we can dry him off a bit in the tub before we try and move him. But first, would you mind laying out the blanket in front of the fire?"

Aubrey had to keep the momentum going; if his dear wife was compelled to focus strictly on the calf, then she would be less inclined to focus on him. When she was back, he made his second smart move in the same minute.

"Keep an eye on the calf, will you, and I'll go and get these boots off and turn up the fire." He mentally blessed the previous owners of the house for installing a natural gas fireplace. He gave her no time to argue, but his actions did call her attention to the state of the carpet, not that anyone could miss the greenish blobs of manure already embedding themselves deep into the pile. And yet for all that, his wife seemed strangely serene.

They dried off the calf as best they could, Sabine actually bringing in some of her better bath towels for the job. Then Aubrey picked up the calf and carried it off into the living room to place on the old blanket before the fire, now on full blast.

"He needs an hour or so to get completely warm," he announced. "Then I'll have to take him back out to his mom. You'd best go to bed and I'll see what I can do about cleaning up the bathroom."

Sabine said not a word. Giving the calf a last little pat on the head, she shuffled off, the wisp of a smile on her face convincing Aubrey that she could be much more into this animal thing than he had previously thought. After all, anyone has the right to a certain smugness if they have just saved a life, any life.

It was only when he tried to get the stains out of the carpet that he realized the probable reason for Sabine's equanimity. The more he tried with scrubbing brush and paper towel to remove the blotches, the paler and wider they became. He knew after fifteen minutes that his wife would be getting the new carpet she hankered after. Oh well, white was an impractical colour anyway. He would have to start lobbying for black.

He returned to the living room. To all intents and purposes, the calf was fast asleep; its body literally sucking in the warmth. He went into the kitchen and attempted to clean up his jacket, making a mental note to take it to the cleaners the next day for good measure. Then he lay down on the couch to catch up with his thoughts, leaving all the lights on so that he stayed at least partially awake.

The crash of breaking glass awoke him with a start. Apparently, it also woke Sabine who came sweeping into the room. Both were greeted by the sight of one bemused calf now on his feet, his muzzle through the glass door of the curio cabinet, Sabine's treasured collection of Ukrainian Easter eggs in some disarray, if not in extreme jeopardy.

It was then, clearly, that both of them knew that she would be getting a new carpet for her bathroom and that it would be the best in town. And not a word passed between them.

As for Nellie's new baby, it was back out to the barn. His excursion into the curio cabinet had made the minus 28 Celsius temperature somehow irrelevant. Nellie's reaction when she saw her baby was unexpected to say the least. Here came farmer Aubrey, so full of pride at having rescued her newborn, and quite ready to accept her unrequited gratitude. But Nellie's attitude was altogether different and totally unambiguous. The instant that her little one was back safely in her territory, she was all set to drive Aubrey into the ground. Fortunately, the calf had found himself a tit and went about his business with gusto, which held his mother back. This, in turn, allowed Aubrey a few seconds to retreat with a modicum of dignity, though painfully aware that he had just been bested by the two favorite females in his life, and that neither of them would be magnanimous in victory.

Chapter Two
HIDDEN TREASURES

*T*he greatest, many would say the only teacher in farming is raw experience. Yet experience can be a hard and sometimes vindictive taskmaster. Like a thief in the night, it can steal up on you and ambush you. It can go on to toy with you, to torment you, and then slink away with a mischievous grin. It can be malicious and disarming, petulant and melancholic, all rolled into one. Whatever it does to you becomes a learning process seared into the mind, a process distilled into your own rustic mythology. Farming makes a point of never repeating itself, no matter what anybody says to the contrary. It is a constantly changing landscape; it transforms itself from the pastoral to the surreal, from the sedate impressionist to the radicalized cubist, from simple caricature to outrageous graffiti. Always, it is a dancing kaleidoscope; the farmer ever caught up in a swirl of variables, suddenly struggling to react to the latest vista paraded before him or her. For all of these reasons, farming should never be entertained by the weak in spirit or the faint of heart; innocents such as these invariably fall as grist to the banker's mill.

Like most local farmers, Aubrey Hanlon purchased his cows at Cole's Auction Mart in Rocky Mountain House. "Cole's" is a veritable institution in Rocky. At the regular Saturday sale, you can find yourself bidding on everything from a Nubian goat to a Muscovy duck, from a full dinette set in imitation oak to a plastic toilet seat that has strayed far from its throne, from a worn-out manure spreader to a brand new fence stretcher still in the original wrapping. So not only does the auction mart function as the ultimate in recycling, it serves as the finest source of instant needs and sudden wants for any farmer starting out in agriculture—or staying in agriculture, for that matter. Yet it goes beyond even this! The auction mart is the place for hidden treasures: the builder's level that you didn't need; the bottle jack that you got for seven dollars and transported behind the seat of your pickup, never to be used for the next ten years; the exercise bike that you snagged for your wife in a fit of unthinking generosity, as if she needed that kind of message anyway. Going to the auction is perhaps the modern equivalent of attending the country fair of yesteryear. An important social gathering place, the atmosphere is always jovial, warm and welcoming, even on the coldest of days. Nor is the trade that occurs here confined only to goods and commodities; "Cole's" is nothing if not a bazaar in an unrestrained commerce of knowledge and banter, advice and tall tales, a place where the old saw, "buyer beware", is particularly applicable, as with any auction. The entire composition is put to music by the constant patter of the auctioneers. Very soon, you are comfortably immersed in a melee of humanity all hunting for that elusive bargain. Your guard drops and you find yourself drawn inexorably into the heat of the chase.

"Going once, going twice, gone to the gentleman over there in the straw hat". Did Aubrey really need a piece of chain with a hook on one end for eighteen dollars? And did that term "gentleman" come with a slight hint of sarcasm? Not at all, he soon realized, for this was the kind of gathering where to take offence would amount to nothing more than a petty indulgence.

It was not long before Aubrey Hanlon became a regular. "An addict" scoffed Sabine, until such time as she herself became addicted, whereupon she modified the description to the less disparaging "aficionado". Pretty soon the Cole clan recognized them, eventually even remembering their names, off and on.

"Good eye Orb", Clayton would shout, and Aubrey would revel in the acknowledgment that he at least was making his contribution to the local economy. That sense of nobility was short-lived when a fellow standing near him announced loudly to his buddy that Aubrey had just paid ten percent above new price for a roll of barbed wire that had already been partially used up. It was about this time that he began to appreciate he also came to the auction to enjoy certain people, "the real characters" he called them, and to despise and even hate certain others; those who were clearly there to ambush him and bid him up on those things that took his fancy. Over time, he learned when to hold and when to fold, when to wince and carry on as if he was in great pain, but not before he had acquired an extensive and useless inventory of grain shovels, frayed rope, assorted mismatched wrenches, and half a dozen shaky power tools. In mitigation though, the cost was little and the regrets were few, except perhaps for Jack, the one-eyed rabbit complete with cardboard box that he bought for three dollars.

He knew that Jack's purchase did not augur well as soon as he picked up the box. Jack had peed in it, so as he picked up the box, the sodden bottom fell out of it, releasing the startled creature inside to a freedom that he was not about to ignore. The ensuing sideshow, complete with colourful commentary from Wes the auctioneer, featured a breathless Aubrey chasing his new acquisition around the lot, cheered on by a crowd of onlookers who deliberately hemmed the entertainment into a big circle. The spectacle only ended when one enterprising fellow grabbed a fishing net from the array of goods to be sold and saved the hapless Aubrey from having a heart attack by trapping the rabbit beneath. This was the first time that Aubrey had ever heard the shrill squealing of a rabbit in distress. As he grabbed it by the ears, it squealed so robustly that he dropped it in alarm, inaugurating the comedy one more time. Once again, Fishnet Fred came to the rescue, only now Aubrey held on despite the noise and carted the rabbit away, dropping him without further ceremony into the back of his station wagon. It soon turned out that one-eyed Jack was a masterful manure spreader, depositing his pellets in every nook and cranny of the vehicle like the maestro bowel-mover he was. Aubrey was still finding evidence of that rabbit's existence eight years later. For a while after that, Aubrey was famous among the auction crowd as "the Funny Bunny Man", a name not easily endorsed by a macho ex-cop. Worse still, as soon as Jack was let loose in the yard at home, he made an almost immediate beeline to Sabine's vegetable patch where he munched on the good things of life for three days. It was the threat of separation and divorce that called for assertive action; using an old publication entitled "A Peasant's Guide to Basic Butchery", Aubrey was constrained to assassinate Jack and then to eat him. At least he went out in a blaze of glory, cooked in Sabine's high society recipe of "Lapin a la Campagne". Moreover, all present agreed that he had been a culinary delight.

On the actual day that he purchased his cows, Aubrey was only a couple of steps on his way to becoming a recognized regular. Had he been truly pressed, he would have freely confessed that he was no connoisseur of livestock, although when it comes to buying cattle generally, beauty is in the eye of the beholder. So his first mistake was not to team up with a local rancher; that way at least, he would have first checked out the feet, the udder, the overall disposition, taking a more systematic look before he leapt. His second mistake was to dragoon Sabine into coming along. She had been quite happy, lost in the "miscellaneous" hall where the patriarch of the business, Russell Cole, was working a jam-packed crowd through trays of brown eggs, cast-off Barbie dolls, quilts, lamps, and an electric guitar, before embarking on an odd assortment of furniture from today, yesterday, and prehistory—some of it begging the question of whether the notion of good taste had ever existed. Had Aubrey had a mind to leave her there, his wife would have been burdened by her own guilt at buying an eggbeater with an intermittent motor and a swag lamp that somehow lost its luster the moment it left the assistant's hand. In fact, close up, it was only half a degree above hideous Sabine decided. She resolved then and there that she would donate it to some worthy person by dropping it into the back of a stranger's pickup truck on her way out through the parking lot; Aubrey would not even need to know of its existence. But alas, her world was not going to unfold without complication. Aubrey arrived unexpectedly on the scene and insisted that he needed his wife by his side for moral support: his way of convincing her that what he was about to do was something of a joint venture. He realized too, though he would never admit it, that such a move would allow him to spread the guilt if he was to make a foolish purchase. Wisely, he said nothing about the grotesque lamp that she had acquired, though he did wonder if her usual discerning eye had deserted her when he put it into the back of the car with his purchases—a pile of "miscellaneous" that included a truck tire with a hole in it, a pail of assorted bolts, and a half-used ball of baler twine—before they headed over to the livestock ring. However, deliberately leaving the car door unlocked, he did find himself hoping that some enterprising fellow might find it worth stealing. Little did he realize that his wife was thinking exactly the same thing.

He knew immediately that he had made a tactical error, if not a major blunder, bringing Sabine along when the first of the live animals were ushered in: six spotted piglets cavorting around in ecstasy in the fresh wood shavings on the sale ring floor. Totally oblivious to the chuckles of the crowd, indeed to the crowd itself, they were a comedy all by themselves.

"Oh, look Aub, aren't they cute," Sabine gushed. "Oh, they're so sweet".

At that moment, Clayton Cole's gravelly voice rattled the walls and brought the audience and his clients to heel. There was a momentary hush, the air charged with expectation.

"Ah, Aub, they're so cute and cuddly". Sabine was quite unable to contain herself. And to Aubrey's acute embarrassment, everybody in the place heard it, the seasoned veterans staring in some wonder at this china doll of a woman sounding off about the cuddly nature of a common pig.

To make it even worse, Clayton was not one to let such an opportunity slip past him. He looked over at Aubrey and lectured him through his microphone. "Now you make darn sure that you buy a couple o' them piggies for the lady, you hear me?" His good-natured chuckle echoed around the sale hall. Instinctively, Sabine froze, horribly aware that she was the undisputed center of attention in a crowd of people, none of whom looked like her.

Aubrey himself could only sit there and grin foolishly, thanking God that Clayton was now rattling on about some upcoming farm sale out west before returning to the items on offer before them, the six spotted piggies. Even though they fetched a paltry six dollars apiece, and even though Clayton harangued him to "grab a couple for his missus," Aubrey graciously declined such an obvious bargain. By his side, Sabine dared not even look up, let alone scratch the back of her neck; she was sure that such a move would make her the new owner of the six little pigs. Soon the ongoing buzz of the sale immersed her back into her anonymity, and she was able to reconnect quietly with what was going on around her. Nobody could remain detached for long, not with such an exotic collection of livestock passing through the ring: more piglets; a couple of young boars whose physical endowments were, at least to Aubrey's unschooled mind, obscenely huge; a massive sow that lumbered in and lay down in the shavings as if deciding that this was the spot where she would deposit the evident litter of babies that she was carrying. Next came a diminutive, eight-year-old Bo-Peep shepherdess armed with a nursing bottle and leading in a pair of lambs. Sadly, all the "oohs" and "ahs" in the world could do nothing to resuscitate a comatose sheep market, for the lambs fetched only a miserable twelve dollars each, but the little girl seemed happy enough. Then, in came a tall woman leading what was evidently a pet llama by a bright red halter. Clayton wisely handed her the microphone, and while she launched into a long spiel about how good it was at keeping coyotes and stray dogs at bay, Sabine could only find herself wondering why it was that so many livestock enthusiasts resembled the animals that they raised. Tall, aristocratic, aloof to the point of overbearing, the two creatures before her were interchangeable as far as she was concerned; certainly any dog or coyote interested in its own self-preservation would give them both a wide berth and run. The red scarf around the animal's neck—matched, of course, by the same thing around the neck of its owner—did nothing for it in the economic aspect ; it sold for twenty-five dollars despite Clayton's prolonged efforts.

Then a string of fall calves came through, many bawling pathetically for the mama they had left behind. Sabine was not to know that they had just been weaned; this was very fortunate for she would have doubtless been tempted to step in and bid on them in a fit of misplaced maternalism. She simply found them "sad", she said, and for somebody as uninitiated as she was, this was enough to explain away their crying. Finally, it came down to the bred cows. In ones, twos, and threes, they were ushered into the sale ring, a fierce-looking cowboy type prodding them now and again with a cane so that as they moved around, prospective buyers could get a better look. Some of the animals were as wild-eyed and shaggy-looking as the cowboy and ready to bolt instantly through the door if it opened even the slightest crack. Others seemed to enjoy sashaying around the ring, almost preening for prospective suitors among the buyers, apparently reveling in such exalted company. One great big Charolais mama came thundering in, baying for blood. First, she sent the cowboy ring-man up the escape ladder bolted to the wall, causing him to lose his hat in the process. Up until this point, Sabine had been mildly attracted to him as "the craggy virile type"; but the appearance of a bald pate with its sparse ring of hair on the lower slopes suddenly whisked away any notions of mystery or machismo. That, and the fact that everybody was calling him "Newt". There were no redeeming features in a name like "Newt" as far as she was concerned. The cow, in the meantime, had changed its focus and began charging at the high steel wire fence that contained it. At once, Sabine's meanderings of the mind were transformed into the more primal instincts of self-preservation. She stood up and began to yank urgently on Aubrey's sleeve.

"S'all right lady", Clayton's microphone intervened. "It's her first trip to town, that's all. Let 'er out boys, let 'er out. And sit down lady, please, she ain't goin' nowhere. Eight-sixty, eight-sixty, eight-seventy, eight-seventy...."

Sabine, now suddenly terribly conscious of both Aubrey reefing down on her sleeve, and of the two hundred plus sets of eyes staring at her, sat down, or rather she collapsed herself down in utter mortification.

"S'all right lady," Clayton's microphone returned, this time to put her at ease. "Not a critter has ever gotten outa here yet, and we've had plenty wilder'n her, let me tell you. So you just sit back and enjoy the ride." Clayton was now well on the way to becoming Aubrey's latest hero: as he felt the tension melt away from his mate beside him, he knew he was escaping from a week's worth of the silent treatment for coaxing her along in the first place. As always with any active auction, the next item on the block diverted everybody's attention.

Charitably described by Clayton as "a bit feisty", she too had no qualms about sending poor old Newt back up his safety ladder, once again to the good-natured hoots of the crowd.

"Now here's a girl with some spirit", Clayton chimed in. "Bred Red Angus. Due in.....'er, what's that sticker on her back say Newt?"

Newt was not about to get down off his perch. He craned his neck and spotted the large label with an "A" on it. "Says April, boss", he responded in a reedy voice that dispelled for Sabine what remained of his manly image.

"There you go boys, due in April. What'll you give me on this one? Thousand? Thousand, anywhere? Nine hund'ed? Nine, anywhere? Eight? Eight hund'ed? Boys, oh boys, what's the matter now? Good feet, good bag, plenty of good calves in 'er yet. Eight hundred, anywhere? Okay, okay, you boys are gonna make me go the hard way. Guess I need the practice. Six hundred, six hundred anywhere, six hund'ed?" Sabine nudged Aubrey in the ribs, a move that a seasoned auctioneer like Clayton would never miss. Aubrey nodded as he had seen the other bidders do. Of course his move now prompted those other bidders to join the chase, taking the one horned mama back up to eight hundred and fifty dollars in less than a minute. Finally the bidding wilted with Aubrey holding the edge at eight hundred and sixty-five.

"Going, going, gone to the gentleman with the lady who thinks our little piggies are so cuddly. I'm sorry sir, what's your name again?"

"Aubrey, Aubrey Hanlon".

"Audrey? Did you say Audrey Hampton?" The buzz in the crowd made it difficult to hear.

"No. Aubrey. Aubrey Hanlon".

"Thanks Audrey. Good eye. Bobbie, that's Audrey Hanson". Bobbie, the sale clerk for the day, hurriedly scribbled down the details on the sale slip. "Let 'er out boys", Clayton boomed. "Put her in a separate pen for Audrey Hanson. Good eye Audrey".

"That's Aubrey Hanlon," Mister Hanlon muttered to his boots.

Next to file in was an old girl who must have been "a veteran of the Korean war," opined the grizzled old rancher sitting somewhere up in the seats behind Aubrey. Even the latter could see that the hooves were so overgrown that she might as well have been in a snowshoe contest. She shambled around the ring like an aged granny who had mislaid her spectacles and was very briskly shuffled out when the bidding stalled at four hundred and eighty dollars, assuredly destined for the meat packers. Happily, Sabine was not to know this at the time, or, undoubtedly, given her extreme empathy for the old and the sick, she would have purchased the old dear as a founding member of an "Old Cows Geriatric Resort Ranch and Spa" to be established at her farm in Rocky Mountain House, Alberta.

The next cow that Aubrey bought was a big white Charolais from "the north country", wherever that was. "Says here, could be bred back to Charolais, Shorthorn, Angus or Gelbvieh, so take your pick boys," commented Clayton. "Kind of a Lotto 6/49".

Maybe it was because of this implied loose morality, or maybe it was the doubt about with whom she had consorted, but Aubrey snagged her for an even seven hundred dollars.

"Good deal, young fellah," commented Grizzly Adams behind them.

"Let's call her Snowflake," announced Sabine to her husband in the second unexpected silence to occur that day.

"Boys," announced the Cole public address system to the packed hall and to the yardmen out back, "put Snowflake into Audrey's pen. Thank yah!"

Sabine literally wilted as the crowd chuckled at her expense, yet nonetheless she could sense the overwhelming good nature of the patrons and their lack of any mean spirit. Instead of feeling wretched for the rest of the day, she began to warm to the crowd in a manner that she could never have anticipated.

A batch of three cows now trooped in. All came from the same home, and all were a deep red in colour, possibly from an Angus or Saler background, though such fine details were way beyond Aubrey at this stage of his agricultural career. At any rate, he had learned enough not to start the bidding, forcing Clayton to take the initial asking bid to a measly four hundred and fifty dollars.

"Boys, oh boys," Clayton harangued his audience, "where in heaven's name would you find young, bred cows for even five or six hundred? Why, we're way below meat price on these girls. So if you need bred cows, now is the time to jump on the wagon."

Aubrey jumped, followed by several others, but he still finished with a final bid of six hundred and ninety.

"Good eye, Audrey," Clayton congratulated him.

"Yeah right," old Grizzly Adams again put in his two cents worth. "That one girl in the middle of them three, she only had one good eye to start with. She's doggone blind in the other one". Sure enough, Aubrey was to find out later that he had bought a half-blind cow. But then she went on to be perhaps the most productive cow that he ever bought, raising him three sets of twins over a span of ten years—this beyond the singles that she raised every other year. All this in spite of Murphy's Law which stipulates that if ever you buy a cow blind in one eye, within a week of purchase she will endeavor to destroy the other one on a tree stump or in a fight with a corral mate.

By the time he had purchased his desired ten cows, Aubrey was a Clayton favorite for the day, although Clayton clearly intended that he take a minimum package of at least twenty. Realizing that he could be too easily tempted from his initial target, Aubrey stood up ready to leave.

"Thank yah, Audrey, thank yah very much," echoed Clayton's gravelly voice. "It's bin a real pleasure doing business with you, and with you too Ma'am," he lifted his hat in old world courtesy. Sabine smiled back demurely, Aubrey mumbled a "Thank you to you, too."

Now the problem was how he was going to get his girls home.

Chapter Three
"...EVEN TO THE BEST OF US!"

*B*ig time cattle buyer that he now was, how was Aubrey going to get his ten cows back to the "ranch"? He resolved to ask Gladys Cole for advice when he paid for his purchases. Gladys was the matriarch of the Cole Empire, the keeper of the books, the fount of all knowledge, and the custodian of the lost and strayed. There had never been any need for high-speed technology here. Gladys orchestrated hundreds, nay thousands, of bits of paper, sales slips, cash receipts, and delivery notes all into one manageable, intelligible stream. Computers may crash or have their glitches, may see themselves become infected with a virus or a worm, but not so Gladys. You could count on her presence at every sale: winter or summer, snow or ice. Beyond all of this though, she knew everybody who was anybody, and others who were nobody in the agricultural world; more often than not, many of them did not even know her. Sabine took herself off for a coffee while Aubrey joined the lineup of people waiting to pay for their purchases. When it finally came to his turn, he made out his check and then asked Gladys if she knew of someone who might be able to truck his cows home.

"Oh sure, you need 'The Flying Zube'," she said without even looking up from her paperwork.

"Pardon me?" queried Aubrey, not sure if he had heard correctly.

"You need 'The Flying Zube'," she repeated, busy stapling his receipt to the sheaf of sales slips he had accumulated. "Go find Lawrie Zuberbier, 'The Flying Zube'; he'll fix you up right away. Next!" The busiest person in the Cole's organization had clearly dismissed him. On Saturdays, the regular sale day at Cole's, there was never any time to spare for loose chitchat as the line-up behind Aubrey attested. As he sauntered off, he spotted a man whom he knew to be a regular at the auction standing up at the coffee counter.

"Say, can you tell me where I might find 'The Flying Zube'?" he asked, feeling quite foolish and very self-conscious.

"Oh, sure. The Zube always sits in the mart during the sale. Bottom row, far right. You can't miss him."

"But how will I be able to recognize him?" asked Aubrey dubiously. "I mean, what does the fellow look like?"

"He looks like what you'd expect any regular trucker to look like. You'll know him as soon as you see him." The man went back to cleaning out the grime from beneath his fingernails with a jackknife.

Well, Aubrey had no idea what "a regular trucker" was supposed to look like. It was not as if they wore some kind of a badge or a uniform after all, was it? Oh well, what the heck, he would go and take a look anyway. But he was a little apprehensive about trusting his new purchases to some fly-by-night trucker, particularly one named "The Flying Zube".

He entered the cavernous sale hall from the bottom left side, the better to appraise the collection of characters situated at the bottom of the banked seating on the far right. Sure enough, there was a jovial-looking fellow who Aubrey knew at once would be The Zube. In animated conversation with his neighbour, an old farmer who was laughing so outrageously his scarcity of molars became a fascination all of its own, The Zube proved to be everything that Aubrey feared; his image certainly did not project anything that would inspire confidence in a yuppie ex-cop with only a passing understanding of the livestock world. The greasy ball cap Aubrey had expected, but the loud, raucous laughter, the somewhat unkempt appearance, the seemingly laid-back attitude, so laid-back it was almost horizontal did not denote a diligent attention to business as far as Aubrey was concerned. Clasped in the trucker's grimy hand was a hamburger dripping relish indiscriminately over the immediate surroundings. Aubrey was about to turn away in some consternation when The Zube caught his eye. He may have seemed a bit disheveled, he may have been unkempt even, but he was alert; far more alert than Aubrey had given him credit for. When it came to transporting cows, his very livelihood, The Zube proved to be an inveterate hustler. He had seen Aubrey buy his stock and had fully intended to broach him for his business.

"You looking for me, young fellah?" He mouthed the words over the heads of a crowd focused on the three brindle steers now in the ring before them.

Aubrey nodded.

Instantly, The Zube was up on his feet and making his way over to this potential new client.

"Hi, I'm Lawrie, Lawrie Zuberbier. Let's get outa here. I'll buy you a coffee. Come on." They made their way out just as Clayton's gravelly voice closed out another successful bid.

"So you need to get them cows of yours hauled home, do you?" The uncomplicated smile left Aubrey totally disarmed.

"Well, yes. I bought ten cows at the sale, and I've got to get them out of here today."

"I saw you buying them. A nice package of critters too, I have to tell you." No trace of the expected sarcasm, just a genuine pleasure at Aubrey's success. "And that girl with the one eye, don't let anyone tell you any different; she's a darn fine cow. But you make sure and watch for that little Red Angus you bought, the one with the single horn. A nice cow right enough, but she's the sort that will take you to the cleaners if you start messing around with her calf. Those Anguses can be a mite feisty when they calve." It was only months later that Aubrey realized how much of a good cattleman The Zube was in his own right.

"Yes. Actually, we're pretty pleased with what we got."

"Okay now, so where do you live? I can probably get 'em out of here right away if it's not too far to go. Then I've got a long haul out east of Ponoka."

"Er, but, er, hold on a second. How much, er, how much will it cost?"

"Oh, you don't have to worry about that. I'll give you the best rate in the business because you're a beginner, and I need you around to support me in the long haul."

"Oh well, I'll just have to trust you I suppose. I live down highway 22, about nine miles south, then two east, and then three and a half miles north."

"Man, oh man, I'll never be able to find the place with directions like that. Who are your neighbours, tell me that?"

"Well, John Upham lives just to the north and, er..."

"Oh, you're the retired cop that bought McGregor's old place. Yeah, I know where you hang your hat. Here's your wife, by the way."

"Sabine, meet, er, meet 'the Flying Zube'...."

"Pleased to meet you, ma'am," The trucker raised his cap in an old-fashioned courtesy that Sabine had not encountered in years. "You sure picked up a nice little grab-bag of cows today."

"Why, thank you," responded Sabine warmly, allowing herself once again to be taken by surprise by the genuine humanity of the local people she had met this day.

"You know, the livestock side of the sale is pretty much over. Why don't we go and find your cows and load 'em up. I'm not gonna do much more business today so I can drop yours off and then get on my merry way to Ponoka. How's that sound?"

"Good deal," said Aubrey. Sabine had already been distracted by the "miscellaneous sale" still going on in the adjacent sale hall. Aubrey encouraged her to rejoin it after he accepted The Zube's invitation to ride home with his cows.

"You can ride in the cab. You don't have to ride with them in the back if you don't want to," he said, a twinkle in his eye.

Once inside the maze of alleys and interconnecting pens, they ran into the foreman, a ferocious looking cowboy type with the name of Bill Hockenhammer; "Hammerhead", they called him behind his back.

"Where's them Hanlon cattle?" asked The Zube.

"Hanlon, did you say? We ain't got no cattle in that name. We got some for Brown, Smithfield, and some guy, I think it's a guy, by the name of Audrey…."

"Audrey, that's the one. Where's them Audrey cattle?" The Zube asked. Aubrey saw it as futile to correct anybody at this late stage.

"Pens 23, 13, and 7," came the response. "Get that useless bugger Newt to help you. He'll be back in the check-in shack, sucking on that bottle of rye that he thinks nobody knows he's got in there."

Newt was there all right, but no sign of a bottle of rye. Not a visible sign at any rate, but there was plenty of sign the moment you came in range of his breath—something you did not want to do too long if you wanted to stay on your feet. Newt was very obliging, however, as those with a guilty conscience often are, and he certainly knew his job. He grabbed his pink cane, and shutting and opening various laneway gates on the way, he led them to pen 23. There were four cows in the pen. Four clearly stressed animals that to Aubrey did not seem quite as impressive as they had been in the ring. The little Angus with the horn was there, and she was already eyeing Newt with some resolve.

"Now don't you start smacking these girls around with that damn stick of yours, you hear me?" ordered The Zube. "This gentleman did not buy these cows for you to beat them up so that they can turn on him at calving time because they hate people. He's got to work with them, you know."

The look said it all. Clearly there was no love lost between these two. But Aubrey was thankful because he had already seen enough of Newt to know how he had a penchant to use his stick when he could get away with it.

"I'll go and bring up the truck. You give Newt a hand here to get all of your group together, and make sure he doesn't take it in his head to beat on any cow that sent him up into his roost, especially that little Angus," Lawrie chuckled. Newt turned his back on them.

Loading the cows was routine, and since there was room for a good fifteen, there was plenty of extra space for them to move around in.

At the other end of town, one of Aubrey's least favorite people, Brett Logan, was strutting his stuff as only Brett Logan could strut. One of those sales types whose very pores seem to ooze with artificial charm, he could only be described as a pain to all who knew him.

Like so many others, Brett Logan had profited hugely from the boom in oil exploration. Rather than possessing some innate natural ability to do well in business, he had simply been in the right place at the right time. Owner of the leading real estate company in town, he had amassed a small fortune buying and selling the property needed to accommodate the droves of oilfield personnel transferring in and out of town.

"Sure, I've made pots of money. I admit it. I don't see why that's so bad." That was true.

"But I deserve it. Don't forget how hard I had to work for it." Not so true.

Trouble was, like so many specimens of the nouveau riche, like so many of the so-called "self-made" men lucky enough to catch a wave in the boom economy, he was too inclined to flaunt it. It seemed that everybody had to know what he had, and he had plenty. Among other things, his passion was collecting classic cars: a 1970 Mustang convertible, his favorite; a 1968 Ford Fairlane; a 1953 Jag that he had wheedled out of an old widow on a remote farm deep in the foothills of the Rockies; and a 1980 Corvette. He did not do any of the restoration work himself. Why would he when he did not have to? But he paid very handsomely to have it done and was always very happy to accept any and all compliments about the superior workmanship that had gone into all of his cars. More than this, he would love to tell anyone who would listen, anybody within earshot really, the life history of whatever car they happened to be looking at—a history where truth could easily become an early casualty, depending on the need to charm or to impress. Some, no doubt those who under-appreciated his achievements, suggested that he had picked up his wife, Savannah, as just another item to add to his collection. His chief rival in real estate, and a classic car aficionado to boot, old Jack Donahue, concurred.

"Well dammit," Donahue said, "she's got more curves than a Corvette, bigger headlights than a Rolls, and a trunk bigger than a Bentley." But then in all honesty, it had to be said that most found her as garrulous as her husband and equally as loud.

"A matched pair," said Mr. Donahue uncharitably.

One of the days in all of the year that the Logans looked forward to with great excitement was that special Saturday designated as the "Western Show and Shine Day" for their local classic car club. Members would gather together in their cars and parade through the streets specifically closed for half an hour for a very popular local occasion. Once through town, they would congregate at one of the supermarket parking lots to "show and tell" and to compete for various prizes. For the past two years in a row, the Logans had run into bad luck. They had missed one parade altogether because they had suffered a flat tire just as the parade was about to begin. On the second occasion, a perished radiator hose had burst leaving them in a cloud of steam and embarrassment right where the crowd was thickest. So this particular year, Brett Logan intended to make a splash and gain the recognition that a man of his standing in the town so rightly deserved. By virtue of some fancy footwork, and by harnessing the sympathy vote for his past mishaps, he got the nod from fellow members to lead the parade. Sadly for him, it was on the same Saturday as Aubrey had bought his cows.

Since it was "to be very much of a western theme", Mr. Logan and his wife had bought the most elaborate western duds money could buy; matched white leather tasseled jackets splattered with rhinestones, identical fancy jeans, the requisite worked leather belts with buckles the size of a combine, dude boots inlaid with a Texas Longhorn motif, and western shirts, of all things, made in silk. Scarlet Stetson hats completed the most garish and expensive dude package ever to be seen west of Manitoba. Of course, Brett made very sure that his wife exposed enough cleavage that much of her most impressive credentials were on display.

"When you've got twin carbs like that, you gotta make sure they get enough air," he retorted loudly when the parade marshal indicated at the club breakfast that morning that a little more modesty and decorum would be appropriate. "A little more cover," he suggested. Savannah just giggled and gobbled up the extra attention. The marshal could only shake his head and go on to explain where and when they were to assemble for the start of the parade.

Meanwhile, back at the auction mart, Aubrey and the Zube were ready to set off with the cows.

"Sure a lot of folks in town today," said Aubrey, trying to make conversation as they pulled into the main thoroughfare through town.

"Well, they've got their classic car show on today, haven't they? A pile of people always come into town for that," said The Zube, shifting up into the next gear.

Aubrey was already anticipating the traffic lights ahead changing from green to red. He need not have worried. An experienced hand such as Mr. Zuberbier had already begun to shift down through his gears, conscious that a sudden slamming on of brakes would not be kind to his load and would probably not endear him to his new customer either. They ground to a halt at the stop line.

While they were waiting for the lights to change, first an old half-ton pickup loaded with square bales of hay pulled up in the lane alongside them, and right behind it, what appeared to be a Mustang convertible— surely one of the cars that had been in the parade. The Zube could not help noticing from his rearview mirror that the occupants, a man and a woman, were dressed in a western get-up that would have put Glen Campbell and all of his rhinestone cohorts in Nashville to shame. Then he got a second look at the woman.

"Will you get a load of that chick!" The Zube spluttered. "She's got more groceries on her top shelf than you've got in the whole of your fridge. Holy macaroni!"

As Aubrey turned to look, the lights changed. The Zube began to pull away in first gear. The fellow with the hay bales who had pulled up alongside of them, realizing that he was in the wrong lane decided to wait and then to switch lanes behind their truck. It was at this precise moment that a liquid stream of bright green manure spurted through the slats on the sides of the truck. The effect could only be described as cataclysmic. The utter consternation caused by the spate of green muck shooting into the open Mustang and on to its occupants saw the Mustang surge forward and smack into the pickup ahead. The pile of bales teetered for a second and then cascaded on to the hood of the Mustang. As their truck pulled away, all that Aubrey and The Zube could see was the bemused old driver of the pickup climbing out to confront a wild-eyed cowboy and his chick, both covered in fresh manure and gesturing wildly at the back of the departing cattle truck.

"Shit happens, even to the best of us!" said The Zube dryly. He had been duped by the realtor some years previously and had no love for the man. "Couldn't have happened to a nicer fellow," he added. Aubrey could only agree.

Chapter Four
THERE GOES THE NEIGHBOURHOOD

*O*ne of the greatest pleasures of country living is the absolute privacy most homes afford their owners. If you are inclined to being a naturist, then be nobody's guest and hang out. If you have to emulate your Swedish cousin and go charging off into the fresh snow in the buff, all the more power to you. If you must dance around the silver birch chanting all sorts of wondrous incantations, there will be nobody watching to crimp your loincloth. If you wish to practice Tai chi, yoga, levitation, or bunny hopping, feel perfectly free. Moreover, the general aura of silence is wonderful: aura because birds will always punctuate the silence in summer, and if not birds then the occasional crow making his solemn dissertation from a tamarack in the muskeg. You might even feel compelled to talk back to him! For some people, however, the silence is too intimidating. It suggests to them a lack of security. They far prefer to cling to the womb of the city, complete with the clamor, the tooting and the honking, all of which seems to cocoon their fears in a blanket of noise. They cannot abide the silent isolation, the lack of that frenetic urban pulse constantly driving their commerce forward, constantly fueling their acquisitive instincts.

After condominium living in south Edmonton, Aubrey and Sabine embraced the solitude of the country like a long-lost friend. For sure, winter was not that friendly. Indeed, it could be downright hostile, but the warmth of a sunny Chinook day more than made up for it. Gradually, because they came to depend more and more on agriculture, they both tuned into and harmonized with the cycle of the seasons. This meant that a rainstorm was no longer something to be cursed. Now it was to be blessed as a source of life, the source of life, within reason of course. If you were confined to your gumboots for too long, your feet quickly caught cabin fever and refused to go anywhere without aching. A hailstorm now took on far more sinister implications than forcing you off the twelfth tee; it had the capacity to wipe out a year's work in mere minutes, seconds even. Drought was no longer some phenomenon that happened somewhere out there in the dark continent of Africa; it was now something that could have you and your cows scrambling for any and every morsel of greenery to stay alive. It could decimate and desiccate your hay crop—your feed for the winter—playing havoc with the protein content and the palatability. So, pretty soon, the Hanlons found themselves falling into that constant harping on the weather practiced by every farmer in the world, for there is no such thing as a perfect equilibrium when it comes to sun and rain, wind and snow.

The other dimension that was deeply affected by country living was the whole business of dress and image. Now it simply did not matter. You were not going to be seen in that yellow jacket with the great big red wine stain that refused to come out. It did not matter much whether Sabine ever got around to repairing Aubrey's pants, the ones with the hole in the crotch: there were no spectators, and he could probably do with the extra air conditioning anyway. You could go ahead and form unrestrained attachments to an old coat or a dog-eared pair of shoes. The message was unlikely to be decoded by anyone of any importance. As for colour coordination, that went straight out of the window. On occasion, it seemed that Aubrey came out of the house dressed for the circus. Red clashed with yellow and purple, and that hideous yellow and black baseball cap proclaiming the merits of somebody's prize Gelbvieh herd did nothing to soften the tones. Even the cows sometimes thought he was too garish, choosing to look away from him as if from the dazzle. All this, in turn, led to a refocusing of buying preferences, with Aubrey at least quite happy to make all his clothing purchases at "Value Village", the apparel recycling store in Red Deer. Truth be told, Sabine even found the odd item there, but for her it would always be a touch "infra dig", sort of below her dignity. Any garment that she purchased for herself would have to go through the laundry at least three times before she would consider wearing it, and even then it seemed to develop an itch all of its own as if to remind her that somebody had worn it before her.

Increasingly then, both Sabine and Aubrey tended to wear what was both comfortable and practical as they both metamorphosed into agriculturalists. Sabine's world in particular expanded into the world of gardening, largely because John Upham, their wonderfully gregarious neighbour to the north, appeared one day in spring with his garden rototiller outfit.

"Where d'ya want your garden, missus?" he barked at Sabine without any of the conventional formalities of "hello" and the like. "I've come over to dig it for you."

Totally taken aback, Sabine really had no idea what to say. "I er, I er, I don't have a garden yet," she blurted out as though she should seek absolution for her sins.

"Good, good, all the better. We'll put one in, you and me. Now, where would you like it?"

"Well, I er, I er, I'm not sure that I want a garden." She looked fixedly at her feet.

"What are you talking about?" laughed John. "Everybody who lives in the country has a garden. Where are you gonna grow your potatoes and your carrots?" Evidently John was not a man given to dwelling on image either; not with the industrial-size suspenders holding up his soiled blue jeans, nor yet with his faded cotton shirt with its ratty collar, nor with his baseball cap smeared so liberally with oil and grease. But, as always, when somebody met John, it was not the attire but the genuine smile that warmed you to him. His eyes were so full of life, brimming over with vitality and humor, and his banter totally unpretentious.

"Well, I er, my er husband is not here right now. I er, I er should really talk to him about it."

"What do you need to talk to him for?" John laughed out loud, never one to be denied of his good deed for the day, not when he could play some more with his favorite toy, his Yanmar tractor and rototiller. After all, there was a limit to how many times he could till his own vegetable garden, now with a tilth as fine as talcum powder.

"You're not one of them women who has to ask dear old hubby permission to do something, are you?"

That did it! Even though she could feel the mischief behind his eyes, the very suggestion was offensive.

"You're darn right I need a garden, a real down home vegetable garden." Her vehemence surprised even herself. "Yes, by George, I need a garden where I can grow my own radishes, and lettuce and cucumbers, and, and other things. Trouble is, I haven't the faintest idea where to put it."

Aubrey showed up about an hour later to find his most friendly neighbour tilling up a square patch of lawn a mere two hundred feet from the bay window of his living room. Try as he might, he could not get the old fellow's attention, what with the tractor belching and farting in its own manufactured cloud of blue smoke, its operator head-phoned in his own private version of diesel heaven. Finally Aubrey picked up a clod of earth and tossed it at John, striking him on the shoulder. Grinning wildly, John stopped his rig and shut down.

"What the hell are you doing to my lawn?" Aubrey bellowed.

That sanctimonious grin again. "Why, we're putting in a garden, me and your missus. Now what's so bad about that?"

"The missus? My missus? Are you out of your mind? My missus does not know one end of a carrot from another. As far as she knows, a cucumber grows in a plastic bag on some back shelf in the vegetable section of the supermarket."

"Not any more," Sabine's voice yodeled behind him. She had just returned from the house with "a hat", an affair that could only give broader meaning to the Easter bonnet concept. "Your missus is about to launch her career in gardening, ably assisted by her friend Mister John Upham here. So, if you don't mind, step aside and let the man finish what he's doing." John now grinned ecstatically, the stubbled chin and the two missing front teeth reminding Aubrey of an Irish leprechaun.

"Well, there'd better be something worth eating out of this, this garden, that's all I can say," he retorted lamely.

Actually, Sabine's new venture into gardening now gave her a focal point outside of the house. She soon became an avid gardener, although Aubrey had to come quickly to his own rescue by reiterating a score of times that he was not to be seen as a digger of soil nor a drawer of water for his wife, nor would he ever be. So she learned to work within herself. And of course, she wore whatever she liked. At first, she would trundle out in shapeless pants and sweater, graduating next to bilious shorts and billowing blouses. But as the summer came into its own and the weather grew hotter, and because her privacy was more or less assured since it was rare that people drove by on the road, she began to wear less and less, and to revel in it.

Of course, Aubrey was not one to put a damper on this delightful turn of events; he still found his wife far too attractive to do that. Finally she took to wearing the bikinis that he knew had lain in a drawer for the last ten years, preferring a turquoise one from her youth that now struggled a little to contain a more bountiful crop. If the odd soul passing by on the road did happen to catch an eyeful, well, that was their good or their bad luck as the case may be. Sabine was going to be free to do her thing her way; that's all there was to it! That approach almost ended in catastrophe one sunny day when she was bent over her tomato sets, her Sony Walkman making her oblivious to the noise of a tractor barreling down the road past the house. Suddenly, a tremendous rumbling sound coming out of the ditch broke through Neil Diamond's "Kentucky Woman" and caused her to look up in alarm. Dear John, who, it must be said, always had an eye for the wild life, had caught more than a glimpse while towing his partially loaded manure spreader down the road in high gear. With his mind so willfully distracted, he parted company with the road and found himself careening along in the ditch. Sabine straightened up to catch an image of her kindly neighbour thundering by in the bushes, fighting mightily to regain control of his rig. How he did it, she would never know; how close to disaster he had come, she did not dare to think. For sure, she did have a substantial twinge of conscience, but then she was still secretly glad that she could still turn a male's head even if it was only old John's. Needless to say, Aubrey had to know when he came home why there were major tire tracks in the ditch past their home. Far from the jealousy that Sabine thought that he might display when she told him the story, he laughed wildly and commented that she'd better not ever let John catch a glimpse of Mr. Hanlon's wife in her entirety.

So that was something of how Mrs. Hanlon got into gardening. How she got into ducks also produced its share of mythology.

It began when Sabine got one of those useless spring catalogues from one of the hatcheries in Central Alberta. They would arrive every spring and get tossed into the garbage, unopened. But this one day, while mulling through her morning coffee, she casually picked one up. She had always been one of those women who, if she took a fancy to something, would circle around it until it became her prey, or until it vanished into the thin air of whimsy. It was the pages on ducks that got her going; specifically, the picture of a gaggle of bright yellow ducklings. Her mind zeroed in on the section about Rouen ducks.

"Rouens have the same feather colouring as their cousins the Mallards, but are about twice as large and cannot fly, so you need have no fear of losing them". Her imagination began to work its magic. She read some more. "The drakes have green heads and silvery feathers on the breast. The ducks are brown, with a silver penciling effect and a blue wing patch". There was no question now, for Sabine they were positively exotic; she was hooked. "A small flock of Rouens looks nice wandering around the yard for the summer and they make excellent ducks for the freezer when fully mature and fattened in the fall". Well, they could forget about that last bit, nobody was going to eat Sabine's ducks, but the first part sure sounded glorious.

In his attempt to deflect her first offensive, Aubrey got himself even more work. In trying to explain to her that a flock of ducks wandering loose would be somewhat incompatible with her unfenced vegetable garden, he earned himself the duty of building a duck pen that, he grumbled, was nearly as big as Vancouver Island—complete with its own version of "sculpted" pond. But now he was infinitely more savvy than he used to be.

The project would only be undertaken if two fundamental conditions were agreed upon. (a) Once the pen was built, since the ducks were not his pleasure, they would not be his responsibility; not the feeding, not the cleaning, not anything. (b) Seeing that the ducks themselves were going to be strictly ornamental, Aubrey and Sabine would acquire a flock of chickens, a dozen laying hens and a score of meat chickens, to be housed in the old granary up by the cowshed and to be tended exclusively by Sabine. That way, at least they would have fresh eggs for breakfast, if not for baking, and an occasional chicken for the pot. Otherwise the deal was dead, never to be discussed again, he said. Feeling like a Yankee hard-nosed negotiator for the free trade deal, he was convinced that poultry would not become a new dimension of their agricultural enterprise; that Sabine would never consent to such terms. How wrong he was! Sabine accepted them unconditionally, without the merest whimper. How like a Canadian, he mused.

Even though it was no labour of love, Aubrey constructed an elaborate affair that would accommodate as many ducks as Sabine could ever want, or so he thought. An old pig waterer mounted on a still solid wooden platform dominated the center of the pen. Around it there was a large, apparently natural wallow. Maybe some of the previous tenant's pigs had made themselves comfortable here. At any rate, there was certainly an extended flood plain. All he had to do was to get the water going, said Sabine.

Murphy's Law—the one that states that all tasks should be attempted at the most inopportune moment—intervened: the whole duck pen undertaking needed to be complete within a week, otherwise it would have to be shelved to allow for critical farm operations like seeding and fertilizing to go ahead when they should. Sabine understood and accepted that. Aubrey saw some potential here but said nothing other than stating that the first goal was to sort out the water situation. Sabine, the power behind the throne when she had to be, was remorseless. "Then sort out the water situation, don't just talk about it as if we need an environmental assessment or something."

To get to the pig waterer, Aubrey was forced to traverse the mini-lake left by the major rainstorm of the previous week. With the current forecast threatening more of the same, his initial attempts to negotiate postponement were seen immediately as task evasion, and rejected out of hand by Sabine. First he lost his gumboot, sucked off by the heavy mud to disappear below the surface; he never did find it. But in his floundering while trying to locate it, it was probably inevitable that his increasing rage caused him to topple over into the ooze with a mighty splash. There ensued an enigmatic silence where, for one split second, Sabine had the awful thought that she might have to wade into the ooze herself and rescue her husband. But then, like the legendary Ogo-Pogo, he arose, skeins of sludge and slime dripping languidly off his body. Sabine could hold it no longer. Bursting out in gales of laughter, she had to resort to the nearby fence for support, the tears streaming down her cheeks. Like a spluttering volcano, Aubrey made his unsteady way back towards her, but the stench of stale mud and ancient piggy business drove her off instantly to a spot a further ten yards away where she continued to giggle insanely.

"Damn you!" Aubrey bellowed. Then suddenly realizing that there was not a soul in the world who could see him, he made the snap decision to strip off; he had to get away from the clamminess of his clothes, if not the stench. That accomplished, and now determined to finish what he had set out to do, Aubrey picked his way back through the sludge armed with an assortment of wrenches. For Sabine, the sight of her husband bare-arsed to the world and slogging his way through the mud was simply a continuation of the show. He finally made it to the platform and climbed up on it. Back on track now, he pried off the lid only to discover that somebody in the past had disconnected the inlet pipe and capped it. He should have known better. He took a pipe wrench with a view to testing how tight it might be. He bent over the contraption, his pallid buttocks exposed to sun and wind, and gave a small jerk. In an instant, a jagged stream of ice-cold water struck him unexpectedly amidships. The shock launched him backwards off the platform, landing him the most perfect back flop into the ooze. Sabine was rolling on the ground now, her sides aching. What else could she do?

"Sabine!" Came this mighty bellow from the ooze. "Go switch off the water."

Realizing the potential for her husband to slip into an uncontrollable rage, Sabine readily found swiftness of foot and headed over to the main control valve down the well. When she got back, her husband was truly a sight to behold. Mud and sludge dripped off him as he inspected the damage. Even his hair was now matted with the gooey substance.

They both heard a car door slam, first one door and then another. Sabine glanced down the driveway to see an impeccably dressed older couple striding out towards her, both of them smiling righteously, both clutching a sheaf of pamphlets. She had just enough time to motion Aubrey to sink down into the mud before they came up to her, neither one of them aware of her husband squatting in the sludge not thirty feet away.

"Good morning. How may I help you?" smiled Sabine.

"Isn't it a lovely day?" chirped the woman.

"What a precious gift the Lord has given us," bolstered the man.

"That's for sure," commented Sabine, wondering at the same time why it was that the Jehovah's Witnesses always arrived at the very moment when they were least needed. Murphy's forty-sixth Law perhaps?

"We came to talk to you about the terrible state our world is in," ventured the woman in her syrupy tone.

"Yes, and what we can do about it," added the man. "Now, this pamphlet here explains it all in black and white." The man handed her the item and continued on. "Yes, we are all of us in the midst of so much evil, don't you think?"

"Yes," echoed his better half. "It all seems so out of control. You see so much sex and nudity on television," her voice trailed away as her eyes suddenly registered the fact that there was a man squatting in the mud looking at them, one could almost say curiously, and the man appeared to be naked. Now that he had been spotted, and since his nether regions were getting unbearably cold, Aubrey G. Hanlon casually stood up and stretched, fully aware that he was giving his now speechless audience a full frontal. Not that he could say it was an unobstructed full frontal, mind you, because he resembled more of an impressionist version of the statue of David sculpted in mud, although to his own chagrin, he was not proportioned quite so exquisitely as the Florentine.

The couple stared in awed fascination until finally the lady broke away. "Oh dear," she said and turned her head.

The man said, "Hmph, I see that you have a lot to do. Have a nice day." They scurried off like a pair of ruffled grouse.

"There goes the neighbourhood," Sabine commented dryly.

Chapter Five
MISTER BIG!

For most retired policemen, the mechanical world would likely be an alien world especially when it comes to farm machinery. For types like Aubrey, mechanics were a necessary evil, somewhere on a par with plumbers and electricians. These were people who practiced their own form of voodoo, surrounding everything that they did with a ritual of mystery and mumbo-jumbo so that the layman just threw up his hands and thankfully paid the bill. Who else could come up with terminology like "the zirk on the wobble box"? Who else could concoct such convoluted calculations for flow rate and pressure values that you gladly paid your money without a whimper? Who else could threaten you with circuit overload and ground-fault interrupters? But Aubrey could not simply avoid the use of machinery in agriculture. Not unless he wanted to dance with wolves and bring in the custom boys to do it all for him, which is what he did in his first year on the farm because he had no machinery at all. They cut and baled his hay, they worked up the back thirty for next season's barley crop, and they sucked up his precious dollars like a high capacity grain vac. Even Sabine asked uncomfortably where all the money was going: sanguine Sabine, for whom money had always been an endless source of magic beans.

What was to be a long and tempestuous affair with machinery began modestly with, as he called it, "my M-F with a wooden leg." He bought himself a well-seasoned Massey-Ferguson 1100 with a front-end loader from a dealer in town. The "wooden leg" aspect came from a bent front rim on the right hand side, which gave the impression of the tractor having a limp as it trundled down the road.

"I'll take a look around for another rim. Should be no problem," asserted the chain-smoking salesman for whom going outside of the blue fog in his cramped little office meant going home at the end of the day. He reminded Aubrey of one of those Moray eels that one sees periodically on nature films on television, lurking in its lair waiting for the next tasty morsel to come floating by the door. At least the tractor had what some humorists might have called a cab. It was more like a tin cage with a cracked glass window, but nevertheless it did a fair job of keeping the cold, and more importantly the acrid blue diesel fumes, out of his face. Actually, Aubrey took a sort of perverse pride in the smoke that "Old Bertha" emitted. It was his signature, his proclamation to the world that he, Aubrey G. Hanlon, was making his very own significant contribution to a thriving Alberta economy.

Then, at his very first on-the-farm auction, he purchased a haybine, his first ever implement—a New Holland 488, the decals said. Although it made more noise than a vintage Israeli tank on the move, it clanked and clattered its way through his hay for several seasons without so much as a chain breaking. His "new" square baler proved far less generous of spirit; indeed, it took on a personality that was both scheming and vindictive. When he hooked it up to the tractor and first put it in the field, it produced twelve picture-perfect bales in a row, so Aubrey saw no further need to twist himself around like a contortionist to study its every move. He got to the end of the field only to turn his head and find that it had spat out five broken bales in succession. He felt the blood coursing up through his cheeks, he felt the dreaded curse bubble up to his lips, but he controlled himself and reached for the "Owner's Manual". He located a section entitled "Trouble-shooting", read up on broken bales, and, very proud that he could follow the instructions, he pulled a wad of jumbled-up twine from the left-hand knotter.

He recommenced: one, two, three, five perfect bales. Man, he was good! Then two more broken ones, only this time it was the other knotter casting who knows what evil spell over his endeavors. He adjusted this, fiddled with that, checked the other, and began again. One, two, four, eight, nine, even ten perfect bales, then two more dog's breakfasts dashed his hopes. Try as he might, he could not coax the machine to play his tune, which is a short way of explaining that this was why he ended up buying a round baler, the square one being confined to a shed for the occasional foray when his patience level was high and square bales were an important item on the agenda.

The round baler, the John Deere 530 that Pete had advised, he bought at another on-farm auction. An old-timer down Didsbury-way was getting out of the business, his two grown sons much too smart to forego their nine-to-five prospects for the unlimited hours and the hard labour of the agricultural gulag in which they had been raised. Besides, Aubrey got a zinger of a deal, or so the kindly folks standing around him led him to believe. It was old Art Zimmer, his neighbour to the east, who unwittingly burst the bubble.

"You know them belts are all screwed up and plumb wore-out, don't you my boy? That's why you got it as cheap as you did."

"Er, well, er, well yes. I saw that. But belts are not that expensive, are they? I mean, they wouldn't be more than a couple of hundred bucks, would they?" Aubrey asked innocently, his mind casting about frantically for an appropriate prayer.

"Oh shit, no! Think again, my boy. A set of belts for a 530, that'd be around two thousand."

Aubrey about choked on his hamburger.

"Them burgers sure ain't up to much now, are they?" Art fired back. "Them new caterers these auction boys are usin' don't much know what they're about, do they?" He sauntered off, totally oblivious to the consternation he had caused in Aubrey's little world.

Two thousand dollars! Two thousand smackeroos! Well, maybe he could hang on for a year or so, he thought, now spotting for the first time a big gash at eye level in one of the belts. Somewhat disconsolate, he took home what should have been his grand prize, curiously silent about all its wondrous attributes when Sabine asked all about it. Sabine still did not yet think that a farm auction was her kind of social outing so she had stayed at home.

The upcoming hay season promised great things. The rain came when it was supposed to, he had spread his fertilizer when he should have, and the hay grew as it was meant to. Aubrey could hardly believe the transformation that took place in his fields, from the nothingness left behind by winter to the lush hay nourished by the warmth of summer, all in the space of a couple of months. Even Sabine commented that her husband was becoming "a real hotshot farmer". Aubrey's confidence soared, but not to the point of cutting down his hay crop, even though he had convinced himself that it was past ripe. Rather, he watched and waited for his neighbours to come to life first, because he conceded that they were more likely to know what they were doing than he was.

That, of course, did not stop him having his haybine hooked up for days on end. He must have given it a test run ten days in a row, engaging the power take-off and scaring himself half to death with the noise. Everything seemed to go round and round and back and forth, so it was easy to believe that he was all set. Better still, Pete dropped by for a coffee one day, so Aubrey gave his machine a whirl to see what his good neighbour thought.

"Should work a treat," Pete commented shortly. "Bit noisy, but everything looks okay. Say, you do know how to open up a field don't you, what with you being an ex-cop and all?"

Open up a field? You just drove in and went round and round, didn't you? What on earth was the man talking about?

"Er, no, well no, not really. I mean don't you just drive in and start cutting?" By now, Aubrey was not afraid of appearing too ignorant in front of Pete; not if he could avoid becoming the laughing stock of the whole neighbourhood.

"Tell you what. I'll set you up and show you what to do, how's that?" Pete said patiently. "Now, have you got a length of rope, say about fifteen feet?"

"What the hell for?"

"Well you need some rope to tie to that spring-loaded pin there. Then you need to run it through to your tractor so that you can get your haybine out of transport mode".

"Pardon me? Did you say transport mode? What the hell is transport mode?"

So it was just as well that Pete showed Aubrey how to get his machine into operating mode and how to open up a field by going "the wrong way around" on the first cut. Not only would Aubrey have gone the other way, he would have done it in transport mode, that was assuming that the haybine would have stayed in one piece long enough to complete the round. He made a pact with himself there and then to make sure that he got an "Operator's Manual" for every machine that he owned, and that he would read it.

The first field of twenty acres went very well, the heavy crop laying itself down in neat swaths to cure in the sun. He even got used to all the clattering and banging, sensing that the noise maintained its own comfortable rhythm that told him that somehow everything was doing what it was supposed to. It was when he was opening up the thirty-acre field near the house that he spotted Sabine walking briskly across the adjoining pasture towards him. Gosh but she looked so feminine and so pastoral in her summer frock; like little Bo-Peep off to find her sheep; he smiled to himself as he realized that he was in danger of veering off course. He stopped the tractor when she got up to him, she knowing that her husband would be delighted if her visit was prompted by an interest in what he was doing rather than by some urgent situation that he had no real desire to address right now.

"Hello darling", she greeted him. "I came up to see how you're getting on".

"Great, my dear, just great!" He climbed out of the tractor and kissed her on the cheek, thrilled by this surprise, as she knew he would be.

As Aubrey came to know well, it was always that innocent little question that slayed you. It was almost as if the spirits of the land did not want you getting too comfortable on their time.

"Honey, what's all that mess behind the machine?" asked dear Sabine, staring down the windrow.

"Huh?" Aubrey turned. Hanging away from and being dragged by the haybine was a mess of wire with at least three fence posts mixed in for good measure.

"Son of a bitch," he yelled wildly. "Some damn fool must have left a pile of bloody wire and posts in the middle of the field. What kind of a stupid s.o.b. would do something like that?"

Sabine did not think that this was quite the right time to tell him that she could see a hole in the fence just about where her very own s.o.b. had veered off track when he had spotted her. Sometimes it is better that your mate discovers his own inadequacies by himself she thought.

But Nellie and her cohorts had no such qualms. Sequestered in the pasture that Sabine had just crossed, she had already spotted the hole in the fence, and the lush cut hay that lay beyond.

"Oh glory be!" Aubrey groaned as the simple truth dawned on him. "I must have hit the fence down there when I saw you, and I didn't know it. But that dear Nellie bitch sure as hell knows it." At that he yelped a despairing "come and help me" at his wife as he set off for the hole like a demented rabbit. Down the field he blundered, leaping over a swath where he had to and yelling like a banshee. Evidently, Nellie relished the idea of a challenge. She kicked up her heels and led her troops on a charge through the gap. A sixty-minute sideshow ensued, with Aubrey almost apoplectic, finishing up a deep crimson, his sides heaving. But it was his bride who was more of an arresting sight. No longer so pastoral, her pastel frock not only sported a large green stain from where she had fallen into a swath, it also gaped immodestly where the seam had parted in some form of surrender on the one side. Her mood was not improved when she was ordered to stay and "see if you can get them back in," as if she was going to run after them like a rabid cattle dog. Aubrey stumbled off to get his fencing tools, muttering "expletive deletives" all the way as he tried to remember where in hell he had left his fencing tools anyway. Sabine was convinced Nellie had a sadistic sense of humor the way she had defied her owners to get her back in, but she decided that even Nellie realized that maybe her sporting instincts were getting to be too much of a good thing for her master. Maybe she knew instinctively that he was capable of going back to the house for his gun and that he was even more capable of shooting them all. Maybe that was why when she was done baiting them, she lifted her head demurely and led her little herd back through the fence without any further prompting. Sabine appreciated then that farming could take a year or two off your life. Not that she had any qualms about capitalizing on Nellie's generous gesture.

"I got them in by myself," she said modestly when her husband returned. "No big deal, really." But Aubrey was still too mad to be impressed.

Baling with his "new" round baler was the ultimate in pleasure as far as Aubrey was concerned. The great big round bales just kept on popping out of the machine, the hay perfectly cured, and all with the ratty belts that he should have changed. The one thing that his friend Pete had warned him to do, to get himself a fire extinguisher and keep it in the tractor, was far from his mind as he worked his way through his fields. He had not bought one yet because they were not on sale at the local Co-op. Currently, there was a good deal in the Princess Auto flyer, but he would have to take a trip to Red Deer for that.

Now it so happened that every Wednesday, old Jim Brassard and Gina, his wife, would come cruising down the road at precisely 3:25 in the afternoon to pick up the two old ladies who lived down by the river. Norah Barker and Sarah Campkin, both nudging seventy, made up the foursome that headed into town to the old folks' drop-in center for their weekly bridge session. Jim was retired now, had long since rented out his land, but still took a lively interest in whatever was going on around him. He spotted Aubrey's baler working away, but more importantly, not missing that telltale sign of smoke coming from a shaft at the top of the machine.

"Jumpin' jellybeans, that young fellow's about to catch fire," he yelled in alarm. "We've got to turn round and warn him before it's too late. He doesn't seem to know he's got a problem. Hang on ladies!"

At the very same moment, Aubrey's keen sense of smell caught a whiff of something burning. Panicked, he shut down the tractor immediately and jumped out. At once he saw the smoke billowing out from around a bearing on the topmost shaft of the baler. Without a second thought, he clambered up onto the machine and worked himself up into a standing position above the offending shaft. Steadying himself, he dropped his pants, underwear and all, and began to pee on the overheated bearing. The ensuing sizzling and the awful stench were enough of a surprise in themselves, but the sight of a van full of people careening down the field came as a total shock. As he reached down desperately trying to retrieve his modesty, he overbalanced. There was something of a "splat" as he dropped a full ten feet and landed flat on his back on the soft ground. He was completely still as the van pulled alongside. All of the occupants bundled out to help so that when Aubrey finally opened his eyes, he saw four old people, four goggle-eyed seniors staring down at him.

That was when dear old Norah added her major contribution to local folklore. "Oh my," she said out loud, "but he's big. Isn't he big Sarah, my dear? I bet your Fred wasn't as big as that!"

"Ladies!" Jim cut in. This last was Aubrey's call to reality. In a flash and crimson with embarrassment, he was up to recoup his dignity, hastily making himself decent.

"Yep," Sarah picked up the conversation. "We had a bull hung like that once. Didn't have much libido though, just like my Fred."

"Ladies!" Jim imposed decorum, but the damage was done; the story was born, and likely to get taller with every telling.

Chapter Six
'TIS THE SEASON

For all the years he had been a policeman, Aubrey could never quite grasp how anybody could get excited about the weather, and yet it seemed to be a national Canadian obsession. For him, if it was going to rain—or dump ten feet of snow on top of you for that matter—it was not as if there was anything you could do to stop it. In other words, there was nothing mystical, nothing supernatural about the weather; for Aubrey, it happened and that was the end of it. Or so he had always thought before he tried his hand at farming. The more of an agriculturalist he became, the more he realized that the atmospheric conditions had their own spiritual dimension. He began to appreciate why it was that supposedly more primitive cultures could view the weather with such awe and superstition. He could see why some cultures might resort to a sun feast or a rain dance to placate the gods and bring on the requisite weather. He could see why the God of Thunder might have to be appeased or the Goddess of Snow and Ice be supplicated. In the first major drought he ever experienced first-hand, he would have been quite happy to have pranced around the weeping birch tree in the garden clad only in a thong and bow tie if he had thought that this would bring an end to the scorching of the land, his land in particular.

Like every farmer, he very quickly learned to shade his eyes from the sun and glance knowingly up into the sky. He could not help but curse the weatherman on Radio CKQX when the latter announced so jauntily that they were in for another beautiful day. Didn't the fool realize that all the farmers were burning their buns off out there in the country while all the city folks were busy smearing themselves with their sun-block and griping about the air-conditioning? And was there ever a lot of whining and bleating if it did decide to rain! Boy oh boy, you could tell it wasn't them who had to slop around in the worst-ever item of footwear ever invented by man, the gumboot. For one thing, the gumboot cannot breathe which, for a man like Aubrey, made it excessively aromatic. Murphy's Law decrees that at least one member of every pair of gumboots shall develop a leak on the second day of agricultural usage, while it is also decreed that each member of every pair shall compete unreservedly with the other to retain the most sweat. So there they were, these "townies" complaining mightily that they could not wear their plaited leather sandals nor their blue suede boots for fear of a mud stain or a dirt spot.

"Get a bloody life!" Aubrey would yell heatedly over the noise of the tractor engine.

When it came to weather, then, every day started out a pristine page, unblemished until the weather gods gave you their latest take on life. On one day they might present to you a vista of unspoiled beauty; not just the reds and the yellows, but also the pastels and the azures. The sky might be an artwork of delicate filigree, or a surrealist creation that you could not quite believe, or a creation so outlandish that were you to reproduce it faithfully on canvas, the critics would be all over you for "your distorted perception of reality". On another day, the gods might be moody; they would attack the page like a petulant child finger-painting dollops of snow, globs of mud, and a deluge of water, all in a peevish swirl of uncoordinated colour. To Aubrey, the weather became primarily visual, and because now it was so vital to what he did for a living, he learned to respect it, to be humble before it, to work with it as occasion demanded. You could not simply pick up your marbles and go home if you did not like it: not when your animals might need feeding or your fields fertilizing.

On top of this, he could no longer envisage his life without the seasons. How could those people out there in the tropics do without the cleansing extreme of winter or the newborn renewal of spring? How lacking were their lives that they had to forego the hues of autumn and the sense of those lazy summer days being so precious before they flew off south with the sun? The seasons were always something to look forward to rather than to wish away. They marched on inexorably, with you or without you. At its height, winter was winter and there could be no denying of it!

Ah, farming in winter! This is the one season of the four that can have you crawling on your knees in supplication: the season that on one day knows no compromise, yet on the next has you believing that there is room for negotiation, that maybe a peaceful coexistence is possible. The first real cold snap Aubrey endured on the farm was a prolonged ten day stretch when the nights plunged to a resolute minus thirty Celsius, the daytime relenting just a little to a high of minus twenty-five. Almost appropriately, the deep freeze struck in the two weeks leading up to Halloween. First, the cattle waterers froze: not just one of them, all five of them. Aubrey had the brilliant idea of thawing out the first one with a propane torch. It was bad enough having to remove the metal cover without gloves and freezing his fingers right to the bone because otherwise he could not hold the screws. It was even worse when he succeeded in melting the molded plastic fittings, thawing not only the ice but melting the plastic as well. The water came gushing out, drenching him spitefully as he tried vainly to control the flow. Within minutes he resembled a malformed mobile popsicle, standing there thoroughly bemused until his frigid brain kicked in to urge him to switch off the entire system at the well by the house. Then it was a trip to town to purchase a new unit some hours later when the stores opened. That was when he learned of the versatility of heat tapes and other such devices.

Two days later, Halloween afternoon to be exact, all water pressure dropped off in the main corral. Actually, it was Nellie's pawing of the ground that let him know that she was somewhat displeased with her current living conditions and that water in the waterer would be nice. The weather had improved to a balmy minus fifteen, so what could have gone wrong? All the waterers had been thoroughly checked over and heat tapes had been installed in every one of them. Wait a second, was that not water apparently welling up out of the ground between the corral and the well down at the house, fifty yards away? His heart sank. It was water all right, and plenty of it. The pipe must have ruptured, though for the life of him he could not fathom why. It was minus thirty a few days ago, why now at minus fifteen? But he did know enough to know that the pipe would be buried at least eight feet underground, and this called for nothing less than a backhoe.

"Have you any bloody idea how hard it is to get my old girl to start in this weather, even if it is only minus fifteen, and I ain't talking about my missus neither?" wheezed old Ed Tilley who ran a backhoe business from his yard, four miles down the road. "I ain't got her plugged in."

"Oh, I am so sorry," said Aubrey innocently. "If you can't come, I'll see if I can find somebody else. I can't leave things as they are, that's for sure," he finished lamely, anxious to restore some normalcy to his disordered world.

"Hold your horses, young fellah, hold your horses!" Ed snorted down the phone. "None of that kind of sassy talk to me, you hear. I'll be down there within the hour, even if I have to bring my missus with a pick and shovel." He was not about to let the prospect of some extra beer money slip through his fingers that easily, no sir. And an ex-cop would likely pay him cash on the spot. Yeah, he would do it, although he might have to light a fire under "his old girl", literally a fire, courtesy of his propane tiger torch, to get her going in this weather. She'd been idle a bit too long in the cold.

"I've got Ed of Ed's Backhoe Service coming down," said Aubrey to Sabine when he got off the phone. "But he reckons it'll take him at least an hour to get here."

"Thank heaven it's not calving time," commented Sabine. "Sit yourself down and have a coffee. You can't really do anything until the man gets here."

Ed rolled up two hours later, his backhoe chugging away on the back of his trailer. "So where's your problem, young fellah?" said this real life caricature of a backwoods Canadian working stiff, the splitting image of Air Farce's "Mike from Canmore". Small in stature, clad in outsize coveralls topped off with a greasy CAT ball cap, his brusque manner could not conceal a big heart that more than made up for any deficiency in size.

"Yup, you've got yourself a break all right, a bad one by the looks of it," he pronounced when he saw the site. "And this baby ain't gonna be no fun, no sir. That water lyin' there is gonna make for a lot of digging. We gotta have a big enough hole around the break so that the whole darn shebang doesn't cave in on us while we're fixin' the pipe." Ed wanted to make sure that his client understood very clearly that this was not one of those "instant plumber jobs". Aubrey was past caring; he wanted it over with so he could go and sit by the fire.

They were still digging when the sun skulked its way over the mountains to the west, but at least they had located the pipe, and Ed's machine had more lights on it than a Walmart Christmas tree to light up the work in progress. Aubrey had not been terribly impressed by the looks of the man on his arrival; in fact, he was downright apprehensive. But as he watched the man's skill with his backhoe, his perception changed a full one hundred and eighty degrees. Ed was obviously a pro of long standing: he could make his machine dance and skip like a newborn lamb. He seemed to sense the foibles of the soil and was not the slightest bit intimidated by the mush that he encountered below the frost line. And as he came closer to where the water line should be, he did not dig so much as stroke the soil away, suddenly laying bare a stretch of black poly pipe lying inert at the bottom of a huge hole, more like a bomb crater than a hole. Gently he worked the machine's giant scoop towards him, and there it was: the break. Seemingly, a joint had let go.

Now, Ed was very much a man of the real world. He knew in advance that if he had to wait for his client to actually get down and fix the line, particularly an ex-policeman, he might have to camp out the night. What might an ex-cop not know about repairing a pipe? How good would he be at minus fifteen, at zero for that matter? No, wily old Ed had brought along an array of just about everything a person might need in the circumstances.

Both he and Aubrey made their way into the hole just as the first "trick or treaters" were starting to show up. In any farming community, a paltry minus fifteen was not enough to keep the kids away from the spoils of Halloween; they were all hardy farm kids, and even the smallest of them were used to doing chores in this cold, anyway. Aubrey always enjoyed seeing the kids in their various costumes, always got a kick out of them by making them parade before him before they departed with their loot. But this night it was not to be; Sabine would have to look after it all. It was probably just as well. She always complained he was far too generous with the candy. Which was also good because he would have a week's worth of surplus candy to chew on.

By the time they had repaired the pipe, Ed was Aubrey's newest and latest hero. Ed had of course guessed correctly: Aubrey had neither the tools, the know-how, nor even the requisite bits to effect more than a temporary repair, so Ed had brought along an assortment of connectors and clamps to make sure that this was a one-shot deal. But Ed was also impressed that Aubrey was willing to get right in and get himself dirty, that he remained undaunted when he slipped in the mud and got himself half covered with a black ooze that froze instantly to his coveralls.

In the meantime, the parade of Halloween trick or treaters had begun arriving in force if the headlights coming in and out of the drive were any indication. Aubrey did not get to see the two ninja turtles, not the goofiest giraffe in the world, not Minnie Mouse, Bugs Bunny, or Donald Duck—or maybe that was Daffy Duck? But at the same moment he came down towards the house, his features streaked with grime and his hands black with frozen mud, the unlikely trio of Elvis Presley, a rotund butterfly with huge plastic wings, and a bright yellow banana were just approaching the light by the house. As if to heighten the macabre effect he presented, Aubrey's silhouette was lit up by the backhoe moving along some distance behind him. His attempt at some sort of civil greeting was pre-empted by a high-pitched shriek as the butterfly reacted inhospitably to this ghoulish creature coming out of the night. The panic was both instant and contagious. The banana preferred not to wait, shedding much of his skin as his two spindly little legs took off down the driveway to find Daddy waiting in his nice warm car at the bottom of the drive. Elvis had more spunk. Up came his guitar in defense of his little sister butterfly, but she was of the same mind as the banana. Oblivious to her brother's chivalry, she spun around on her heel only to put her head through one of her gossamer wings and come crashing to the ground. Aubrey got to her just in time to take Elvis' guitar full over the head. Noble Elvis was not about to abandon little sister butterfly to the mercies of this evil monster of darkness. The ensuing ruckus brought Sabine out of the house at precisely the same moment as the banana arrived back from the truck with his big, bemused daddy.

"It was a not great meeting of the minds," was how Aubrey described it later, and that was all that he would say.

It was hard to say which of the two men at the scene of the crime took the most flack: Aubrey from his Sabine or the man from his wife when he got home with two howling kids and a still defiant Elvis Presley.

Sabine was altogether predictable. Why on earth did he have to come in when he did? What was the matter with him? Surely he realized that his ghastly appearance would scare the living daylights out of any rational adult, let alone a bunch of little kids? What was he thinking? Now the neighbours would all get to thinking and talking. Aubrey, good policeman that he had once been, had learned long ago to tune out anything extraneous to the case. The other man was not so lucky.

"You're so lazy, you sat there in your nice warm truck and sent your kids up some stranger's driveway to some stranger's house all by themselves," the wife was shrill. "Are you nuts? How could you do that to your kids?" Then came the nub of the problem, "And that guitar that Charlie had, you realize that it once belonged to my grandpa, don't you? Do you have any idea what it was worth, and we're not just talking sentimental value either? Do you?" Not that the tirade could accommodate any sort of answer at this point. "Two thousand dollars is what I had it appraised at. Two thousand dollars. And poor little Sarah. She's traumatized out of her mind, never wants to go out on Halloween ever again. Do you know how many hours I spent working on that butterfly costume? Well, do you?" Again, no room for an answer as the barrage continued unabated. "What have you got to say for yourself, eh?" Even then the man could say nothing; it seemed that the woman had to say it all for him.

Isn't that always the way, he thought to himself numbly.

But the real thing about winter that bugged Aubrey the most was the whole business of clothing. First of all, you had to have insulated coveralls if you had any intention of working outside, and of course they cost you an arm and a leg. Then there were the boots. A good pair cost almost as much or more than the coveralls. "Good to minus fifty," the label would proclaim. But what if the flesh and blood inside them is only good to minus ten, what then, Aubrey would think sourly. This was quite apart from the fact that one's mobility was reduced by a minimum of fifty percent, a fact that Nellie seemed to have stored in her tiny mind. Even that most Canadian of all the clothing items, the lowly toque, was beset with issues of quality. If there was too much polyester or polywhatsit in the fiber, Aubrey's head would itch insanely, and if he was to exert himself at all physically, it would sweat obscenely. Then when it got too cold, he had to resort to what Sabine referred to as "the bandito toque", the sort preferred by bank robbers and the like because they could cover up their incriminating faces leaving just eyes and nose showing. Oh, and mouth! Aubrey hated it. For him it was "the snotsicle toque" because of buildup of fluids from nose and mouth that always iced up around the openings.

As for the "layering", that was another hated story. In frigid conditions, undergarments would have been better named as "subterranean garments", given the sheer volume of material layered over them. And inevitably, you had just finished dressing up to head out the door when Nature called: not just tentatively so that it could wait, but loudly, urgently.

Where winter tended to be more of a season of inertia, spring was the season of optimism and hope. Every farmer, Aubrey included, wants to think that this will be the year, the year of the bumper crop, and the first one among many where the rewards will properly compensate you for all those wasted efforts of the seven lean years gone by. It is the time for renewal and new life: Aubrey loved it for the calving, for the new leaves bursting out on the trees, and for the flowers driving off the drabness of winter. Of course, he had appreciated none of this when he was a policeman on the beat; nature then had always been just an incidental.

Inevitably though, spring could be the start of a string of broken promises, too. A farmer could get the scours among his calves and watch almost helplessly as one after another succumbed to the ravages of dehydration. That much needed, much heralded moisture required to kick-start the crops might come all at once in one great big dollop, or not at all. The main tractor might throw a tantrum and blow the transmission to put you and your cash flow a couple of thousand dollars behind the eight ball. Aubrey quickly learned not to take his hopes too seriously, and never to count his calves before they had been weaned and trucked out.

Everybody who has ever raised cattle has had a calf that arrives on the scene firmly clutching an express ticket to heaven. Yet others seem to arrive on the scene without any ambition, their brains stuck doggedly in neutral. After his first encounter with such a critter in his second calving season on the farm, Aubrey labeled them as "SBS calves"—Squashed Brain Syndrome calves. Even after a no-stress birth, an SBS calf would lie there with absolutely no inclination to get up and go foraging for a tit, which meant that Aubrey finally had to intervene and find one for it. That would have been quite okay had the mother on one occasion not been the meanest cow in the herd. She was coincidentally the prettiest cow, which was why Sabine had insisted that Aubrey bid on her even though she had sent Newt smartly up his escape ladder at the mart. "Matata" they called her, Swahili for "trouble" as every kid who ever watched "The Lion King" could tell you. It was the last time that Aubrey allowed any animal to be called anything that could turn out to be a self-fulfilling prophecy. Make no mistake, "Matata" loved her baby dearly even if she showed no concern over its lackadaisical attitude to life. But she brooked no interference, and to her, all of Aubrey's best efforts were simply that—interference.

"All right, my girl, it's the head-gate for you," he told her severely. "You've got to let me work on your baby one way or another."

As if! As if talking nicely to a cow named "Matata" was somehow going to magically change her disposition!

"So you wanna dance?" she challenged him, beckoning him with her head to come within range. She followed this up with a vicious kick that would have smashed Aubrey's kneecap had he been a few inches closer. Up until this one day, he had always sworn off striking one of his cows in anger, an unspoken code of honour you might say. Trouble was, on this occasion there was a short piece of 2 X 4 conveniently at hand, testing his very best intentions to the limit.

"Matata", on the other hand, made it clear that she was bound by no such good intentions. Her calf was strictly her business, and if he just wanted to lie there, then that was just fine by her. Just as Aubrey found himself picking up the piece of wood, his brain took over. Of course! A bucket of chop would surely seduce Matata into the head-gate. Just as Sabine could be bought with a plate of fine seafood, so the world would stop for a bucket of rolled grain as far as "Matata" was concerned. The ruse worked like a charm; she went into the head-gate without a second look back. But the moment she realized that she had been trapped, that she had been betrayed, she bellowed high treason and lashed out with her hooves, all to no avail. Aubrey gave her time to wear herself out and to rediscover the chop, then he approached with the calf which he had to half carry because it was so weak. As he got close, "Matata" let him know in no uncertain terms that the gloves were off, her antics only succeeding in terrifying her own offspring for whom all this was being done in the first place. But now Aubrey's anger was equal to that of the cow. Feeling very hurt that one of his girls could act like this with her benefactor, he seized the piece of 2 X 4 and whacked her hard with all his strength across the behind. Call it an act of revenge, or of retaliation, or merely of discipline, the result was completely unexpected. She stood stock still, at least long enough for him to gingerly feed a rope around one of her back feet and tie it to a post.

"You bloody well try and kick me now, my dear," said Aubrey breathing hard, "and see where that bloody well gets you!" He sat down on a square bale of straw and coaxed the lethargic baby up to the grocery department, a perfectly shaped udder with four perfect tits. Nothing, nada; the baby was not the slightest bit interested. Aubrey squeezed some milk into its mouth as the calf stood there helplessly, milk dribbling out of its mouth.

"Peace brother! Peace be with you!" Aubrey always found it very soothing to talk thus to himself when in extreme frustration. "Let not the beast triumph over thee," he intoned as he felt a more reasoned calm coming over him. The calf had ideas of its own, however. Having decided that even standing up was just too much of a chore, it insisted on collapsing into a shapeless heap in the straw. Exasperated with such behavior, Aubrey grabbed a hold of it and straddled it across his knees, forcing a tit into its mouth. It chewed the tit a couple of times and then went inert.

"Suck the damn thing!" yelled Aubrey furiously. "Don't chew on it, suck it!"

He was doing his absolute best not to explode into a hopeless fit of temper when, lo and behold, a sudden sucking sound pierced his manmade fury. Aubrey held his breath, did not dare to breathe for a full thirty seconds, praying all the while that something positive was happening. The calf's tail burst into life, swishing madly in an ecstasy of its own as baby sucked with unbridled enthusiasm. Aubrey still had it cradled over his knees; he could not afford to have it fall down because it might not have the strength to get up again, or it might lose concentration and not be able to re-access the grocery department. He need not have worried; baby was now on a roll, sucking madly from a second untried tit. Tail wagging furiously, it was oblivious to everything except this wondrous source of goodness flowing into its mouth. That was when Aubrey felt a warmth, not an unpleasant one necessarily, spreading outwards in his lap. It took him a couple of seconds to realize that for the calf, some "output" was required to accommodate the "input"; the calf had peed on him. The association of ideas being so powerful, his first instinct was to recoil in disgust. He and the calf and the bale landed in an inglorious heap at the back end of the cow; happily her foot was still tied so she could not have exacted her revenge even if she had tried, thought Aubrey somewhat smugly. Oh yeah? She arched her back instead, and let loose a cascade of very liquefied bright green manure that splattered him from head to toe. Not that the calf cared; it floundered to its feet and was back to the tit in a matter of seconds. Yet for Aubrey somehow it had all been worth it. Never before had he experienced this degree of contentment, or gratitude, or whatever it was. He sat there in the straw for a full minute, "smiling bucolically" as a man of letters might say. So much for spring and new life!

If winter was the season of extremes, summer was always softer and more mellow in the lee of the Rockies, although the "mellow" might more often be applicable to one's mood. For sure, there were those days when the heat could be extreme, especially in the infamous drought of 2002, but with heat there was always some way of cooling off. Grab a cold one. Jump into the pool, the dugout, the fishpond. Wear enough only for the sake of decency, and discard even that if decency was not an issue. The big plus for Aubrey, who hated the protracted business of dressing in winter, was that dressing for summer was no business at all. Moreover, physically attracted as he ever was to his mate, Sabine beat them all when it came to "under-dressing in style". It was as if she came into bloom in summer, along with her pansies and her begonias, although he knew for certain that this view of her mate was not reciprocated on her part. But then he had never been photogenic.

Early summer was the time to relax. The crops were seeded, the crops were fertilized, and the cows were out to pasture. Even when you made your weekly check on them on the rented pasture out west, they would turn a bored eye upon you and question your presence. Aubrey always felt like an intruder, but then his girls always had a welcome for him if he brought a sack of mineral or a salt block, or if they thought it was time he moved them to a fresh pasture. This was also the time of year to squeeze in a holiday. So too, it was the time to fix the fence, repair the machinery, replace the boards on the south side of the main corral, spread some of the piled up manure, or build a calf shed; the jobs just clamored for attention. Trouble was, there were always so many of them, you could easily feel overwhelmed, and take the day, or the week, or the month off, succumbing to the joys of procrastination. After battling the elements all year, the attraction to a lazy day or three meant that some of the jobs simply did not get done, and you always paid a price for that! You had to prioritize concluded Aubrey, harking back to one of the most hated words in a policeman's dictionary. Then that ugly word "discipline" reared its malevolent head. Being an ex-policeman, Aubrey was no stranger to discipline, but then as custodian of the law, he was applying it to others, often with gusto, more than it was ever being applied to him. No, he had left the police force to get as far away from words like "prioritize", "discipline", even "uniform". After his first year of lazing around on the farm making his own contributions to the excesses of summer, he learned to temper judiciously such "lazings around".

Of course, as summer becomes full-blown, mature, laziness on the farm becomes nothing more than gross self-indulgence. The plants and the bees have been quietly doing their thing, hay now has to be cut and baled at its prime— not at a time of your choosing, not if you want your cows to have the best, your best. Machines need to be maintained, not haphazardly with a drop of oil here, a dab of grease there, but systematically so that they do what they were meant to do with a minimum of problems. Ah, the English language intrudes again; the word "systematically" implied a modicum of discipline to Aubrey, a sense of tidiness that to him represented an alien way of thinking.

Farmers can be assigned to two categories: those who are tidy and those for whom even the notion of anarchy implies a certain level of organization or sophistication they simply do not possess nor intend to possess. Indeed, these latter types tend to label their more ordered counterparts as "tidiness freaks" as though their tidiness is some sort of blight or affliction, a kind of "psycho-obsession" that is best left to a practicing psychiatrist. Not that the "freaks" do not have their own jaundiced view of their less evolved neighbours, perceiving them as much closer to the apes than they themselves could ever be. Aubrey saw himself as somewhere in between, with a definite list towards the more disordered. Yet he did retain enough "system" to ensure that every machine had a ball pein hammer and a crescent wrench designated to it, though he sometimes surmised that the hammer was only there to let him vent his frustration on whatever was troubling him at the time. Somehow, summer finagled the notion of "responsibility" into the equation. Aubrey could not sit out in the deck chair with a glass of wine and a juicy novel without more than a twinge of guilt. And naturally, the more Sabine became conversant with the vocabulary of the farm, the more she tended to ride shotgun on her husband, making sure that everything was attempted if not completed—sometimes with a zeal that Aubrey had to insist to her was misplaced.

"You said that you needed to grease your crutch, dear. Have you done it yet?"

The statement stopped him dead in his tracks for a moment as he considered this new proposition. Then it dawned on him what she was talking about. "That's clutch, honey, clutch not crutch."

"Oh, whatever!"

"And you said something about tightening your fanny belt on the Massey. Did you get to it, dear?"

"What do you mean you've got to bleed it? Can you make a tractor bleed?"

This was after Aubrey had neglected to change the fuel filter on the Massey. Understandably, the old girl suddenly spluttered and died, not in some anonymous back field—that never happens—but right there on the road past the house for everybody to see and laugh about. At least he was able to diagnose the problem immediately, even if it did mean a quick trip into town because, of course, he had no spare on hand. Then, and much to his pleasant surprise, he got her going again by following the step by step procedure outlined in the Operator's Manual; the first set of instructions in a long time that did not seem to have been translated from three other languages into a pidgin English incomprehensible to a native English speaker.

By high summer, too, Aubrey had pretty much rounded up most of the tools he had left lying around in various exotic locations, only to be caught by the onset of early snow the previous winter and removed from sight for the next five months. Despite all of his best intentions, however, he never seemed to learn that his practice of flitting from one half-completed job to another only set himself up again for precisely the same thing.

As the business of summer took over, those deck chair days receded into memory as the hay was put up, the bales moved and stacked, the crop of barley liberally augmented by stinkweed was harvested, and on and on it went. Then one day, Aubrey would look up to discover that the trees had started to change colour, announcing that fall, that season of "mists and mellow fruitfulness", was on its way. Fall was another favorite for Aubrey, usually because he had the time to enjoy it, to breathe in its serenity and warmth. Maybe because he knew it was the last hurrah before the uncompromising chill of winter, he deliberately made time for himself, and nobody, man nor beast, nor wife begrudged him. All too soon it was over, and he was back into singing to and feeding his cows, and peeling the endless yards of frozen twine from the bales with frigid fingers. The cycle had begun again.

Chapter Seven
NOT SINCE GRANNY WENT TO PASTURE

Machinery, the vices and vicissitudes of such, became the bane of Aubrey's agricultural life. In today's farming, unless you wish to beat a retreat to the hard labour of peasant subsistence agriculture, you will require a whole range of specialist machines to cope with different phases of the growing and feeding cycle. Unfortunately, the relentless march of technology always conspires to assure you that the item you just purchased with so much pride and hard-earned cash is suddenly not only outdated but also immediately inferior for the job you intended. For Aubrey, the whole business of machinery presented him with a steep learning curve; a curve so steep that at times he felt himself spinning out or even going backwards. No sooner did he become adept at using a particular implement or tool, he found that either it broke irreparably or it slid its way so far into antiquity that it belonged in a museum. For the sake of simple efficiency, his favorite old sickle mower simply had to be replaced with a haybine, and his haybine absolutely had to be replaced with a discbine if he was to tackle the new clovers with any success. Experience, as ever, came with bumps on the head and bruises to the ego, and always with that surreptitious look around to see who might be watching the latest fiasco.

Aubrey was especially glad that nobody other than Sabine saw the incident with the old Farmall M. It was a 1952 model, one of those versions that model collectors and restoration buffs adore; the same ones that have belt buckles and calendars with their very own name. With its high rear wheels and its tricycle front axle with the two front wheels side by side, and its seat way up in the air, it resembled something of a giant three-legged spider. Perched up there, Aubrey saw himself as "King of the Prairies", master of all that he surveyed—well, maybe with some concession to the bank. He bought the old girl at an estate auction near Sundre and was crazed enough to drive it the thirty something miles home. His opposite bidder at the auction was good enough to point out to him that there were only two bolts intact holding the seat to the main frame, but Aubrey dismissed him as a sore loser and decided to chance it anyway. Once home, he promptly forgot about the problem.

It was in the early days on the farm, at a time when he still had that old manure spreader of indeterminable age and indecipherable origin. He decided to be adventurous and hitched it up to the Farmall, intending to get rid of some of the mound of manure piling up near his main corral. Getting smarter by the season, he connected up and made sure everything moved and turned the way it was supposed to before he loaded up and headed out to the field. Once he was lined up, he tied the heavy rope that engaged the trip mechanism to the seat; that way, all he had to do was to reach down and yank on it when he was ready for action. He took a deep breath, let out the clutch and heaved on the rope.

Within seconds, he found himself assailed by "clods and clumps of cow shit", or at least that was how he put it to his cronies later on at the coffee shop. But strong of character that he was, he gritted his teeth and bore the barrage with great courage, happy that the bulk of the manure was spreading out behind him the way it was meant to. Indeed, he found himself grinning with delight that his experiment was proving so successful, that is until a small stone shot out from beneath a flail and bounced off his head. He turned around, cursing like a trooper. That's when a great wad of manure caught him full in the open mouth, a sort of divine retribution for his language, perhaps. It did not taste all that good, either. Furious now beyond words, he came to a grinding stop before deciding to empty out the little bit left in the spreader. Still flushed and angry, he elected to unhitch the machine where it was in the field, figuring that it would be much wiser to hitch it up to the other tractor because it had a cab on it which would give him some protection at least. He pulled the pin, climbed back on to his high seat, and set off for the yard at full bore. Within a split second he was flying through the air to end up sitting on the stump of his seat in mid-field, the tractor chugging off without him.

It took only a couple of seconds for him to realize what had happened. That darn rope! He had forgotten to untie that damn rope from his seat. When he had set off, the rope had tightened enough to shear the two remaining bolts on the seat and he had come off his machine like a Flying Wallenda. But right now, this was the least of his problems. There was his tractor, his old antique pride and joy, now driverless, putt-putting its ungainly way across the field like some alien contraption run amok. He jumped up and tore after it, running as fast as his rarely-exercised legs had ever carried him, praying first that he would actually reach it in time, and second that he would be able to climb up and switch it off, or at least pull it out of gear, all before it crashed through the plank fence that separated the field from the vegetable garden and, God forbid, the house! Panting like a winded moose, he was closing in nicely on his target when he tripped. Down he went in a scramble of arms and ears, a cacophony of curses bluing the air and giving vent to his frustration. He looked up from full horizontal only to see the front wheels of the tricycle axle catch the only rock on the entire ten-acre field. Oh God! Oh no! Oh hell, the rock had nudged the tractor from its current relatively harmless line to redirect it straight for the old glass greenhouse now only about thirty yards away. Destiny had declared its fate, of that there could be no doubt. The greenhouse was an eyesore that Aubrey and Sabine had inherited with the farm; they had mutually agreed to tolerate its seedy presence in the southwest corner of the garden only because they got great tomatoes and bountiful zucchinis from its micro-world. They would demolish it sometime down the road, they decided, some day when the farm was making enough money to pay for one of those instant packaged greenhouses that even the village idiot could put together. Destiny was not to be denied this day.

Aubrey was still flat on his belly when the tractor breached the fence into the vegetable patch. He saw his dear wife, so engrossed in weeding her carrots, look up with startled uncomprehending eyes. He saw her abandon "The Claw", Canadian Tire's latest whiz tool for geriatric gardeners, and run like a frightened deer for the refuge of the caragana hedge. He watched more in fascination than in horror as the tractor took the greenhouse end-on. It was a visual experience like no other as the entire structure disintegrated into showers of falling glass. The tractor did not hesitate for a second; it bumbled on through until seemingly a shard of glass caught the kill switch, stopping it dead in its tracks. Suddenly there was silence, a prolonged, even blissful silence. Then came an eerie wail from the caragana hedge, a sound that prompted Aubrey to stand up and immediately to resume walking. When Sabine spotted him, the wail mutated first into a shriek of delight, and then into a demonic peal of laughter that made the hairs stand up on Aubrey's neck.

"Not today," she could only wheeze at him. "Not today, I didn't mean you to demolish it today," the words struggled out between tears of laughter and relief as Sabine fought to regain her composure.

The tractor was a sorry sight. Festooned with tomato plants and shards of glass, it sat there; the proud champion of its very own demolition derby. Only when Aubrey was sure that his wife was not particularly upset did he confess what had actually happened, that he had forgotten to untie the rope and it had pulled the seat off. He did not see the sense of going further, admitting that he knew that there were only two bolts holding the seat on in the first place.

"But the spreader sure works well," he added in mitigation.

Nonetheless, the episode was an object lesson in safety that he never forgot. Never again did he ever unhitch an implement without assuring himself that all connections between tractor and implement were severed.

The machine that showed the strongest tendency for drama, however, was the swather, certainly initially anyway. Aubrey and Sabine were at one of those farm auctions where money was tight and interest was low. Being too early in the year, nobody showed any interest in the swather, a badly faded Hesston 520, whatsoever. A troop of Hutterites from the local colony was in attendance, but they were interested only in the big-ticket items, the combine the size of a house and a fancy big grain truck. It was a Clayton Cole auction, so Aubrey was in familiar territory, so to speak. If Clayton had not spotted him in the crowd, there would have been little doubt that he would have returned home empty-handed, although he was sure Sabine would have done her bit to keep prices from rock-bottom.

"Hey Orb, c'mon now," Clayton hollered at him. "You need a swather, and don't say that you don't." He was exasperated that nobody showed any sign of making a bid. "This baby is hydrostatic, for Pete's sake. And it's even got a cab so you can keep your buns warm. You all know that if it was any nearer to harvest time, none of you would touch this baby for less than a couple of thousand. C'mon now, where's a thousand? A thousand, anywhere?"

No response, the crowd was dead.

"All right then, if it's gonna be a slow day, then we'll take it slow. Give me five hundred. Five hundred, anywhere?"

No takers anywhere.

"Well, we've gotta start somewhere. Who'll start me off? C'mon Orb, here's your chance."

"One hundred," Aubrey was too ashamed to look at Clayton directly, preferring instead to stare at the ground when he said it. And he had no idea at all what Clayton meant when he said the machine was hydrostatic.

"Thank ya' Orb, thank ya'. Now, someone give me a hundred and fifty. A hundred and fifty, anywhere, one hundred and fifty?"

The crowd was comatose.

"Sold," said Clayton impatiently. "She's all yours. You stole it at that price, let me tell you. Sheesh, you couldn't even buy a tire for it at that price!"

Now, Aubrey had harbored every intention of buying a swather in the future, but up until this moment he had been quite content to get one of his neighbours to come in and do what little needed to be done, although it always seemed that whenever he was ready, the neighbour could not come because he was busy doing his own. Inevitably then, Aubrey's crop was never swathed at quite the right time.

"Say, what's he mean when he says the swather is hydrostatic?" he asked one of the more knowledgeable-looking bystanders.

"Oh, all he means is that the machine moves through hydrostatic pressure. You remember learning about hydrostatics at school, no? You know, the study of fluids?"

"No." Aubrey was loath to admit that he did not remember anything he had learned at school, least of all something as abstract as the study of fluids. No, he was always too busy raising hell, chasing girls, and playing on every sports team there was.

"Well, let me put it this way. When you get in and push the steering column forward, the machine moves forward. Pull the column backwards and the whole darn thing will go backwards. Then all you have to do is turn the wheel when you want to go left or right. Simple, yes?"

"If you say so," said Aubrey, hoping desperately that he had understood enough to drive it home. "And thanks a lot. By the way, my name is Aubrey, Aubrey Hanlon."

"Henry Tarbuck. I live right next door to this place. Say, if you want to borrow my swather mover to get this baby home, you're more than welcome. I'll even help you load her, seeing as I'm about done with buying anything today".

"Oh, that would be a huge help. I'll get my wife to bring up our truck and I'll be up there just as soon as I've paid my bill."

"Great. I'll just go take one more look at the junk they're selling right now, and I'll head out."

Aubrey was happy to see Sabine emerge from the direction of the house where the second ring was well into auctioning off the household goods. A matronly Hutterite woman appeared at the same time, shooing her flock of young maidens ahead of her. Aubrey arranged for Sabine to go and pay, and he went back to his latest acquisition. He did a general check around the outside, and satisfied that nothing appeared to pose a hazard, he stepped up into the cab. He looked over the controls. "Looks simple enough," he said to himself. "Ignition switch. Throttle. Choke. What more do I want?" He switched on and pressed the starter button. Instantly, the swather came to life, the motor purring smoothly. "Great," he thought, "for once I've got me a real good deal." At that moment, Sabine reappeared, so he got out and told her to bring the truck and to follow him up to the Tarbuck place.

"Hubris: Overbearing pride or presumption" is how the dictionary describes the feeling. Aubrey should have known better, should have known that to make any sort of prediction or to have any anticipation that the swather would move from point A to point B without complication was extremely presumptuous. He leapt back on to the step and grabbed the steering wheel, inadvertently pushing the whole column forward. Oh yes, this old Hesston girl was full of enthusiasm and raring to go. She took off with Aubrey half-hanging out of the door, fighting to stay on board as it were. Thankfully, his weight pulled the steering wheel hard over so the machine was cruising around in a tight circle; the throttle, too, was set not too far above idle so progress was still relatively slow, a sedate five miles an hour. Alas, not slow enough for the Hutterite mama who was shepherding her little flock out of danger before her. The crop divider at the one end of the table, a sort of metal spike, hooked into her black floral skirt and whisked it off like some trophy from a medieval jousting match. She remained behind, standing there in utter bewilderment, her voluminous pink bloomers so reminiscent of the Victorian era on view for all to see. Her language, someone muttered something about it being Low German, was very guttural and completely unintelligible, but all present judged it to be as severe as her demeanor. At any rate, the message was clear. She didn't stand for long, couldn't stand for long as the swather made its way around for its second offensive, prompting the apoplectic old mama to take to her heels and seek sanctuary inside an empty grain bin that had just been sold. Of course, the attention of the main crowd had not only been deflected by the commotion, it was now riveted to the drama unfolding before them. A horrified silence engulfed them.

"Haven't seen a pair of bloomers like that, not since granny went to pasture," commented one old dear, herself not a year under seventy, breaking the tension completely.

"Reminds me of a half-plucked chicken," added her husband uncharitably. "Feathers on the top, pink on the bottom."

The comments left the rest of the crowd in hysterics; even the Hutterite brethren had to resort to holding each other up, they were laughing so hard.

A body lunged past Aubrey and forced its way into the cab. It yanked the column back to neutral, pushing Aubrey off the machine with the other hand as it did so. The machine stopped on command, purring as sweetly as ever. The man inside switched it off.

"Better let 'em all settle down," Henry Tarbuck said, tears of laughter still coursing down his cheeks. "And next time, don't leave the old girl running unless you are actually in the cab. These things can be a bloody hazard. By the way, you need to get the neutral safety device looked at; it doesn't work".

Mother Hutterite would not come out of the granary to accept Aubrey's apology, though the door opened just enough for a hand to snatch back the proffered skirt. Aubrey did what he thought was the next finest thing, he apologized loudly to the metal bin and then to all of the others. Judging by another spasm of unbridled laughter, his apology did not make all that much of an impression. Then, even though he was now terrified of his new purchase, he started it up and got it over to his new friend's place where they loaded it front wheels first on to the swather mover which Mr. Tarbuck had hitched to Aubrey's truck.

"Don't be pushing it lad; no more than about forty clicks an hour. You've only got ten or so miles to go, so take it easy and listen to the radio or something."

Aubrey and Sabine started out for home. "Switch on the radio, will you hon?" Aubrey said. A string of numbers that they had danced to in their courtship days came on. Both became mesmerized, lost in the mists of time and memory; neither one of them felt Aubrey's foot grow heavy, gradually increasing their speed. Tom Jones' "Daughter of Darkness" was playing when the truck began to shake, imperceptibly at first, but gathering momentum as if in time to the music. As the tune ended, it dawned on Aubrey that the truck was doing a jig all of its own, shuddering as if it was about to implode. With that realization came another one, that the rear wheel of the swather was shimmying crazily along behind on the highway. The very moment that he looked down at the speedometer to see what speed they were doing, ninety kilometers an hour as it turned out, was the same moment that swather's back tire chose to explode with a mighty bang. They slewed to a stop, Aubrey fighting the wheel like a mad thing. Sheepishly, he opened the door and got out to assess the damage. Sabine, wise in the ways of her husband, saw fit to stay put. All that was left of the swather's rear wheel was a mangled tire with slivers of tube hanging obscenely out.

"Shoot, I was going much too fast," was Aubrey's muttered admission to his wife. "Oh well, we're only two or three miles from home, we'll just crawl slowly along on the rim until we get there."

The first kind soul to pass them on the highway flagged them down to tell them about their flat tire. Then the second, and the third and fourth.

"Reach over into the back, dear, and give me that old toque that's lying in the junk there," Aubrey asked of his mate. She pulled out an old grease-stained creation, scarlet in colour, with a big hole on one side. It had lain there for a good three years, Aubrey reckoned later. He put it on, deliberately pulling a clump of hair through the hole on the window side of his head to better the effect. The driver of the next car that slowed up alongside to tell them of their wheel took one look at this freak driving a truck, shook his head, and drove off. It was the same with the next car. Even the uniformed occupants of the police cruiser spared only one glance at this moron in a toque and decided that their time would be better spent at Tim Horton's, drinking hot coffee and grazing on donuts. So it was that Aubrey made it home: sadder, maybe wiser, and thoroughly intimidated by their new swather.

The scariest experience of all came when he left the handbrake on by mistake when he went off disking in the old Massey 1100 tractor. It was one of those hotter than Hades spring days when the barometer was pushing at over thirty Celsius. He was feeling very satisfied with his progress on a field that he had been working at for the past couple of days. As always, he had the radio cranked up, and, as was his wont, he was singing along at the top of his lungs to the likes of Tom Jones, Roger Whittaker, and the great Engelbert. But man it was getting hot in the cab, even though he had every vent and every window open. It was so hot, in fact, that he stripped down to his under-shorts and battled on. But where the heck was Sabine with his lunch, he wondered; she was always so good and so prompt at keeping him fed and watered when he was doing his field work. Aha, there she was, the good lass, trundling through the field on her bicycle. He jumped out of the tractor to meet her as she drew up.

"Dear, why are you near naked? And look at those under-shorts. You can't walk around like that. Why, there's almost nothing left of them. What if someone sees you like that?"

"Oh sure, like every traveling salesman is going to drive in and sell me a paint brush and see me in my under-shorts. Besides it's bloody hot in there, let me tell you."

"What on earth is that smell?" she said, ignoring his comments.

"Smell? What smell?" responded Aubrey, eyeing the flask of iced tea that she carried in her hand.

"That smell of burning," she said, still clutching on to Aubrey's lunch in her concern.

"I don't smell....Holy sheep shit!" Aubrey exclaimed, as he turned around. "There's a bloody great fire going under the cab. No wonder it was so hot in there."

With that, he leapt back into the tractor, rammed it into top gear, lifted his disk out of the ground and tore off down the field leaving his wife becalmed (bemused?) in the middle of the latest storm.

Pete and his wife happened to be coming down the road to the east of the field at that particular moment. What he saw made him pull up in awe and amazement. There was his neighbour, that crazy damn cop, careening down his field at full speed, a disk bouncing wildly behind him, smoke billowing out from beneath the cab of his tractor.

Aubrey had remembered that there was plenty of water in the slough at the far end of the field. It was just that he had not planned ever to enter it with gusto. As he approached the slough, he hammered on the brakes. Nothing. Zip. Zero. What the hell… oh damn, the fire must have burned through the brake lines. Okay, throttle back, semi-fetal position; the rest would have to take care of itself.

Pete saw Aubrey hit the slough with a huge splash. Then he saw the tractor settle comfortably into the ooze, the smoke transforming itself into a sudden cloud of steam as the water doused the flames.

"You know my dear, some people are born never to have a dull moment, and our neighbour is one of them," Pete said to his wife, Jeannie. "Now I suppose we'd better go rescue him."

As they pulled up to the site, Aubrey was just exiting the cab. "What if someone sees you like that?" Sabine's words echoed in his mind as his eyes took in the fact that he had an audience. That's when he decided to settle comfortably down into the ooze alongside his tractor and conduct any conversation from the sanctuary of the slough.

Chapter Eight
MAY YOUR CIRCUS ALWAYS HAVE A CLOWN

*P*erhaps it is the wrong approach to take when raising your own livestock, to see all of your animals as individuals if not fully-fledged personalities. Agribusiness demands otherwise, that you see them as commodities to be bought and sold as supply and demand dictates. Once again, Aubrey and Sabine ignored conventional wisdom only to find that the moment they began naming their cows was the same moment that they began to develop an emotional attachment to them. As they built up their herd, slowly the cows came to know their names, many of them seeming to conform to what was expected of, or associated with, the name they were given. So it was that Nellie was as feisty as Nellie McClung, Snowflake was as gentle and soft as her name implied, and Pixie was just that—a pixie. They also quickly learned not to call any of their girls anything that might be derogatory in any way, nor anything that could turn out to be a self-fulfilling prophecy. Their experience with the cow named "Matata", for example. "Matata", the Swahili word for trouble certainly seemed to have convinced the cow to live up to her name. Most farmers used tags with numbers, but that idea was vehemently opposed by Sabine until such tags became law in a world obsessed about tracing the source of its food. "Where was there any lyricism, any poetry in a number?" she asked. "'Come in, seventy-four' was infinitely more boring than 'come in, Mirabella'. It's so damn pedestrian," she insisted. "Besides, you can't sing it," Aubrey would add, thinking about the infinite number of ways he could yodel with a name like Mirabella.

Other farmers, the more progressive types, chose to see their animals as neither their pets nor even as their friends. Instead, these people saw nothing but dollar signs. If a cow lost her calf, even if it was through no fault of her own, she would be culled from the herd immediately; it was economic common sense that you should not have her consuming too many dollars worth of hay or grass if she was not going to make any economic contribution in return. They said such thinking made Aubrey and Sabine's operation less efficient. But then again, "they" said a lot of things. "They" had always maintained that an ex-cop like Aubrey did not stand a chance of making it; that he had nowhere near enough experience. "They", the enlightened "they", were still saying that after he had been at it for twelve years. "They" all forgot that although a little knowledge is a dangerous thing, starting with no knowledge whatsoever means that you start with no preconceptions.

"And take a look at that wife of his", they said, "the one with the fancy high-falutin' name. Now how could a china doll like that ever expect to become a genuine farmer's wife?"

But Sabine, too, evolved with the Hanlon spread. Moreover, she had always retained the capacity to laugh at herself, never taking herself too seriously. She characterized herself as "stylishly impractical with a flair for the dramatic and the artistic." The local vet was would soon endorse that particular view, although he might have replaced the "artistic" with "comic".

When you raise livestock, you know and expect that you will encounter problems. Like people, cows get sick, they play the hanky-panky, and get pregnant too. Of course, there are those farmers who fondly decree nature must be allowed to do her thing, but that is their way of saying that they have no intention of getting up at night to check on a might-be-calving cow, no intention of doctoring a sick animal unless its mobility is so compromised that they can walk right up and stab her with a syringe full of the latest wonder drug. "Cowboy boots were never made for running," they pronounce sagely. On the other hand, Aubrey was nothing if not conscientious. The decision to go into beef had not been taken lightly, and he was not about to lose any animal for a lack of attention: not after that incident with Nellie's beautiful baby. Sabine very soon got drawn into the act because she adored babies.

Their very first encounter with the vet was an illustration of another aspect of Murphy's Law; "two unrelated activities can be thrown together fortuitously to give rise to curious, even unwanted, perceptions."

It was the very day that they had been invited to a costume party at the community hall. Everybody of any consequence and humor was scheduled to be there. Aubrey, the retired policeman was going dressed, of course, as a pig. Sabine, who had eagerly been looking forward to the event all week, was set to go as Coco the clown. In the meantime, Aubrey had been monitoring little Petunia all afternoon. She was a small, gray cow who liked to keep to herself so much so that Aubrey had taken to singing, "I'm a lonely little petunia in an onion patch" to her every time he paid her a visit to see what was happening. He knew from the calendar she was about due; they had actually seen her bred nine months ago. But as much as Petunia seemed reluctant to settle and get down to business, so Sabine was reluctant to delay dressing up and heading out for their party. It was getting on for dark when she insisted that Aubrey change into his piggy suit and forget his cow. She would be fine, anyway. Sabine, of course, was fully dressed right down to her bright red bulbous nose.

"Well, I'll just take a quick hike up to the barn and have one more look. We just can't afford to lose a calf, especially when we don't have to. Be back in a minute." Damn, but did he ever feel foolish wearing this crazy suit. The tail that Sabine had made out of a piece of garden hose felt like a hammer half falling out of his pocket. Just as well he didn't have to wear the head too, that would surely have had an interesting effect on the cow!

Before this day, Aubrey and Sabine had never encountered a calving problem, per se. Aubrey had picked up a book that he had found in some hippy-looking bookstore in Penticton, B.C., called "The Fundamentals of Raising a Cow". What had attracted his attention was a series of diagrams illustrating all of the ways a calf might be presented on its way out into an uncaring world. Written in 1935, the prose was quaint, but Aubrey surmised that the information would still be applicable; after all, babies, calves, lambs, had all been coming into this world the same way as they had always come, right? However, he was soon to find out that there was "a gap in translation" between looking at a black line diagram and an actual hands-on, hands-in physical exploration of a cow.

By this time, it was pretty well dark. One solitary bulb in the barn struggled to illuminate this micro-world, but it was quite enough for Aubrey to see a very unsettled Petunia, and more than enough for an irascible Petunia to see him. As soon as he stuck his head around the door, she turned to face him, the threatening gestures with her head informing him that any interference would be considered an invasion of privacy. Every time Aubrey moved to try and get a better look at what might be going on at the tail end of things, she insisted on moving with him, always facing him, her mood becoming increasingly truculent. Finally in utter exasperation, he slipped back out of the door, pretending to shut it and then peering through the partial opening. Confident that the prying eyes had gone, Petunia turned and went back to her business, whatever that was. That was when he saw not only the remains of the water bag but also a single foot protruding from her rump. A single foot? Then where was the other one? There were supposed to be two, right? He racked his brains trying to remember the diagrams in his book, though somehow they did not look quite as confusing as this. It was no good; he would have to get involved. But what should be the next move?

Now, all the books and articles he had ever read counseled him not to move too quickly. But what was "too quickly"? She had been playing around now for about four hours. Well, he would have to talk it out with a wife who had set her heart on going to the costume party; a wife who had not read any of the material on calving—this being early days in her agricultural career, a time when she was maddeningly ambivalent about her involvement in agriculture.

Sabine was surprisingly amenable. Why not go up to the barn together and take another look? Then if it was necessary, which it would not be, they could call the vet, which they would not have to do. Sabine was quite confident that Aubrey had misread the situation, that Petunia would probably be nursing a beautiful little calf by now.

"Maybe we should change into some work clothes?" said Aubrey, not terribly confident about working on a distressed cow while dressed in a pig suit. Sabine smelled a rat. Her husband was angling to get out of going to the party, the devious coward.

"No, no, there's no need to do that," she said. "After all, we're just going up to take a quick look, aren't we?"

"As you wish," said Aubrey heavily and about ready to rip that damn tail right out of his suit. They headed up to the barn together. "Thank God it's only minus one," he said by way of conversation.

"I'd better not get disgustingly dirty," warned Sabine, now second-guessing the wisdom of coming up here in costume. What if there really was a problem?

The moment they entered the barn, two things were instantly obvious. One, Petunia did not have a beautiful little calf nursing at her side. Two, her attitude had soured demonstrably, perhaps because there were now two weirdly-dressed human beings apparently interested in interjecting themselves into her business. It was as if she dared them to come and make their examination. Aha, make an examination he would, but not on her terms, thought Aubrey. She would have to be coaxed quietly into the head-gate at which point he could take a more reasoned scientific approach at checking out what was going on. One thing was certain; they were way over what the book stated was a reasonable amount of time before intervening.

Armed with a bucket of chop, he made his way cautiously over to the head-gate, not one of those commercial wonders that snapped shut on the cow as soon as she ventured near it, but a homemade contraption where you had to pull on a rope when the cow put her head into it, hoping that the dog clicked into place to prevent any reversal of fortune.

"Come over here and pull on the rope as soon as Petunia puts her head through it," Aubrey instructed his now very hesitant wife.

Maybe it was Sabine's attire that held Petunia back. A bright scarlet toque over her hair, a beige, or was it azure jumpsuit splattered liberally with large maroon polka dots, her red bulbous nose that for some reason she had elected to leave in place, and a pair of Aubrey's giant gumboots spray-painted a gaudy yellow and sporting ladybug stickers all over them. At any rate, Petunia hung back, giving Sabine time to get into place.

Aubrey's initial attempts to maneuver Petunia into the head-gate were singularly unsuccessful, but then his maneuvering was taking place over too much distance. It was a remote control sort of thing in that neither Sabine nor Aubrey was physically in the pen with the animal. Trouble was, the cow knew that she intimidated her handlers, and she intended to make the most of it. That was, until the moment that Aubrey's temper raised its ugly head.

"We're not gonna stay here all bloody night playing waltzing Matilda with you," he shouted suddenly. Armed with his "extreme measures motivator", the short length of 2x4 that he had used with Matata, he climbed into the pen with her. Sabine, although now terrified about what could happen, knew enough not to say anything. Petunia put her head down and charged; there was no bluff to this move, not this time. Aubrey connected her as hard across the muzzle as he dared, side stepping as he did so. Petunia stopped dead, a puzzled expression on her face. The move had been pure self-defense on Aubrey's part, but it had the desired effect. If Petunia had decided to get really aggressive at this juncture, she could have easily rolled and stomped on her master, but she didn't. She just stood there like a child who has discovered that every father has a point of no return. She shook her head a couple of times, more perplexed than angry, and then walked calmly over to the head-gate. She stuck her head tentatively through it and began munching contentedly on the chop. Sabine pulled on the rope and Petunia was secure.

"You could easily have hurt her," said Sabine accusingly.

"Could have," Aubrey agreed, "and would have if she hadn't cooperated. But then again, she wanted to hurt me, so don't worry about it. Anyway, she now knows who's the boss."

"What do we do now?"

"We check her out. We try to figure out what is going on inside her. Pass me that plastic glove in the ice cream bucket up on the shelf and the bottle of mineral oil."

"What's the oil for?"

"Well, the book says to put on a glove, coat it with oil, and then conduct an internal inspection of the cow." Aubrey was paraphrasing the book now. At least he had possessed the gumption to buy these things ahead of time and have them available, thought his wife.

"What do you want me to do?"

"Right now, nothing. Oh, hang on a second; you can hold her tail to one side so that it doesn't get in the way."

"I thought you said I wasn't going to get dirty," she complained, as she gingerly grabbed the tail.

"Look dear, if it bothers you, take your clothes off. Or do you want to run down to the house and change?"

"Oh, go ahead," she snapped.

This was the moment that she discovered that the cow's tail answers to no man nor woman for that matter. It suddenly swished out of her grip, splattering generous green flecks of fresh manure over both of them.

"Aubrey Hanlon," she said between gritted teeth, "you are an unmitigated bastard." She lunged for the errant tail, caught it, and held it tight.

"Just look at it as a giant exercise in character-building," mumbled Aubrey. In the circumstances, it was not the best thing to say to somebody who has a longer memory than any elephant, someone who could hold a grudge longer than any camel. He plunged his hand deep into the cow, a move that was truly character-building on his own part. It was all quite mushy inside but he finally felt a leg and then another and maybe, maybe, was that another? One thing was for sure, it was downright chaos in there as far as he was concerned. Everything seemed to be intertwined.

"I'm going to call the vet," he announced. "Or do you want to have a go and see what you can feel?" he asked Sabine, a token gesture really because he knew she would be revolted.

"Sure. You come and hold the tail. Thanks to you, I'm already covered in cow poop, what's a bit more among friends? Have you got another glove?"

"In the box, over there by the door."

Sabine went right to it, not an instant of hesitation. She too felt legs, "millions of them" she said, and then a head, or no, was it....? No it was a head, had to be a head, didn't it? "Hold on, hold on a sec," she cried out excitedly, "I've found its penis. It has to be a penis. It's a little boy. Petunia's going to have a little boy."

"I think we should call the vet," said Aubrey imposing his authority on her misplaced jubilation. He did not want this to turn out like one of those high school biology experiments he recalled, his wife on her own wayward journey of scientific exploration that would probably lead to a totally incomprehensible result. "Do you want to go down to the house and phone him, or shall I?"

"You go. I don't know who he is."

"Well, you hang on up here with the cow in case there are any further developments. The book says you should pull a calf downwards by the way." Surprisingly, she had no trouble with that.

Aubrey was agreeably surprised to hear the vet's voice almost immediately after he dialed the number and said he lived on McGregor's old place. God bless Alexander Graham Bell.

"Well, actually, I live just down the way from there. I've just come back from a C-section down at Fred Kosinski's. So what's the problem, laddie?"

Aubrey so enjoyed listening to the man's Scottish accent, he almost forgot to respond. "Well, we're kind of new at this game, so keep that in mind. We have a cow that has been trying to calve since, oh about lunchtime or so."

"And why didn't you call sooner?" the voice gently admonished him.

"I said we're new at this game."

"Okay laddie, now have you checked her oot? Have you had a wee look at what's going on?"

"Well yes. She's in the head-gate as we speak."

"And?"

"Well, to be perfectly honest, I haven't a clue what I'm supposed to be looking for. But my wife reckons that she can find… oh, it doesn't matter."

"Can find what? What doesn't matter?"

"Well, she says, she says she can feel a penis." Aubrey regretted it as soon as he said it.

"A what? What did you say?" the voice asked incredulously.

"I know it sounds funny, but she says she felt a penis."

"Oh dearie me, oh dear, oh dear. You folks need all the help you can get. I'll be there in five minutes. Have a bucket of hot water ready and a couple of drams of good Scotch handy."

Back at the barn, Sabine was now in sole charge of a world that neither she nor her husband understood fully. When Aubrey had gone out of the door, she had reinserted her hand into the cow. Yes, there were plenty of legs all right. And yes, there it was, a penis. But now where had the head gone, the one she had felt before? She pushed her hand in further, as far as it would go. The whole thing became even more incomprehensible. She came back to a leg. It kicked.

"He kicked," she squealed with delight. "He kicked. Oh Aubrey, my love, hurry up with that vet, our little fellah is still alive."

As she withdrew her arm, a great glob of amniotic fluid came with it to drop mostly into her left boot, an occurrence that should, by rights, have sent her into some sort of yuppie hysteria save for the fact that Petunia posted a mighty contraction coupled with an agonized bellow. Maternity and motherhood seem to elicit their own form of mutual understanding and empathy between females that by virtue of what they are, exclude the male. This understanding, this empathy, has no trouble crossing over to another species. Sabine found herself almost heaving in tandem with the cow as if to take on some of the load. She launched into a "coaching monologue", alternately coaxing and caressing her patient whose response was to quiet right down. Petunia sensed, somehow knew, that she was in good hands, while Sabine never did figure out how long Aubrey had been gone, so engrossed was she in what she was doing.

Aubrey met the vet at the gate, Doctor Gordon Clark, an unrepentant Scotsman with a fiery reputation. And like everyone else, Aubrey had heard the story, too. "Ye look like a wee haggis, ye smell like a wee haggis, and be damned if ye dinnae dance like a bloody big haggis too," was the apocryphal line yelled out by the good vet's wife as she endured his attempt at the Eightsome Reel at the last Robbie Burns night. She too was vintage Scot, Edinburgh rock, she claimed with pride. Apparently, the doctor had just grinned and poured himself another double malt, his way of trying to improve his waltzing capability with his wife.

It was pitch dark by this time, with no moon to lessen the blackness. The good doctor's headlights picked up a man standing by at the gate holding a bucket of steaming water. "What the hell is that laddie wearing for God's sake?" he asked himself aloud. "Be damned if he hasn't got a tail and all!" He drove on up to the barn.

He grabbed his calving equipment from the passenger side of the truck and stepped out just as Aubrey came up. "So your wee wifey had a hold of a penis, you say?" he addressed Aubrey, the faintest of smiles on his face, a smile that expanded as he registered the entirety of the pig suit.

"Well neither one of us has ever done this before so we really don't know what we are doing."

"I gathered that, laddie. I gathered that. Gordon Clark, at your service."

"Aubrey. Aubrey Hanlon. Thank you very much for coming out," he added as he ushered the venerable doctor into the barn.

Doctor Clark always said that he would never forget the sight that greeted him; a perfect story for his memoirs if he ever got around to writing them, was his immediate thought. If James Herriot could make a fortune from his experiences, then dammit, so could he, so could he. In the dim light given off by a single bulb, he was presented with the picture of a woman dressed, well, like a clown—at least that was what he got from the scarlet toque on her head, the red bulbous nose, and the polka dot suit down to the technicolour yellow gumboots with the giant red ladybugs on them. The woman was so focused on the birthing process, she did not even hear them enter. Indeed, he actually saw her heave when the cow heaved, heard her groan when the cow groaned.

"So you got yersel' a hold of a vital organ, did you?" he announced his presence.

Sabine gave a start and jumped back from the cow, the goop in her boot sploshing as she did so. Only now did it dawn on her how she was dressed. The realization left her totally speechless, rooted to the spot.

"Gordon Clark," he proffered his hand. "And you must be Coco," his eyes twinkled.

"Sabine Hanlon," she said numbly.

"Well, if ye'll step aside lassie, I'll take a look myself." From here on, he was all business. He pulled a glove from his coveralls pocket, oiled it liberally and inserted his hand into the cow's vulva. "Aye," he grunted. "I thought so. Ye've got yourselves a set of twins, that's the problem. A wee bit tied up, you might say, but both of them are still alive at least. Now get yourself over here lassie, and let me show you."

Sabine's total embarrassment was completely forgotten as she was ordered to put her hand back into the cow while the doctor explained what she might be feeling.

"Aye. And you won't find that penis again, let me tell you, because that penis was probably a tail. The one is coming backwards, the other is underneath coming forward. Trouble is, the wee 'un on top has got one back leg facing the wrong way." Sabine said that she thought she could visualize what the vet was saying. Aubrey didn't even get in on the lesson.

"Time to get the wee 'uns out," said Dr. Clark as Sabine retracted her hand. She watched in fascination as he pulled a set of calving chains from his coveralls. Expertly he manipulated the baby to a satisfactory position. "Aye, you've got a set of twins all right. The first one we'll pull out is backwards. Here, pull on this chain someone." Sabine was there before Aubrey had even registered what the vet had said.

First one back foot appeared, then another. "See how the feet point downwards. That should tell a person that the wee one is backwards." Without more ado, Dr. Clark pulled together with Sabine and out popped a beautiful brindle calf to drop with a thud in the straw. Its panting announced a healthy set of lungs. "Now it's your turn laddie," he directed Aubrey. "Stick a piece of straw in its nostrils and clear its mouth. That'll really get the breathing going." Sabine was right there before Aubrey could even take a step. Dr. Clark sighed. "Ach, that young lassie of yours wants to do it all. Okay, come and give me a hand with the second one. That lassie of yours is just too quick for you."

Once again the vet went in and hooked the calving chain on the front feet of the remaining twin. "Hang on to that lad, and pull like hell when I tell you. I'll keep an eye on the head." He seemed to do some further manipulation, then came the call to heave.

Aubrey, charged with a desire to do his part, and saddled with the enthusiasm of inexperience, heaved with all his strength.

"Steady on lad, steady on. This is no brick you're pulling on; it's a live animal." Gradually, the legs came out. "Now pull downwards lad, downwards." A lolling tongue appeared, then a nose.

"It's dead, isn't it? The damn thing's dead," Aubrey bleated in exasperation, fully primed to take it out on his self. That's when a large eye opened and appeared to look him over in a sort of dazed curiosity.

"He's no dead, just having a last wee nap before coming into the world," said Dr. Clark. Further downward pressure eased the calf out on to the straw where it was subjected to the same care and attention as its twin.

"Now, did you remember the whisky, laddie?" asked the vet.

"Well yes, but it's only half a bottle," said Aubrey wondering why he would be wasting it on a cow. Or maybe he intended to stimulate the calves somehow.

"Good lad. A man after my own heart. Okay, thanks for the water by the way." He walked over to the bucket, washed his hands thoroughly, as if he was about to do some surgery, and then reached for the bottle. He unscrewed the cap and put the bottle to his lips taking a large gulp. "Medicinal purposes, medicinal purposes. Here help yourself to a wee dram." Before Aubrey could react, Sabine took the proffered bottle from the vet's hand.

"My Lord, but you're a lassie with some spirit," he commented. He bent over the second calf, pronounced it to be destined for greatness, and made his closing remarks. "Unfortunately, I've got to run; otherwise, I'd be finishing the whisky among new friends. I can see the wee 'uns are in good hands. Now, let the cow out and leave her be. She'll know what to do. Good night to the both of you, and may your circus always have a clown." He winked and was gone.

Aubrey went over to the head-gate and released the catch. Petunia backed out like an express train, turned on a dime, smelled both babies, and immediately began to lick them—first one and then the other. Aubrey and Sabine were hooked, permanently, on the miracle of childbirth.

"How can any costume party come up to this?" Sabine whispered, flicking a piece of straw off one very soiled clown suit as they left Petunia to do what she knew best.

Chapter Nine
CHEAP LABOUR, RAW ENTERTAINMENT

It was inevitable, really, inevitable that such urban stereotypes as Aubrey and Sabine would hold a curious fascination for their city friends when they abandoned the pulsing, frenetic flow of the city for the turgid waters of the boondocks. Most of their kindred city folk saw it as a move so alien it was as if Aubrey and Sabine had "gone native" or suddenly turned to naturism or something. Some of them secretly envied the couple their courage, especially those who saw themselves as trapped by image, career, marriage, inertia, or a combination of them all. Others felt obliged to counsel them in case there was an underlying psychiatric or psychological need they had all missed. Others again applauded them for following their dream, however bizarre and far-fetched that dream seemed to be. And in the early years on the farm in particular, many of them contrived a visit to see if this romanticism and "going back to nature" was all that it was cut out to be, although some of them had rather a tenuous grasp on what nature actually was.

Aubrey very quickly realized that here was a ready source of cheap labour and raw entertainment, given their skill level. It also assured him of a welcome, if sporadic, replenishing of his wine stocks, although it seemed that consumption readily kept pace with supply, for nobody ever showed up from the city without a sample of its bounty—the fruits of the local liquor store. Most of the men-folk demonstrated an enthusiastic need to role play machismo; in lieu of suits and ties and uniforms, they strutted about in western gear, primed and ready "to get on down and lasso some of them dogies."

For Sigmund, the professional trumpet player with the Edmonton Symphony Orchestra, it was the roar of the tractor and the reek of diesel that put him in macho heaven. Siggy's wife Sybil, on the other hand, was never happier than when she could return to her hippy roots of muslin and seersucker, which tended to put rather too much of a now homely silhouette on show, but that was Sybil. Her passion was to dig a bit in the garden, don a red apron and go collect the eggs six times a day, harvest and can fresh beets; all the things she would have done had she made it to the commune or the kibbutz to which she had always aspired. Then there was Ernest "the mechanic" who loved to put his considerable technical knowledge into tinkering with Aubrey's machinery, an area in which he could only do more good than harm, given the antiquity of it all. His wife, Mavis, was a self-confessed bookworm whose sole motivation for accompanying her husband to the farm was so that she could sequester herself away from "all that noise." Most of what she read seemed to go by weight for she never had a book that was less than a thousand pages. Rarely did anyone know she was there, that is until the first wine bottle was uncorked. Mavis was more than partial to a glass of white wine. Then there was the garrulous Dick Conley, a displaced, many said a misplaced, Brit and all-the-time-party-man. Indeed, he was such a party man that his wife had long since sought more serene pastures where she did not have to witness her husband's latest virtuoso performance. Dick, Mister Conley, threw himself into whatever was currently being done, usually with much pranksterism and always with too much gusto. Nellie, for one, had no love for the man. Every time he appeared, she angled to get him into a corner; the only female of any species that deliberately followed such a strategy. There was a delightful French-Canadian couple, Jean-Claude et Pierrette Moreau. He was the cerebral type ever needing to know the dynamics of why; she was the consummate chef who came down to cook and make noise at every get-together.

Ah yes, the labour may have been cheap, but when you factored in what the likes of a hungry Dick Conley could eat and drink, coupled with the cost of repairing the swather after he had rubbed noses with an unyielding fence post, the equation was not so one-sided. Yet when all was said and done, Aubrey and Sabine always finished up on the plus side of the ledger, and they never lacked for lively company, especially on long weekends. Jobs that required bodies, preferably those jobs requiring more brawn than brain, were deliberately scheduled for such occasions. Branding and vaccinating, chicken plucking and dressing, weaning the calves or bringing the herd home from pasture, all went so much better with additional manpower. Various individuals became very skilled at certain tasks. Sig always came down in the spring to do field work; that became "his territory". Dick Conley became "master of the squeeze", able to work the head-gate on vaccination day like any professional cowhand. And it was Ernest who figured out the best possible seeding pattern for sowing grain so that Aubrey could avoid all those unsightly "misses" that all the neighbours chuckled at.

One of the yearly activities that went on to become an annual tradition was "the chicken harvest", as Mister Conley called it. He would not miss the occasion for the world, especially seeing that he had cast himself in the role of The Lord High Executioner. Sig, the musician, never missed it either because he literally slavered after free-range chicken. His wife Sybil, far from being the probable squeamish airhead flower girl everybody expected her to be, turned out to have by far the best credentials. Having grown up on an acreage in the country, she was the one who showed Sabine how to draw and then dress a freshly butchered chicken. It was amazing how this changed the perceptions that people had of Sybil: far from being seen as no more than a flighty butterfly, here was someone who possessed down to earth practical skills that even the men around her would have preferred not to know; someone who also got down to business without any great fanfare. Moreover, she quickly made it clear that she brooked no sloppy plucking, that was until Ernie went and sabotaged that aspect of the whole operation.

The first year that Aubrey and Sabine raised meat chickens on shares with their city friends, the "execution day" was nothing short of a riotous affair. The Saturday morning breakfast saw a lively discussion about how to dispatch the chickens to Conley's "Chickie Heaven" as humanely as possible. The consensus settled on a chopping block with Mister C wielding an axe, a skill with which he insisted he needed no direction. It turned out that his sense of direction was rather more wayward than he boasted, which was no consolation for the first bird on the block.

"I just can't do this very well when the intended victim is watching me go about my business," said Mister Conley apologetically. "Maybe we should put a paper bag over the next one's head, kinda like a blindfold."

But Ernie the mechanic had seen enough. "I'll head on into town and pick up some beer, anything to avoid this. I'll even pay double for my share of the chickens. How's that?" Ernie's wife, Mavis, had long since announced that she had no desire to play her part, any part, in such primordial activities. She had isolated herself somewhere out front with Anna Karenina.

Sigmund arrived with the next chicken; one that had contrived to excrete forcefully up his sleeve upon capture. A great big ten-pound rooster, its action had not endeared him to his captor whose efforts to solicit sympathy only elicited ribald laughter. It was at this precise moment that every living thing around, including the chicken, was startled by an outburst of song in an admittedly very striking baritone voice.

"Defer, defer, to The Lord High Executioner. Defer, defer, to The Lord High Executioner!"

"Holy kamoly, can that boy ever sing," Siggy burst out. "Where'd someone like you ever learn to sing like that?" The chicken was impressed enough to void the rest of its bowels up Sig's sleeve, but he was too astonished to notice.

"Don't fool! Someone like me learned to sing many moons ago. 'The Mikado', twice. 'The Pirates of Penzance'. 'Oklahoma'. And now 'The Best Little Slaughterhouse on the Prairie.'" Again he burst forth. "Okla, Okla, Oklahoma where the wind comes howling down the plain, where the girls are freaks.... C'mon Sig, bring forward the next candidate for knighthood, there's a good lad. This one shall be dubbed 'Lord Cretin of Shawinigan.'"

Unhappily, Lord Cretin did not fare much better than the first candidate because the paper bag obscured a clean line of attack. It was decided that they should pluck the dead birds and rethink strategy.

Mister Conley was off again. "My father was a pheasant plucker, and I am a pheasant plucker's son," he intoned. Siggy, on the other hand, was still standing there incredulously, seemingly unaware of the chicken manure seeping from his sleeve. If ever there was a seasoned and versatile musician, he was it, and he knew a fine voice when he heard one. What if he could talk this crazy Englishman into doing some choral work with the Edmonton Symphony Orchestra? But then, would he have the necessary discipline? But then again, with a voice as fine as that at stake, the E.S.O. conductor would put up with a lot.

"Tell me more about your singing," Sig said to Dick. "What have you done? What else have you played in?"

"Don't you start getting any ideas, my boy. I've already got enough on me plate without getting dragooned into Beethoven's Ninth, though truth be told, I wouldn't mind a shot at that some day." That he had plenty on his plate was probably true because everybody present knew that he was some kind of big wheel in criminal investigation, although nobody knew exactly what.

"Oh, so you've been approached before, I take it?" said Sig, openly disappointed.

"More than once, my son, more than once. Let me say this to you, Sir Aubrey, such pleasant peasant pheasant plucking is for the birds, don't you think?" Clearly the conversation was not destined for a deep discussion of arias and high notes. And even more clearly, the plucking of the two chickens was not going as smoothly as Aubrey and Sabine had envisaged it would. Some of the larger feathers stubbornly resisted removal, and when one or more of the unskilled workers became over-zealous, the skin would tear. Sybil seemed to be the only person with any knack. Trying to save face for the men, and trying more particularly to ensure that the end, dressed product did not too much resemble something that had been through the Iran-Iraq war, she elected to finish up the two that they had been working on. This released the men to go and catch another pair.

"We've got to do something different," Sabine said when the men were out of earshot. "These first two birds are so ragged they will probably have to be stewed."

Decapitation continued to be a bit of a hit-and-miss affair, primarily because Mister Conley saw no need to relinquish his role as "chief dispenser of summary justice", not that there would have been any takers for the job anyway. The business of plucking went from being a novel experience to a laborious chore. To make it worse, wasps and bees and other assorted insects were now attracted to the savory smells that accompany any outdoor butchery. Mister Conley suddenly chose to announce that he wasn't sure if he was allergic to bee stings, a clear attempt to set up an escape clause as far as the others were concerned, and they let him know it. Progress was slow, but progress was being made nonetheless, albeit haphazardly. That is, until Ernie showed up with a raft of cold beer, which he generously began dispensing to the plucking crew. The more serious-minded Sabine and Sybil declined any refreshment since they were both working with sharp knives. From there on, quality control somehow took a back seat to a loud camaraderie; as the noise level increased, so productivity decreased. Not only productivity, but efficiency also. The next two chickens coming from the pluckers could only be charitably described as "bedraggled". Sybil pronounced them to be "a spectacular mess". Evidently her sense of diplomacy had fled along with her patience.

Ernest, custodian of cold beer and good cheer, now saw his primary role as keeping the chicken pluckers "lubricated"; maybe his way of salving a guilty conscience for not doing any plucking himself . Whatever the motivation, certainly he dispensed his stores with great generosity and goodwill. The net result was that the next pair of chickens was even more bedraggled, while the pair after that was simply disastrous.

"Looks like a couple of porcupines with a lousy barber," Sybil grumbled to Sabine. Then, quite spontaneously, she lowered the boom on them all. Mild, homely Sybil shut down the whole operation with a vehemence not to be trifled with. Mild-mannered hippy type was replaced with fire-breathing dragon. Even Siggy was all set to make a run for it, only ever having seen her like this the once, when he had run over her youthful backpack with a ten ton truck that he was driving for a living in the early days of their courtship. Probably because there was still a flicker of interest left on her part, her enthusiasm for him only barely outweighed the flattened contents of the backpack; it was a near thing. Here and now, she said, the problem was that there were still another thirty-eight or so chickens to go.

Aubrey had blessed a number of his neighbours many times. Once again, Pete and his wife Jeannie were the "recipients of his beneficence" when they arrived for a social visit. Of course, they would have received a more deluxe blessing had they arrived with their knowledge a few hours earlier.

"So, you're killing a few chickens I see," said Pete. "We won't stay and get in your way, then."

"No, no. Stay and have a beer with us and meet our friends from the big city. Let's just say that we have not been progressing as well as we should have, so we are shutting it down for today. Going back to the drawing board, you might say."

"Oh Lordy be," sputtered Mrs. Pete when she spotted a couple of the finished products. "You'll never make a chicken plucker with shoddy work like that, none of you."

"My father was a pheasant plucker, and I am a pheasant plucker's son," Mister Conley intervened solemnly.

"Ach, away with you, pheasant plucker indeed! Aubrey, how many more chickens do you folks have to do?"

"Well, fifty minus twelve, I guess. That makes thirty-eight," he finished heavily. "Enough to keep this crew busy for three weeks. We had intended to do them all this weekend but we don't seem to be that good at it, none of us except Sybil."

Jeannie looked knowingly at her husband. "Ach, we'll have to come down and show you how to do it right, won't we dear?"

"That we can, and we'll have time to have a brew with you too, but not today, tomorrow. By the way, we'll need a small stack of firewood before we can start." As if Ernie needed further invitation to go and start the chainsaw and put it to work to redeem a somewhat soiled reputation.

The next morning saw everybody on a parade that was meant to be a parade. Ernie had had all night to come up with the conviction that the swather was in urgent need of a full service, so regretfully he would not be available. His wife had now embraced a mighty tome by Alexander Solzhenitsyn, so she had done the wise thing and removed herself as far away from the hustle and bustle of chicken plucking as she could get. She would cook the supper, she said. Pete and Jeannie arrived with, oh wonder of mechanical wonders, an industrial age chicken plucker driven by an electric motor and a mammoth tin tub on legs. Like the seasoned campaigners they were, they had the whole show up and running in no time. The tub was filled with water, a roaring fire burning underneath. And the diminutive

Jeannie took control, making sure that everybody knew about and became familiar with every step when killing and dressing a chicken.

"Take your selves a good look at this, ladies and gentlemen," she called when she produced a container of product called "KwikPik". "Now your plucking will be a piece of cake, and there'll be no need for there to be any pin feathers sticking out of any chicken's rump, will there Mister Pheasant Plucker's son?" There was no doubting the message; even the pheasant plucker's son deemed it politically wise not to respond. She measured the requisite amount of magic powder and threw it into the water. "Time to go catch a chicken," she said, with a twinkle in her eye.

Pete had not allowed Aubrey to stand around idly. The tractor had been rigged up with five thin pieces of rope hanging from the teeth of the bucket. The execution of each chicken was quick and without undue stress, the chickens bleeding out fully as they now hung headless and upside down from the loader. The plucking part was as Jeannie had said it would be: a piece of cake, with Mister C even showing some signs of becoming an expert. The thirty-eight chickens were gone in three hours. Ernie appeared only the once, apparently intent on sabotaging the operation again with his need for "further lubrication". Jeannie sent him packing. He and his beer were publicly banned for the duration of chicken plucking, and if he should come back whining about further lubrication, Jeannie would personally empty a grease gun in his ear.

"What, what er, do we er, owe you?" said Aubrey hesitantly when they finally settled down to a bottle of Ernie's largesse. There was almost an involuntary stiffening on the part of the audience.

"Well," said Pete slowly, "it costs around $35 for World Vision to give a couple of live chickens to a needy family in Africa so that they can raise their own poultry. How about a donation of $35 to World Vision?"

"Thirty-five dollars!" Dick burst out. "Thirty-five dollars. Heck, why not thirty-five dollars per couple? That'll give you four sets of chickens. Jeez, it was worth thirty-five dollars not to have to do the chickens the way we were doing them yesterday." Then came the realization that he had just volunteered the thirty-five dollars from the other couples without even asking. "That's if it's all right with the others," he finished lamely. He need not have worried. They had all had a nightmare reduced to something less than a bad dream, and since they had planned for this exercise to be an annual occasion, they all agreed to contribute to somebody else's welfare; that is, if they could borrow the tub and the mechanical plucker every year, stated the cunning Mister Conley.

"Ach, for that price, you might as well throw us in, too," said Jeannie. "That's of course if you want us," she added feeling very gratified.

"How about a pair of chickens for the use of the plucker and another pair for our services, then everybody goes home happy?" Pete was not one to give the store away to a yappy Englishman. The deal was struck, and everybody felt good into the bargain.

Of course, Aubrey and Sabine and their friends alike soon learned to pay attention to that standard caveat in farming: "Make sure that nobody is watching if you are going to put on a show," if you don't want an audience, that is. Now in the era of the video camera, the last thing one needs is to be caught in full colour in a performance never intended for public consumption. Sigmund learned this lesson first-hand one day when he had come down with Sybil for the weekend to do "a spot of baling for therapy." Sig was one of those types so entranced with forward motion and diesel fumes that looking back now and again to see what might be happening with the implement tended to be an afterthought at best. Besides, he was first and foremost a musician, and musicians could easily float off into another world when they can plug in their favorite music. He was pulling an old New Holland chain baler that Aubrey had picked up for two hundred and seventy dollars at an auction. He figured that if he could ever get it going, he would use it for a backup if his main baler broke down. Sig and Ernie had taken up the challenge, and with a bit of welding here and a couple of bearings there, the monstrosity ran like a dream.

So there he was, Sig the musician—beach shirt and shorts, the very latest in stylish sun-glasses, favorite ball cap on his head, tattered sandals on his feet—comfortably ensconced in the tractor cab, reverberating to the opening strains of Sibelius's "Karelia Suite". The baler had been working well, and the bales, although not beautiful, were very acceptable; the old chain balers just could not make an aesthetic-looking bale according to Pete. But this time, Sig was at one with the crescendo, and nothing, least of all a baler, could come between him and his crescendo. Sig just kept on going when he should have stopped.

The sudden straining of the tractor engine coincided with a quiet segment following the crescendo, and only then did Sigmund realize that he was in some trouble. He stopped everything and got out to take a look. Damn, of course he had to be in full view of the bay window of the sitting room. Oh, but they would be about other business, wouldn't they? Nobody would have the time, let alone the inclination to watch what he was about now, would they? Wrong! "They"—Sabine and Aubrey, and Dick Conley who was also down for the weekend—had decided to stop what they were doing and have a cup of afternoon tea.

"Can't pass four o'clock in the afternoon without a cuppa, that would be sacrilege," pronounced Mister Conley who had spent most of his afternoon filming "Scenes of Pastoral Bliss" with his friends, Mr. And Mrs. Hanlon, courtesy of his brand new video camera. Sybil, Sig's wife, was off on her own somewhere, "probably conducting a séance among the ducks," suggested Dick unkindly.

"Sig must be having a problem. He's stopped," commented Sabine staring through the drapes of the front window. All eyes looked towards the field.

"Damn fool has got himself an oversize bale," said Aubrey surprisingly unconcerned. "It will be interesting to see how he goes about dealing with it. He's going to have quite a job getting it out." Aubrey would know; he had done the same thing the previous week, and it had almost killed him getting the bale out. He had eventually had to tow it out with a second tractor.

Sig, on the other hand, had never encountered an oversize bale before, had never even given it a thought. But damn it, he was mad with himself. Why hadn't he been paying attention? After he had made his examination, he climbed back into the tractor and opened the gate of the baler to maximum. The enormous mess of hay stayed resolutely in the bale chamber.

"Damn! Damn! And be damned!" he yelled at the top of his lungs. He jumped back out of the tractor and tried tugging at the bale with his bare hands; he might just as well have been pulling on the Canadian Shield, for all the effect he had. And in his frustration, he grabbed a clump full of thistles, which really made him hop. Oh, but he was mad! He pulled the cap off the top of his head, that favorite cap given to him by Willie Pless of the Edmonton Eskimos football team, threw it to the ground and began stomping on it. That was when Dick Conley began filming, but of course he had the zoom set to the widest possible angle. The episode was over before he could zoom in on the action.

"Please Lord, let him do that again," he breathed, making sure that only his lens was showing through the curtains; it wouldn't do to give the game away

Sig clambered back into the cab. The ensuing puff of smoke indicated that he was about to move. He went round in a wide circle, braking hard at intervals in a vain attempt to dislodge the bale out of the machine. The bale was steadfast. They watched him climb out of the cab once again, watched him tug uselessly on the bale, saw him reach for his cap and stomp the hell out of it one more time before picking it up and putting it back on his head. He then seemed to rummage around in the tractor for a minute or so before emerging with a crow bar. They watched him stand on the baler wheel and try to lever the bale out with the bar. They saw him overbalance and fall flat on his back on the ground. He leapt to his feet and the whole stomping routine unfolded once more. At this juncture, he disappeared for five minutes, time for his audience to disengage and go foraging disappointedly for another cup of tea. Just as they were about to give up on any further developments, there was their Sig striding manfully across the field, an axe over his shoulder. Evidently he had come down to the garden shed in search of a tool more effective than a crowbar.

Sigmund laid about that bale with a zest that was awesome to behold. Shreds of hay flew off in every direction, but no movement occurred. The bale, now beginning to look as if a plague of mice had been attending a nibble-fest upon it, remained stubbornly in place. This prompted a further and wilder jig upon the cap and another walk down to the garden shed. This time, they saw Sig striding purposefully across the field with the chainsaw in hand. Seemingly, he had some initial problems starting it, too, because the cap took yet another stomping, but finally the motor caught. Sig set about that bale as if he was engaged in mortal combat. First he did his cutting on the far side and then reappeared to begin cutting on the near side. The chain caught on something, probably a root, and stalled, the bar still stuck firmly in the core of the bale. Try as he did, Sig could not budge that saw; it was there for keeps. His cap endured a sustained onslaught this time so that when it made the trip back to his head, it was so covered in dust and chaff that it started a spate of itching that drove him into a state of near apoplexy. Dick Conley was laughing so hard that Sabine was forced to take over the camera to ensure everything was properly recorded for posterity.

It was now that Sybil suddenly appeared in the bottom left-hand corner of the viewfinder. Dressed in a breezy summer getup of shorts and light blouse, she seemed intent on heading over to her husband to see what his problem might be. But unfortunately for her, this was also the year of the grasshopper. They were everywhere and fluttered and jumped away from her every step in a continuous stream. Clearly, Sybil was not very comfortable around (or perhaps with) them, but she was stoic in her resolve to see what calamity had befallen her mate. "The biggest grasshopper you ever saw" contrived at this point to somehow land down her blouse when she was some twenty yards out from the tractor. Her shriek of terror could assuredly have been heard in downtown Saskatoon. Sig turned his head to see his wife frantically ripping away her blouse. Mistaking this as some new wrinkle in the mating game, he came to life, tearing off his own shirt in abandon as he came bounding towards her. She on the other hand had absolutely no eyes for him, concerned as she was with "a grasshopper the size of a bloody locust" that was exerting considerable energy trying to exit the lacy bra that Sybil was hastily removing in her panic.

Sabine was later to claim that she switched off the camera in the interests of Sybil's modesty. Mister Conley insisted that she had switched it off to spite him. Whatever the case, the subject couple exited centre stage like a pair of demented creatures, she yelling shrilly for him "to get away from me you bloody sex maniac. You're worse than the bloody grasshopper." Her laughter hinted at the prospect of a more thrilling conclusion down by the duck house.

Chapter Ten
CONFESSION TO MAKE

*T*hanksgiving! Just another holiday, a long weekend, an escape from the grind of work, work, work: at least that was how Aubrey and Sabine had always viewed it in the city. As with so many of their fellow travelers, any religious significance essentially passed them by. Far from seeing the day as a celebration of their bounty, they generally saw it as their last chance to eat, drink, and be merry before the cold, harsh reality of winter set in. The days had shortened, the leaves had pretty well all gone from the trees, and the changing of the clocks to daylight savings time would soon imprison them all in their acres of neon. But down on the farm, being dependent as you are on the whims of the weather, the wiles of the growing season, the will of whichever gods you worship, you quickly realize that you are not doing it all by yourself. That bin full of barley could just as easily have been half empty, and Nellie's seven hundred pound calf could just as easily have been four hundred pounds courtesy of a bout of pneumonia or scours from a wet spring. As a farmer, you may preside over life, but you certainly do not control it, so even if you are not religious, it is perfectly natural to feel a deep sense of gratitude; a sort of visceral acknowledgment to a greater power that the harvest has been brought in safely. Of course, those who are affiliated with a church have the luxury of not needing to seek an answer; they can give thanks openly, as their beliefs dictate.

Jean-Claude and Pierrette Moreau made Thanksgiving their special day to come down to the farm. Pierrette would take command of the kitchen, and produce a Thanksgiving supper that became famous for its unique French-Canadian flavours, its mouth-watering desserts, and its free-flowing wine. Moreover, most of what was eaten was grown on the farm, as if in recognition of the day itself. If there was no room at the inn, there being only a couple of spare bedrooms in the house, no worries; there was always space in the yard for an RV or two. Dick Conley had staked out a permanent spot in the coziest corner for his battered old tent trailer, and, conveniently it was only about thirty yards from the ancient outhouse that looked as though it had served its parishioners since prehistoric times. However, apart from Aubrey who used it fairly regularly, only the intrepid and the desperate ever felt the need to use it. You had to make a point of brushing away the latest spider's web—and sometimes the spider itself—before sitting down to rewrite the constitution.

"There isn't a building on this place that is not put to some use or other," Aubrey was often heard to say, and he was right.

To digress for a moment or two, many wives really do not like to nag their husbands; too close to approaching the stereotype perhaps. But when it came that time of the year to get a Christmas tree, were it not for the constant barrage upon her husband, Sabine would be lucky to get hers by New Year's Day. Naturally, she was forced to take ownership for part of the problem because she always made "getting the tree" into something of a wilderness adventure. Aubrey would have been quite happy to spend the money and buy one from that unsavory-looking fellow set up in the back of the supermarket parking lot, or better still from the Boy Scouts, but Sabine would have none of it. "It's just not the same," she said, although Aubrey knew it was fruitless to ask, "the same as what?" This was rural Alberta, she insisted, and there were millions of small firs that were better than anything they had to pay money for.

Sabine also knew better than to send Aubrey off to look for one by his self; she knew well that he would surely chop down some scruffy-looking tree at the side of some back road. Not only would it be half-dead, it would also be covered with a fine dust from all the traffic. So, Sabine had to make a mission of it—tree-getting, that is. She would set a date and hold him to it, snow, ice, sleet, or rain. At the appointed day and time, she would make sure Aubrey was armed with his chainsaw, and she would drag him off to a place by the river where firs were plentiful but the terrain was more aptly suited to the training of winter shock troops—or to the more adventurous among the moose and deer that ventured down there.

Aubrey would always find the perfect tree within twenty yards of the truck. Not Sabine. She would tramp off into the heaviest bush in her fancy "Lady Hikers", the ones with the bright yellow laces, yelling sporadically to scare off grizzlies, mountain gorillas, Bigfoot, anything that might be interested in contesting her presence. Suddenly the tone would change. A shrill ululation of "Orby, Orby, where are you? I've got one!" would signal that she was the one who had found the perfect tree, as ever, a mile and a half from the truck by the sound of it. He was never given any say in the matter. His job was to shut up, saw, trim, and carry the tree while pine needles from all the other paltry specimens along the way dropped maddeningly down his parka. Back at the yard, science and exactitude would take over. Precise measurements needed to be taken and acted upon.

"We have to have our little angel just below ceiling height," Sabine would instruct. "It's our good luck charm. The tree has to be eight inches shorter than your measurement from floor to ceiling to leave enough space for the angel to sit on." Aubrey thought the angel was a trifle moth-eaten and frumpish, but wisely he elected to bite his tongue. What the heck, it was what was under the tree, not what was on it, that interested him the most.

Once the bare tree was in its traditional spot, in one nook of the bay window, Aubrey was banished. He had helped with decorating the tree only once, ten years ago, only to be told, "That red ball does not belong here, and that gold tinsel should be moved further round, and why are you hanging the lights like that? Don't you have any sense of balance?" Apparently not.

Christmas would come and go. The tree would be duly admired by all, and then Aubrey would be told to remove it before the thirteenth day blighted their good fortune for the next decade or half century. It would, of course, be freezing outside, so he would simply chuck the tree off the end of the deck, and there it would stay despite Sabine's entreaties that it be disposed of somewhere more out of sight. A dead Christmas tree in the yard looked so tatty, she said. It became something of a game: she ordering, carping, cajoling, begging her man to do the honourable thing, and he not getting around to it "just yet". Eventually, one year this whole performance carried on right up to Thanksgiving. Only this particular year, the train of events that unfolded convinced Aubrey that maybe there was some merit in disposing of the Christmas tree earlier in the year, after all.

Now, Aubrey had made it very clear at the outset of their venture into ducks and poultry that they were to be strictly Sabine's concern. She, on the other hand, started to need "help" with them.

"Because the numbers have gone up so drastically now that they've had so many babies," she explained. "Because the sacks of feed are so darn heavy for me to carry. Because it takes so much time to do it all properly. Because you love me."

So, curiously, Aubrey started to somehow disappear at that critical time of day. Sabine knew he was avoiding her, or rather avoiding having to help her. On some days, he would have "to fix something on the tractor's power steering," on other days, he needed to deal with a leak in some hydraulic pump, but such excuses were not good for every day.

Where was he disappearing to on those other days? When she pressed him, all he could say was, "I'm busy doing stuff. You're not the only one who does things around here, you know," and he would make a big pretense of stomping off to avoid any further inquisition.

It so happened that one day Sabine had to come back to the house from "The Cocorico Hotel", the name given to the chicken house by Pierrette. She needed another egg carton because the hens were laying like crazy at the time. Out of the corner of her eye, she caught a glimpse of her dear husband, "The Globe and Mail" in hand, exiting the outhouse. Evidently, he did not think that she had seen him because he stepped back in smartly and pulled the door to. Aha! So that's where Mister Hanlon was busy "fixing things". Well, she would fix him!

The following day, Aubrey had to go to town. Did Sabine want to come too and try a coffee at the new book boutique and internet café that had just opened up?

"No thanks, honey, I've got so much stuff I had planned to do today. Go have a coffee with Bud at the police station if he's on today. He's always so glad to see you." Aubrey set off by himself.

First, she put on her gardening gloves. She went to the end of the deck, descended the stairs, and grabbed that offending Christmas tree from last December. Now a forlorn dried-up shadow of its former glory, the needles had mostly fallen off leaving a scraggy, undignified skeleton of a tree with sharp branches sticking up all over the trunk. Very carefully, she took it over to the outhouse. Yes, with a bit of modification it would work a treat. She took it around the corner so as not to leave any visible evidence of her skullduggery, and cut it up in such a way that when she inserted it down through the seat, the branches would be positioned for a dramatic effect on whatever might choose to sit above them.

Wouldn't you know it, Aubrey actually did find some genuine repairs that needed attention over the next few evenings, and that brought them up to the Thanksgiving long weekend without Sabine seeing any action.

The guests arrived sporadically, as they always did, on the Friday evening: Sig and Sybil with a brand-new monster of an RV; Jean-Claude and Pierrette in their more modest affair; and Dick Conley in his latest "jalopy" as he called it, a 19-something Dodge Polara that should have been recycled into something more useful years ago. "The damn thing is almost bigger than me bloody tent trailer," he boasted.

"As long as your tent trailer doesn't stink like this," commented Sig, looking it over and noting the three "Fragrant Pine" air fresheners hanging from the rearview mirror.

"Well, the student fellow who sold it to me was certainly no cleanliness freak, of that I can assure you. But let me also say the Scotch Pine times three is a helluva lot better than assorted toe-jam," Dick explained. "Besides, it keeps out anybody who shouldn't be in there," he added enigmatically.

By Saturday morning, everybody was comfortably settled in. As the day wore on, the level of activity increased. By evening, Pierrette, Sybil, and Sabine had commandeered the kitchen and had cracked open the first bottle of wine. Sig was doing what Sig always enjoyed doing, finishing up a last bit of field work in the tractor, while Dick, Jean-Claude, and Aubrey had spent a couple of hours fishing, down at the river.

When they had made it back home, Aubrey decided that he had better jump on the quad and head up to the field to see how Sig was getting on.

"Well, me and Jean Chretien, here, will clean these fish while you're playing at being a farmer, eh J-C?" said Dick.

"Mais, oui, we cannot let these whitefish go to waste. But first I need to make some room in my closet."

"Room in your closet? What the hell are you talking about? You mean room in your freezer?"

"No, room in my closet. 'Ow do you Anglais put it? I need to see a little man about a big dog. I need to go to the toilette, okay?"

"Well my advice to you is to use the outhouse. Don't go into the house; those women will have you peeling potatoes and slicing carrots for them for the next two hours."

"Mon Dieu, you are so wise in the ways of women. D'accord. I am pretty dirty, anyway. Maybe it would be better for me to use the outhouse, as you say."

The howl of anguish pierced the air just as Sybil came out of the house "to check out what those men are up to." What she saw stopped her dead in her tracks, and had her wondering for a second whether she had already had too much wine on an empty stomach. There was Jean-Claude, big, burly Jean-Claude, charging out of the outhouse, slamming the door as he exited, with his pants down below his knees. And he was howling blue murder.

"What the hell is your problem?" asked Dick, the first person Jean-Claude reached some twenty yards away.

"Il.....il y a.....," pulling up his pants, "il y a .....," huffing and puffing like a moose in rut, "il y a .....there......there is a porc-epic inside......et......and he got me on.......on......la derriere," Jean-Claude panted. Since it was unlikely that J-C would encounter a porcupine very often, it was forgivable that he did not know the English word "porcupine". It was equally forgivable that Dick Conley did not know that a "porc-epic" was a porcupine in French.

"Let's see where he bit you," said Mister Conley, never known to shy away from the direct verification of evidence.

But there was no stopping Jean-Claude now. So full of righteous indignation was he that he did not even hear Dick. "I'm gonna get you, espece de cochon. I will teach you not to play with a great Acadian derriere, Monsieur Porc-epic. You're gonna have a talk with Monsieur's shotgun, mon ami!"

Dick Conley had encountered Jean-Claude in action once before, and he now knew better than to stand before a tidal wave of "fin du monde" temper. No, he would be much further ahead to stand back and let the whole thing play out as it would. "Overheated Latin temperament," he muttered to himself as he returned to de-scaling the fish. Sybil was compelled to hurry back inside and tell the others about all this unexpected excitement.

Jean-Claude knew where Aubrey kept his rifle and his shotgun, both concealed in the back of the coat closet in the boot-room. Everybody of significance knew where they were. The coyotes had to be discouraged from coming in to look for a free chicken dinner. And Aubrey had declared death to every porcupine that ventured on to the place after he had paid a four hundred dollar vet bill for the services involved in removing dozens of quills from the muzzles of five of his cows after their altercation with one of the animals.

The first shotgun blast went off just as Aubrey pulled up on the quad alongside Dick.

"What on earth is going on?" he asked, spotting Jean-Claude in typical hunter's stance, the shotgun seemingly trained on the outhouse door.

"Oh that? Jean-Claude said he got bit on the arse by Porky Pig in the outhouse. So, by the sounds of it, Porky Pig is now on his way to Porker Heaven."

"Porky Pig? Who the hell is Porky pig? Oh shit, has one of our freezer pigs got trapped in there?"

BANG!

They both turned. The entire wooden substructure of the toilet was shredded into wooden slivers. The plastic toilet seat had been mashed into the back wall. Sticking enigmatically out of the toilet was......was....... what the hell was it? A dead tree? How did a dead tree get into the toilet? By this time, Jean-Claude had made his way into the outhouse itself and was busy surveying the results of his handiwork, his face creased in total puzzlement.

"Qu'est-ce que c'est?" he kept repeating.

Just then, all the womenfolk arrived. And that was when Sabine, now well fortified by a few glasses of "Blanc des Blancs", had to be held up because she was laughing so hard. Every face turned towards her, but every time she attempted an explanation, she would burst into nothing short of hysterics.

So Pierrette did the obvious, she turned to her husband who had just joined them. "Qu'est-ce qu'il y avait?" she asked.

"Je pensais qu'un porc-epic m'a mordu," he said. "I thought there was, 'ow you say, a porc-epic, porkypine, in the toilet and it bit me on the derriere," he translated for the others. "But it was a tree, a goddamn tree. 'Ow would a dead tree get in there, eh Conley?" Sabine's hysterics took on new life.

Clearly Conley knew nothing, legitimately; Aubrey neither. Quickly, all eyes turned back to Sabine. All she could say when she had regained enough of her composure was, "Let's go back inside. I've got a confession to make."

Chapter Eleven
STOCKING STUFFERS

*F*arming created a whole new dimension when it came to Christmas shopping. Traditionally, Aubrey and Sabine tended to indulge each other with the finer things in life. Sabine would hope for, and receive, the fancy body lotions, the mink coat, the diamond pendant, the crystal wine glasses complete with a bottle of Chateauneuf Du Pape, that sort of thing. Aubrey would look forward to a new leather coat, a suede silk-lined jacket, a bottle of Bushmills Scotch, even a brand new leather golf bag the one year, clubs the next. But it wasn't as if there was any great surprise because dropping the appropriate hints, what politicians like to call "lobbying", was all so much a part of the game. Happiness was more contingent upon quality than it was upon expense, even if the two tended to go hand in hand. The Christmas stocking, and by extension the notion of "stocking stuffers", had always been a non-starter. Two gifts, each, under the tree was as far as this particular family went, and it had always worked well. Neither one of them ever felt disappointed with, nor envious of the other. Indeed, both were decidedly content with the fact that gift giving never assumed the wholesale proportions it did in some households. Not that either one of them was religious mind you, although Sabine always press-ganged Aubrey into taking her along to the annual carol singing at the local Presbyterian church. It was just too bad it was not his cup of tea, she said dismissively; he could take it as time served in Purgatory, if he wished.

Hell, if only she could hear herself sing, thought Aubrey, wisely to himself. Every year the service began with "Silent Night", and every year he would give an involuntary start as Sabine launched herself into the fray like a wounded bagpipe. By the time they had made it to the mightier carols, the likes of "The First Noel" and such, Sabine's Noels were a reminder of why he had a pathological terror of dentists.

Farming changed it all. First off were the endless farm flyers, designed to seduce every farmer, male and female, into panting breathlessly for an endless range of "stocking stuffers". Then came the recognition of how "useful" this array of gadgets and tools would be down on the farm: everything from the enigmatic "nut-breaker" to the wide-view, flip-front welding helmet; from dual scale torque wrenches to winter boots with triple density liners; from halters for heifers to saddles for horses, although for the life of him, Aubrey could never figure out how you could call a saddle a "stocking stuffer". Strangely enough, it was Sabine who succumbed first.

"You know what, Aub," she said. "We should give ourselves a Christmas stocking this year," this after the third year on the farm. "There are so many practical things and little gadgets that could be useful, and all of them are on sale at this time of year. Take a look at this Peavey Mart flyer, for instance. It's chock full of neat stuff. So why don't we allow each other a hundred bucks to fill a stocking, you for me, me for you. It'll be so much fun."

"Why don't we just buy what we need, when we need it," said Aubrey darkly. "If I need a Robertson's number two screwdriver, I'll just go out and buy one."

"Yes, but listen to this! You can have a whole collection of thirty different screwdrivers, and all for $9.99. And a claw hammer for $3.99, regularly $12.00. And a warmer for your boots at $49.99, regularly $80.00. You know how you always curse cold boots in winter. All these things are on sale, a lot of them are really cheap, and so many of them would be so practical." There was no stopping Sabine's acquisitive instincts now; Aubrey was smart enough to realize that he had little choice but to sign on, albeit grudgingly.

"But what on earth do I do for your stocking, then? A pair of pliers or eighty-six bottles of bath salts just doesn't seem to cut it. Or do you want a set of screwdrivers too?"

"Oh Aub, stop being so silly and sarcastic! Anything that you or I can use on the farm would be good. And it wouldn't hurt you to use your imagination either. Let's throw a bit of mystery and romance into our lives for once. Let's have a bit of fun for a change; we only live once!" That line was to pay off in more ways than once, though Sabine could have no inkling of it at the time. So the plot was hatched. A trip to Red Deer was planned to access the greater variety of stores available there. Of course, Aubrey was still looking half-heartedly for a way out of this "new morass" as he called it, but Sabine had decreed that they were going to have fun, and that was the end of it. Things only got worse when she insisted on dropping him off at a large mall where she ordered him to browse, clearly signaling that her stocking stuffers were not coming exclusively from the likes of Princess Auto or Peavey Mart. "Remember, you've got one hour.

And honey, lighten up," she said. "I'll meet you at the door of 'The Bay', the one where they have all that lovely women's wear." Was that supposed to be a hint, Aubrey wondered.

Once she was on her own, Sabine had a ball, a real ball. Aubrey did not know it yet, but he was about to be better equipped, better organized, better directed than he had ever been in his life. Bolt caddies, a set of punches, jumper cables, a flashlight with a magnetic base, and a six- piece carbide router bit set for $14.99. To be sure, Aubrey did not have a router, but when they were regularly $49.99, who could pass up a deal like that? Boy, this was fun! So what if she had spent double what they had agreed on! If Aubrey did not get the same amount of fun out of it as she did, well then he was nothing more than an old stick-in-the-mud.

Now a visit to Canadian Tire was called for; they had sent out a pretty exciting flyer too. The amazing display of Christmas lights that greeted her as she came in through the door, a display designed to seduce any consumer's eye, convinced her that from now on, lights were a prerequisite to every Hanlon Christmas. They were so beautiful, and so Christmassy! And there were all kinds of them: icicles, snowdrops, reindeer, Santa, Frosty the Snowman, they were all there, and they all had to be represented in Sabine's basket. The $118.99 bill immediately convinced Sabine that Christmas lights were outside the domain of stocking stuffer. Up popped that word "requirement", again. However, the Snoopy floor mats for the station wagon, and the digital stud finder were definite candidates for Aubrey's stocking. A lasso and a battery-operated stock prod from UFA put the finishing touches to her campaign.

Meanwhile, back at the mall, Aubrey's browsing was not progressing well. For somebody who loved to hate any mall, being stuck in one for an hour, a whole hour amounted to cruel and unusual punishment. What the hell was he going to do for one full hour? It boggled the mind! One thing was for sure, Sabine had better be on time to pick him up, otherwise she might be paying him a visit at the mental hospital. "Mystery and romance, my foot!" he thought bitterly.

The music store where he bought the "Enya" CD mercifully gobbled up about fifteen minutes. The bookstore where he found a copy of "Gardening for Klutzes" absorbed another ten. The house wares department at "The Bay" served him equally well, providing him with a timer and a pair of oven mitts, and it swallowed up another ten minutes. Now what? He stumbled his way back into the main mall and found himself facing directly into a women's clothing store. Not only that, there in the window was the perfect see-through nightie creation, in "gossamer-silver" proclaimed the label, also proclaiming forty percent off. Moreover, there was not a soul in the place, other than the store personnel of course. He strode in, bursting with purpose and intent.

"Morning Ma'am," he said too brightly to the rather large saleslady. "Could you tell me how much," damn, his voice was faltering but he just could not help it. "Could you tell me how much that 'er, that night dress is that you have in your window?"

"Oh that's a beauty, isn't it?" she gushed. "Are you shopping for your wife?"

As if it's any of her damn business, Aubrey thought sourly, sorely tempted for a second to tell her that no, it was for his eighty-seven-year-old mistress. He was so taken aback, he did not even hear the next question.

"Excuse me, sir," the saleslady broke through his confusion, "what size is she?"

Oh dear, oh God, oh hell, how stupid he had been. He had never thought to ask Sabine her size so he did the next best thing. "Medium, I guess." Surely that would cover all the ground.

"Medium? Did you say medium? I'm afraid our store only caters to larger women. We only cater to image size."

"Image size? What the heck is image size?" Aubrey was floundering now.

"Larger women. The smallest we would have in that particular nightie would be extra-large."

"Oh," said Aubrey in dismay, and very disappointed that he had blown precious time and come up with absolutely nothing. He did not just beat a dignified retreat, he bolted, noting as he did so that the garment that he had so fancied in the window could easily have accommodated both him and Sabine quite comfortably, and probably Nellie too. So, seven and a half full minutes, and he was still empty-handed when it came to the "mystery and romance" department. Oh well, the novelty store across the way would provide an ideal refuge for him to gather his thoughts once again.

The contents of the store grabbed his attention instantly with the weirdest collection of bric-a-brac he had ever seen. It was the perfect store for the likes of Dick Conley, he thought, as he appraised the edible underwear, the whoopee cushions, the calendars so brazen with their exposure of the human form, the tee shirts with utterly outrageous slogans, even a fishing lure in the form of a penis for heaven's sake! But the best of all was an "Inflatable Bonking Cow" for $23.00. Or, if you were not into cows and preferred those more woolly denizens of the planet, you could get an "Inflatable Bonking Sheep" for $12.49! For a split second, a split second only, the devil counseled Aubrey to get a cow for Sabine's stocking but reason persuaded him that her reaction might result in a large, inflated foreign body up his "Land's End" on Christmas day, of all days. Truth be told, Aubrey was fascinated by this incredible array of shoddy goods in the worst of taste, yet, at the same time, there was a sense of revulsion tinged with wonder that people actually paid money for this stuff. And then he realized that he had consumed another ten minutes, again for no gain. Where to now?

His anti-American, anti-big corporation kick precluded a visit to Wal-Mart or Home Depot, so he ambled aimlessly around in the mall itself, looking in the specialty store windows. He slipped into a "house-wares boutique" feeling totally uninspired until he spotted a really neat spice rack in carved oak. Of course with his luck, there was no visible price tag, and the item was high up on a top shelf that Aubrey dared not reach up to for fear of starting a "crockery quake" with all the intervening goods so fragile in nature. Eventually, he contrived to catch the salesgirl's attention: one of those cooler chicks with green hair and an assortment of rings inserted into most, if not all of her visible appendages.

"Oh them," she said tiredly, "they're a hundred and eight dollars each." Her wad of gum continued to be masticated with unschooled disinterest.

"One hundred and eight dollars! What is it made of, gold?" retorted Aubrey sarcastically.

"Nah, just polished oak or something."

"Well, it's er, it's way too much."

"Suit yourself, dad," said this prima ballerina of the retail sector, going back to chewing the cud.

Aubrey was on the cusp of surrender when he spied a branch of "La Senza". The previous week, he had caught a snippet of a business commentary on TV, boasting about how this Canadian chain had been so successful in establishing itself throughout the land. Moreover, and more to the point, there was only a single man in there; otherwise, the store was empty, or, to match the description more appropriately to his state of mind, the coast was clear. The moment he walked in—no, snuck in would be a better way to put it—he found himself bombarded with rack upon rack, and table after table of garish and exotic women's underwear. Clearly, flaming red and magenta passion were the colours of the season. The nighties, too, the ones worth having, not the yards of flannelette infested with bouncing teddy bears, were all in-your-face scarlet and burgundy, and most of them put Aubrey in mind of that welding helmet—that wide-view, flip-front marvel of modern engineering—in Peavey Mart. A younger saleswoman in her late twenties, showing more cleavage than Aubrey was comfortable with at close range, approached him with a knowing smile.

"May I help you with something, sir?" she trilled.

"Well, well er, yes. I er, I'm looking for a night dress for my wife." Damn, why had he said 'night-dress'? That would probably put him slap bang into the geriatric section.

"Ah, we have plenty of those," the young woman preened. "What sort of 'night dress' are we looking for?"

Aubrey found himself wishing that she had not stressed her words quite that way. He wasn't so sure about the "we", either. He glanced furtively over at the other man, now absorbed in reviewing the physics of a lacy push-up bra, before answering.

"Well, just a nightie," he said, hoping that she had picked up on his correction. "Just a nightie, you know, like you women like to wear." How could he tell her that he wanted something outrageously sexy—and cheap, so that he did not end up blowing his whole stocking stuffer budget?

"Well, we have some real nice ones in flannelette. I really like flannelette myself. Like this one here, for instance. What size is your wife?"

The ubiquitous bouncing bears all over the garment prompted Aubrey's hurried response. "Medium, and I don't care for flannelette." No doubt about it, he had lowered the boom on the teddy bears! And the saleswoman had been through too many of these stilted exchanges not to know instantly what the man wanted.

"Aha! So you're looking for something naughty but nice," she winked at him, letting him know that she was now in on the conspiracy.

"Well, er, well yes, if you must put it like that," muttered Aubrey, again glancing furtively around to see who else might be in on the conspiracy, given the robust carrying capacity of the woman's voice.

"How about this one?" she charged on, holding up a bright red creation that consisted of a few strategically placed bows on half a yard of fine mesh. Wouldn't you know it? A couple of middle-aged women chose that very moment to wander into the store. Aubrey felt as though he had just been caught in some nefarious act. He went beet red as he declined the scarlet offering.

The saleswoman re-hung the garment on the rack and began rummaging around for something different. Aubrey should have fled, would have fled at this juncture, but he felt an old-fashioned sense of obligation to somebody who was prepared to put in so much effort on his behalf.

"Are you looking for something in a particular colour?" came her next question, muffled in a half acre of maroon and magenta.

"Well, I er, well blue is my wife's favorite colour." That put the woman back to burrowing once more as a younger couple now sauntered through the door. Feeling almost unbearably trapped, Aubrey was stoic as he struggled to keep his face inscrutable to the end.

"Ta da!" announced the saleswoman much too loudly, and holding up a light blue, well, work of art as far as Aubrey was concerned. It was perfect!

"How much is it?" he asked, desperately hoping to clinch a deal and run.

"Well, it's on at forty percent off, so forty percent of $64.00, what is that?"

"Fine, I'll take it," said Aubrey breathlessly, his vision suddenly arrested by the original man in the store not having any qualms about checking out the mechanics of a wicked-looking masterpiece called a "Merry Widow", if he had overheard correctly.

"Sheesh. If he can do it, so can I," Aubrey thought to himself.

"How about a nice bra?" asked the saleswoman, determined that she was not yet finished.

"Well, I er, I er had better, well I...."

"Go for it, Mister! Get your lady a bra," piped up the younger-looking of the two middle-aged women, now fingering through the wares displayed on the next table. "She'll love you for it, she really will."

"Wish I could get my old rancher type in here," said her companion. "He wouldn't be seen dead in a place like this. His idea of romance is a pair of gumboots from Peavey Mart. Good for you, mister. It's good to see that there's still a bit of romance left in this world, even if it doesn't happen to us, eh Marie?"

"Well," said the saleswoman puffing out her own attributes as if in encouragement. "What do you think?"

Aubrey almost said the wrong thing before he registered what she was talking about. "Sure. What the hell? If I am going to get shot, it might as well be done in style. Sure. What have you got?" he asked, feeling now as if he had just voluntarily walked the plank.

"Well, what size is she?" said the saleswoman, hugely enjoying herself.

"Size? Oh hell, size. Well, let's just say medium."

"No, no, no. We're talking undergarments now, not dresses or nighties. Medium doesn't work with a bra."

"Oh shoot, then I have no idea what size she is."

"Well, do you think that she's about the same size as me for instance?" she said, striking a provocative pose so that Aubrey could not avoid an appraisal of her total cleavage. Needless to say, he was plunged into the most profound sense of embarrassment he had ever experienced. "I'm a 36C," she added as though she was discussing tire size, completely disarming him.

"Or is she my size, 38D?" interjected Mrs. Rancher, puffing out her chest in a bid not to miss out on her own moment of glory.

"Actually, the number 36C rings a bell," said Aubrey almost in panic mode, nevertheless enjoying what amounted to a legitimate close-up assessment of a fine female form.

"I tell you what," said his new heroine. "Normally, we don't allow our customers to return underwear, you know, for health reasons and all that, but for you I'm prepared to make an exception. If whatever you take is the wrong size, you can bring it back as long as you bring it to me personally. My name is Madeline."

"You can't do better than that!" commented Mrs. Rancher, now as much a part of the transaction as the saleswoman. "Go for it. Your wife's a lucky girl, let me tell you. All I'm due for this year is an oilskin raincoat. Now there's romance for you!"

The eventual outcome saw Aubrey buy both the nightie and what he perceived to be a magnificent multicoloured, multi-paneled bra for his mate, for a grand total of $57.00. And he had made a new friend, even counselor, in Madeline the saleswoman. But he was now at least twenty minutes late for his rendezvous with Sabine.

"And where the hell have you been?" she exploded when she saw him. Since she rarely used this kind of language, Aubrey knew that he had overstayed his welcome, overplayed his hand, whatever.

"I was busy," he said flatly.

"Busy, my foot," grumbled Sabine. That was when her eyes took in the "La Senza" bag. Oh, ho, ho, ho, so Santa had been adventurous had he? And for the first time in his life! Ho, ho, ho! Well now, it would definitely be worth her while to back off, seeing as it was all for such a good cause. "Let's go home," she said. "I'm tired and I need a cup of tea."

Perhaps it was an attempt to preserve the mystery, or maybe it was because she was still mad at her mate, but on the way home, Sabine switched on the radio, tuned to CBC 1010. The Christmas music effectively killed any conversation. Not that Aubrey was displeased with that; he had endured enough trauma for one day.

"I've got a job for you," Sabine said immediately as they had sat down to a cup of tea at home. She had decided that the authoritarian approach was the best way to ensure she got her Christmas lights hung up. "This year, you and I are going to have Christmas lights, lots of them, and guess who's going to put them up?" Only then did Aubrey realize that he had climbed into the station wagon without scanning her purchases.

Ah, the lights. Why on earth did Sabine suddenly want lights? The last thing he wanted was a house that looked like Candy Cane Lane. Oh well, a couple of strings might be all right, he supposed.

When it came time for action, he went outside to the station wagon. Surely all those boxes were not lights, or were they? Had she gone nuts? Out came two larger boxes containing string on string of several varieties of lights. Then there was another box that contained a hideously plasticized Santa Claus, and another that produced what Aubrey could only describe as a grotesquely disfigured Frosty the Snowman. And then there was a reindeer. He was speechless, but in the interests of matrimonial solidarity, and because his acquisitions might be viewed as an equally crazy spending binge, he bit his tongue.

Maybe it would have worked out better if he had first laid out all the Christmas lights and planned out exactly how he was going to hang them. But no, even though he recognized the solidarity-with-the wife aspect, he was decidedly unenthused by the sheer scope of the task, and besides, it was too damn cold to be putting up lights. So he simply set about joining one string to another only to discover that Sabine had displayed no more logic in her purchasing than he had in his hanging. What made it worse was that he tripped over the reindeer that was supposed to go up on the roof, leaving it with a permanent crick in its neck. When he presented his ninety minute effort to Sabine, there was a strangled "Oh, I didn't think it would look quite like that," as she surveyed the mish-mash of snowflakes and icicles drifting their way erratically around the house. After that, she was wise enough to clam up; she knew well that criticism from quarters not so close would have a positive effect on her husband. Her intuition was right on, her savior being none other than Mister C, Dick Conley, whom she had always dismissed as an artistic lightweight, even if he did sing in "The Mikado".

"Who the hell is responsible for this mess?" Mr. Conley asked in astonishment when he saw the lights.

"Who the hell d'ya think?" retorted Aubrey antagonistically.

"Well, I've never seen such a dog's breakfast in my life. I hereby pronounce that I shall redo them tomorrow morning before I head back to the big city. You can't possibly leave them the way they are; those lights'll scare Santa and his reindeer so bad they'll abandon the whole of North America."

So it was that Dick created a true masterpiece out of Aubrey's bungling, a masterpiece that Aubrey refused to take down the first year for fear of never being able to reproduce it. "That reindeer will always have a crick in the neck, though. Some idiot must have stepped on it," observed Dick.

"Must have," sighed Aubrey.

A week or so later, December 25 dawned upon a sparkling white Christmas. As he always did, Aubrey stumbled into the kitchen and brewed up a pot of coffee, bringing a steaming cup of the beverage to his wife in bed.

"Did Santa come last night?" she asked excitedly.

"Uh, pardon me, what did you say?" said Aubrey, still half-asleep.

"Did Santa come last night?" she repeated, a twinkle in her eye. "Is there anything in your stocking?"

"Oh shoot, I didn't look. And I know there's nothing in your stocking because I've got it packed away downstairs in a cardboard box. Why didn't you tell me that you wanted it all put out in your stocking?" he finished huffily.

"Well, why don't you go and put it out now? I'll just pretend the noise you are making is Santa coming down the chimney."

Aubrey shuffled off downstairs and retrieved the store of goodies for his wife. Carefully, he took her stocking and packed it, making sure that the more risqué items went to the very bottom.

"Did Santa come last night?" Sabine asked brightly when he got back to the bedroom.

"Yeah, and we must have both been good because there's a ton of stuff by the look of it."

"Let's go and take a look." It was a long time ago that Aubrey had last seen his wife so excited. She was like a little girl as she pulled on her dressing gown over her flannelette nightie, covered in, wouldn't you know it, bouncing bears.

Of course, Sabine had to watch Aubrey unpack his loot from his stocking before she turned to her own.

Well now, Santa had brought him a set of jumper cables. Did Sabine not forgive him for starting a small fire under the hood of the station wagon when he had tried to boost it? The current set was so frayed and threadbare they had shorted out on the frame of the vehicle, setting a small patch of oil alight. Judging by her instant hysteria, Sabine had not been impressed even though he had put it out in seconds. There was also a set of steel punches. How did Santa know that Aubrey already owned a set, but that he had not seen it these last two years? He kept insisting to Sabine that it was still around "somewhere".

"You know dear, you're absolutely right. This is great fun and we shall have to do it every year. I would never have gone out and bought either of these things, and we can sure use them. But this little flashlight is a real find. You can attach it to a vehicle's hood when you are working on the engine," Aubrey was obliged to add, translating the picture on the box for his bemused wife. She was discreet enough not to suggest that if ever Aubrey got to working on an engine, then they would both be in trouble.

"Why on earth did you buy a set of router bits, though? I don't have a router you know."

"Oh, they were such a good deal," she said innocently. "Maybe one day soon I'll have to get you a router for your birthday or something."

A router was the last thing Aubrey wanted for his birthday; he certainly did not want a router to displace the new style golf putter that he had his eye on. He had better kill that idea right now.

"Aubrey Hanlon and wood were never destined to work together, remember that," he pronounced sagely. "But I sure like these Snoopy floor mats, and I know we can make good use of this lasso, or Mister Conley will. But why a digital stud finder? Are we going building or something?" He regretted opening his mouth as soon as he said it.

"Remember that last picture you put up? Remember how you drilled seven holes in the wall before you found a stud? Well, if ever we want to put up another picture in the future, you will only have to drill one hole." As if he needed to be reminded; and with such self-righteousness too.

"Hey, look at this now, a stock prod, and you, sorry, Santa even remembered the batteries for it. Now this I can use." He sat down in his reading chair and began perusing the instructions.

"Can I go now?" asked Sabine sweetly.

"Oh sure, go for it," said Aubrey, watching her start on her stocking. "Enya" was a Sabine favorite so he knew he could not have gone wrong there. But evidently she intended to savor every moment for she began studying what particular numbers were on the CD. Aubrey went back to the stock prod, casting a discreet glance over at his wife to see where she was at. The timer and the mitts seemingly radically upgraded what was already in the kitchen, for Sabine marched off and dumped the old ones and replaced them with Santa's latest offerings.

"You're not implying anything with this, I hope." She had returned and clutched in her hand was "Gardening for Klutzes".

"Not at all, but the cartoons in it are out of this world." Sabine at once began browsing through the cartoons as Aubrey unpacked the batteries for the prod. The thing was supposed to buzz when it was working, but when he pushed it against the floor, there was nothing. Maybe he had got the batteries in the wrong way round. With one eye on Sabine, he deposited the batteries back out onto the carpet. He saw her pull out the bra. He stopped what he was doing and watched her face. It was as if he had just bought her a new car, something so different and so unexpected that she had to spend a few minutes metaphorically kicking the wheels and opening the doors.

"How did you know my size?" came the obvious question. No indication as to whether he had scored a goal or was about to be sent down to the minor leagues.

"I didn't. So I have permission to take it back if it's the wrong size." He regretted saying that because she would surely grasp the opportunity to get rid of it, replacing it with something more utilitarian, more industrial in design.

"Well, it is the right size, and it is very nice. But it is not something that I would have bought."

"Any more than the punches and the booster cables, my dear," he redeemed himself.

"Touché!" she said. "And thank you Santa. It's very different, but I shall wear it just for you," she leaned down and kissed him impulsively before going back for the last item. Aubrey set about installing the batteries into the prod as per the instructions. Sabine's face was a kaleidoscope of expressions as she pulled out the nightie.

"If she throws a fit over this one, it'll be the last mysterious and romantic thing I'll ever buy for her," thought Aubrey dourly. He need not have worried. She held it up to the light, turned it around, studied it from all angles, and then promptly set about undressing so that she could try it on. This was fantasy come true as far as Aubrey was concerned. It was beautiful, she was beautiful, and the creation fitted like a glove. She struck a pose for him, an impish smile on her face, and that brought him out of his chair for an instant hug.

"This is lovely," she whispered in his ear. "How courageous you must have been. Christmas stockings are henceforth a formal institution in the Hanlon household, don't you agree?"

"Only if I can get this bloody stock prod to work," he said, disengaging before his ardor got out of control.

"Let me have a look," Sabine said, taking the prod and plonking herself down on the armchair, leaving Aubrey standing by the tree enjoying the landscape. First though, she looked at the instructions, checking out the section entitled, "How to Operate".

"For safety reasons, the operator must turn the handle so that it clicks out of safety mode." Sabine did that and leaned across to press it unthinkingly against her husband's rump. The reaction was instantaneous. He crashed into the tree, taking it down in a popping of lights and falling tinsel, ornaments scattering everywhere in disarray.

Sabine was smart enough to unplug the tree immediately. Then she was up on her feet and leaning over her husband lying prostrate among the bedraggled branches, tinsel in his hair, in his ears, everywhere. He looked up to see his distraught mate leaning over him in the sexiest get-up he had ever seen.

"Oh, I am so sorry, honey, are you okay?" The tears began to flow.

"I think I've died and gone to heaven," he said. "And they've given me my very own angel!"

Chapter Twelve
THE NUMBERS GAME

Sooner or later, those who dare to try their hand at farming, in whatever capacity, find out that what they are into is not "farming" but "agribusiness", and that agribusiness has an unsavory dimension, economics. As a policeman, Aubrey had never had to give any thought to economics; his pay cheque always arrived on time and usually in the amount he expected it to be. Frugal, but not miserly, he had never had any reason to think beyond his secure little financial world. Besides, with Sabine bringing in a tidy contribution from "The Boutique", the small and exclusive dress shop where she worked part time, they could live comfortably and still enjoy a fancy meal here and there. The fact that they had resigned themselves to Sabine's biological inability to conceive children meant that their standard of living was more assured than most. Moreover, since he had retired from the force, Aubrey was in receipt of a respectable pension which, when combined with their savings, encouraged them to flutter their wings and follow their country dream, leaving an urban lifestyle with which they had become thoroughly bored, if not disenchanted.

But out there on the farm, Aubrey very quickly came to the realization that a farm could easily transform itself into a financially voracious dragon whose appetite could barely be appeased and certainly never satiated. If you did not have a mind to control it, the beast would happily gorge itself on all your life savings and still demand more. The trick, he discovered, was to learn where to draw the line so that his "wants" did not overtake his "needs", although the two notions were entirely interchangeable when Aubrey started out. How important, for example, was the tractor with FWA (front wheel assist) in the whole scheme of things? Very important, actually indispensable, Aubrey decided, after he had been stuck in the spring mud on scores of occasions and marooned just as often on winter's ice; both were situations that defied any and all attempts to move forward or backward. How important was the tractor with FWA, air ride, GPS, stereo-surround, air conditioning, sunroof—all the bells and whistles? Very important if you were something of a hedonist, or you had a passion for toys and gadgets and you possessed the moolah to pay for such decadence. Totally irrelevant if your primary focus was the hard and boring reality of increased agricultural production.

Likewise, if you were to give in to the histrionic bawling of your cows in winter, and you decided to feed them what they wanted, what they constantly hollered for, they could annul your profit margin and leave you destitute in very short order. Aubrey found that he resented having to make concessions to economics. It surrendered too much of his sovereignty, it undermined his credibility, and it gave too much of the high moral ground to those wretched economists who were always spouting off their jargon so earnestly. He came to have quite a thing about "number-crunchers", always so knowing, and so self-righteous with it. As if they really knew any more than he did!

He'd be damned if he would resign himself to being a statistic or a category, one of those "x" per cent that StatsCan (Statistics Canada) identified as a hobby farmer. As if you could call it a hobby when you battled the elements all year—the wind and the snow, the heat and the cold, the mud and the slush—just so you could put an income in your pocket. Hell, even the word itself, economics, was an invasion of his privacy as far as Aubrey was concerned. Yet, as his adventure into the world of agribusiness progressed, he had to become more than just grudgingly acquainted not only with basic economic terms but also with their application. He could no longer see the notion of interest, for example, as "their interest, not mine". He had to admit, finally, that he too derived some benefit, even if it was always secondary. Likewise, the concept of infrastructure moved from the abstract into the rickety reality of his system of fences and corrals designed to keep in whatever was meant to be kept in—except when Nellie decided that an extra-curricular walkabout was past due. Infrastructure was the water well that had to be re-drilled when it silted up, it was the expanding range of antique machinery that he needed to produce more and better from the land, and the power line that distributed his electricity to his workshop, the barn, the waterers, and all the other places where it might be needed.

Almost immediately, unless you are one of those most fortunate individuals who are independently wealthy, your farm will necessitate some form of relationship with one or more of the local bankers. Like everything else, they come in all sorts of shapes and sizes, espousing all sorts of causes and philosophies.

The first portly fellow with whom Aubrey had to deal to get a loan for a baler was a gentleman whose pet peeve was law and order, or rather what he perceived to be a demonstrable lack of it. When the good banker discovered that Aubrey was an ex-policeman, the business of Aubrey's loan became secondary to the man's diatribe about the current crime spree that he assured his client was rampaging through today's society. Aubrey was thankful to escape without a lecture about the need for the death penalty for all petty theft but more especially for loan default and poor creditworthiness. But he did find himself wondering whether the death penalty could serve as a deterrent to self-opinionated bankers and others of such ilk whose hobbyhorses had become rooted to one spot.

The second manager Aubrey had to deal was Fred. Fred was a golf buff first and foremost and a financier second, which probably explained why he was encouraged by head office to shuffle off his banker's coil prematurely for the proprietorship of Fred's Mini-Golf and Go-Carts in Sicamous, BC. Unhappily, this transpired before the consummation of Aubrey's operating loan agreement, and Fred was replaced by a hard-nosed, no-nonsense, upwardly mobile climber from the head office in Edmonton. It was immediately evident that he resented his new posting to "the sticks". Clearly, his self-styled mission was to root out the poor creditors and other such delinquents that he privately labeled as "banker's vermin" prior to moving onward to stardom in a regional office somewhere more cosmopolitan than Rocky Mountain House. He tuned Aubrey both off and down: off because he had the personality of a menopausal grizzly, and down because he said Aubrey had "an exceedingly poor attitude". Aubrey realized, afterward, that he should not have reminded the bear who it was that actually paid his salary. It was a thoughtless statement that called for a change in banks and a new adventure in relationship-building with another financier.

The new fellow across the road was much more hospitable—hospitable, but not accommodating. He too was something of a jargonmeister. Did Aubrey have some sort of business plan? Well no, not exactly, it was sort of in his head. Uh huh, and how would Aubrey rate his cash flow situation? Well, more was flowing out than was flowing in, ha, ha, and that was why he needed a loan. The "ha ha" was not received at all well, so he added that his cash flow was "you know, kinda flat right now". The banker, now apparently in some pain, then asked him what kind of return percentage-wise he was expecting from his investment if the bank was to lend him its money. Ugh, well, to be honest, that was something he had not really analyzed. It was the prelude to the ending of another potentially beautiful friendship.

"You realize, Mr. Hanlon," the man was staring malevolently over his bi-focals at Aubrey as if he was some kind of learning-disabled child, "you realize that it is incumbent upon me to do everything in my power to safeguard the bank's money? You do understand that, don't you Mr. Hanlon?" he confirmed with a smug smile and overbearing attitude.

"Your money? Did you say your money? If you choose to lend it to me, it is my money. Not your money, my money. I am your valued customer, remember? That's customer, not prisoner-of-war. So are you going to lend me any money or would you prefer that I take my business elsewhere?" retorted Aubrey.

"Well of course we value you as a customer", schmoozed Mister Suit. "But I, too, have my responsibilities, one of which is to ensure that our funds are not squandered on some hare-brained scheme like.......like........"

"Building me a calving barn?" Aubrey finished for him.

"Well no, that's not, er, that's not quite what I meant. I'm sure your calving barn is, is a very worthwhile investment, so if you care to work with one of our senior loans officers and develop a proper business plan, maybe we can make something work. Maybe we can put our money and your money to good use."

"Maybe," snarled Aubrey, "but then again, maybe not. Tell me, do people in your position ever take sensitivity training? You know, so they don't talk down to country people as if they are morons?" He did not wait for a reply, but plowed on. "Because even in the RCMP we were trained not to treat our clients the way you do. So keep your money and have a nice day".

The upshot of all this was that Aubrey had to make a point of coming to grips with the basic economics terms he needed to know in order to joust with the bankers. It was a learning curve that made him chuckle as he progressed.

Would his dear friend Nellie be classified as a "fixed asset" or a "current liability"? It depended on her mood, he supposed. If what Nellie ate was clearly an "input", presumably that which she expelled would be an "output", no? The last great jargonmeister with whom he had wrestled had suggested that most small farmers were vastly over-capitalized. Did he mean that most of them ought to be sporting a "Wide Load"sign on their rears, a declaration of how well they dined. Or did he mean that in lieu of buying a more up-to-date haybine, they should be cutting their hay with a lawnmower? As for that wonderful term cash flow, Aubrey found out all about that when he sold his first crop of calves at the auction. The gross income was great, maybe even breathtaking, for Aubrey, but then the cash immediately began flowing away what with the auctioneer's fee, the fee for the brand inspector, the fee for Hartford Insurance (whatever that was), the charge for the Alberta Cattle Commission, and the bill for overnight food and water. The concept that most baffled him, however, was the notion of net worth. In fact, it was offensive: it smacked of a sort of discrimination, as if somebody in the bank could sit in judgment of how worthy he was. Sheer financial necessity eventually forced him to concede that economics would always have to play a dominant role in his farming life, a sort of "evil empire" he could hate at his leisure.

So it was that he finished up as a customer at the local credit union. Chastened by his experiences, he was surprised to find that he had no trouble dealing with the next senior loans officer assigned to him: an officer who made things happen without all the song and dance that he had encountered elsewhere. Good heavens, she even understood farming at the ground level: she was obviously tuned into it if her references to the current CanFax projections on fall calf prices were any indication.

"Oh, but my husband George farms", she said. "He's not that good at it though, which is why I have to work here" she added, perhaps a touch ruefully. "And yes, you have loads of room for your loan because you have bags of equity. Just you go do your farming and leave the paperwork to me. But I will have to come out with the manager sometime and take a look at your operation, if that's all right with you?" she finished apologetically.

"You're most welcome. Come out any time", he said, hoping that he had found a listening ear in the banking world.

When she finally did show up for her official visit the following week, her stock rose even further in Aubrey's eyes. Yes, she came in the requisite shiny SUV that all the yuppie professionals favored these days, but the shiny chrome and fancy fenders were liberally splattered with mud and cow poop. Yes, she got out of the car in her yuppie banker's suit but immediately stepped out of her stylish oxfords into a pair of tatty gumboots, all as a matter of course. He did get a little concerned when she produced a camera. It was not as if Nellie was all that photogenic, and his spread in general would be better characterized as "nineteenth century rustic" rather than "twenty-first century progressive". It was the sort of spread that would yield a bumper crop of snapshots for a calendar titled "Bucolic Yesteryear in Alberta".

"Sorry, the manager could not make it," she said, "he's busy organizing a golf tournament for the movers and shakers."

That puts me out of the category of movers and shakers, thought Aubrey to himself. Probably a hell of a lot cleaner and more meaningful for him than having to spend his afternoon with an ex-cop trying his hand at subsistence farming on the bank's money, he continued thinking uncharitably.

"Oh, no worries," he declared aloud, "just as long as you have the signing authority to make whatever decisions are needed."

"Oh for sure," she laughed. "It's us peons who do the bank's work, you know".

What was even more gratifying was that the banker lady also hit it off instantly with Sabine. The trouble with Sabine was that if she did not much care for somebody, she had a disconcerting habit of letting him or her know it. Whether it was through body language or hostile vibes, maybe a misplaced comment or two, the message was always clear and unmistakable. In this instance, Sabine almost hijacked Mrs. Banker's official visit, insisting that she first join them for a pot of tea to be followed by the grand tour of Sabine's garden, her ducks, and her chickens. Only then was she released to pursue her mandated duty of assessing the productive capacity of the farm. However, it was very clear that an escape from the office combined with a genuine interest in everything around her conspired to make the occasion one of great goodwill.

Oh, so that's what economists mean by goodwill, thought Aubrey, idly. And maybe my wife is my equity?

The outcome of it all—the tour of the cows, the talk of future plans, the vista of productive crop land—was that Aubrey was finally able to establish a solid relationship with a financial institution. The camera that she had brought along still unnerved him somewhat; she was snapping pictures as if she were on some glorious holiday vacation.

"Oh, I'll send you copies." She soothed his paranoia. "This is the only way that I can remember where I've been and what I've seen". Her smile was so disarming he felt guilty for attributing ulterior motives to her behavior. More importantly, as far as he was concerned, she allowed him to push back all of those threatening economic terms to an arms-length arrangement with her and the bank.

Her and the accountant!

Ah, the accountant: that humourless, earnest, little fellow whom Aubrey decided was made of glass. It was quite apparent that he dared not crack a smile. Mrs. Banker had asked him whom he used to do his books and taxes. When he responded that he planned to do them himself, she came up with the only disparaging remark of her visit.

"And what does an ex-policeman know about accounting?" She asked, verging on the scornful.

"Well, I er, I've always done my taxes myself. I was pretty good at math in high school, you know". He regretted adding that last statement as soon as he had said it.

"Well, now that you are running your own business, and that's what it is, your own business, you would be very wise to use an accountant. They are the only ones today who know and understand what government programs are available to help small farmers like you. Besides, there are so many pitfalls that can lose you money and so many mechanisms that can save you money, you'd be a fool if you don't access a professional. Let me recommend Mister Brittle, Wilbur Brittle. He has an office in town".

Aubrey really felt like he was entering the big leagues when he walked into Mr. Brittle's office. Here he was, about to sign up his very own accountant; not that he was totally convinced that this was the right thing to do. His perception of accountants had always been influenced by a vodka advert that he remembered from his misspent youth, when he had sojourned in London, England, for a summer. It was an advert that he saw often on the London underground. It showed a stereotypical accountant first in context, then all disheveled at a wild party, bottle of vodka in one hand, half-filled glass in the other. The caption below read "I'm an accountant and I'm a bore no more!"

The offices of Brittle, Biddle, and Bain, "the three Bs", as they were known locally, were on the second floor of a large office complex appropriately located next door to a bank. Airy and with that clinically neutral welcome of professional offices the world over, it was nonetheless evident that the inhabitants liked to work in some comfort.

"And you are Mister …?" the rather severe-looking receptionist greeted him. A smile was a rare commodity around here, Aubrey was to discover. Perhaps if you didn't pay for it, you didn't get it.

"Aubrey. Aubrey Hanlon," Aubrey smiled at her.

"Ah yes, Mister Hanlon. Mister Brittle is expecting you. Will you please take a seat? I'll go and tell him that you are here".

"Thank you." Aubrey sat down, casting a baleful eye at the array of business magazines guaranteed to bore the hind leg off a dead giraffe. Why couldn't such places ever have anything a normal person might like to read, he wondered. In fact, why did all such professionals take themselves so seriously? Did they have to convince themselves, if not their customers, that they knew what they were doing?

When the man appeared, Aubrey almost could not contain himself. Mr. Brittle would have been the perfect double of the man in the vodka ad if he had not had the moustache. And there was no doubt that he took himself seriously, too.

"Good morning Mister Hanlon. My name is Brittle, Wilbur Brittle, CGA, at your service".

"Aubrey. Aubrey Hanlon." Aubrey hoped that his smile was not much more than a smile.

"Come this way," breathed, Mr. Accountant in a condescendingly formal tone as if the malicious intent to charge him a hefty fee was cause for some great ceremony.

Aubrey could not help it. "Are you a party animal?" he said as they entered the man's well-appointed office. The man stopped as if he had just been struck on the head with a hammer. He turned, his face drained of all colour. What did this fellow know? What had he heard? Damn, that Christmas party threatened to haunt him all the days of his life.

The damnable thing about it was that he was not a party animal, absolutely not. Never had been, never would be. It had not been his idea to join all the professionals in the building—the three lawyers, the small company of surveyors, and a realty firm with a dozen agents, most of them women—for the annual Christmas party. He would have been quite happy if the staff had gotten a luncheon voucher and a box of chocolates, economy size and on sale of course. But no, his partners Biddle and Bain had overruled him. They wanted some real cheer, they had said, as if everybody in the office did not know that "Biddle the fiddle" had his eye on an amply proportioned realtor of the opposite sex who had just recently arrived in town. It was not Brittle's fault that his wife Mildred had got tied up at the church bazaar, she being a bright light in the local Presbyterian church and all. Nor was it his fault that he had loosened up with a couple of beers that had virtually been poured down him by "Bain the pain". Actually, it was the punch that did the damage, "Cranberry Christmas" they had called it, though it had a whole lot more than cranberry juice in it. Maybe it was not even the punch; maybe it was the buxom lady serving it who had been the real devil in disguise. After all, she was the one who had urged (perhaps foisted might be a good word choice here) it upon him while he was distracted by her cleavage.

As the party got into full swing, he was drawn in. In his twenty-seven years in accounting, nobody had ever seen him like this: "The real Mister B," they said. He became a veritable rooster in the chicken dance, crowing madly and ruffling his feathers. He was the rotund limbo dancer whose "limbo wiggle" actually got him below the four-foot mark. Both "antics" became the stuff of Christmas legend. He was the life and soul of the party, and when dear Mildred arrived, she was horrified to find her Wilbur involved in some kind of clothes-swapping caper. Nobody was quite sure where the bra had come from, but it was enormous, black and lacy, and he was wearing it over his head: one cup over each ear like some gigantic toque. Naked from the waist up, at least he was decent where it mattered.

"Greetings from Frobisher Bay," he saluted his wife as a leaden silence descended on the room.

"Wilbur! Wilbur! What in the name of God has got into you? What on earth do you think you are doing?" Mildred shrieked.

The sense of impending doom had not quite struck home. "It's very cold up here in the north", he said. "Would you care to share my igloo with me? It's got two rooms". He lifted one cup of the bra on his head.

The silence broke like a bursting dam. Wilbur, Mister Brittle, was last seen being chased down the street, still semi-naked, by a witch dressed in black and armed with an umbrella that she was apparently using to good effect. It was curious that for every subsequent Christmas party he had another engagement.

But no, this Mister Hanlon standing before him could not possibly know about that party, surely? "Party animal? What makes you think that, may I ask?" It always paid to be cautious.

The story of the vodka ad not only put him at ease, it warmed him to his new client. He also experienced a twinge of regret that he wasn't a party animal; it had been a blast after all was said and done. Business was conducted efficiently, effortlessly, and a bond was formed between Aubrey and his accountant. It was just as well because Revenue Canada had a hand in his future.

The call came after they had been on the farm about four years. It was innocent enough, too.

"It's for you," Sabine said, after she had answered the phone.

"Hello."

"Hello. Is this Mister Aubrey Hanlon?"

"Yes, it is".

"Mister Hanlon, I'm phoning to let you know that you have been selected...." Dreams of a free Hawaiian vacation pierced his mind; lazing on the beach, Daiquiris.... "for a random audit by Revenue Canada". There was a prolonged silence.

"Excuse me. Did you hear me, Mister Hanlon? Did you hear what I was saying?"

"Er, would you mind saying it again?" Somehow, all those thoughts of sunny beaches had vanished into thin air, despite the fact that he distinctly remembered entering in at least three draws where sunny beaches were a principal prize.

"You have been selected by Revenue Canada for a random audit. I have been directed to set up a mutually convenient date. By the way, my name is Eldon Snodgrass".

"I've been selected for what?" Aubrey was incredulous.

"A random audit conducted by Revenue Canada. They're quite common, you know".

Aubrey had heard about them all right, who hadn't? There were countless apochryphal stories of how the Revenue Canada folks had been through a certain farmer's books, and how if he had not been rendered bankrupt as a result, he had been beggared by the process. His immediate reaction was to agree to a date and then to scuttle for cover and consult with Mister Brittle.

"Oh, no problem, my boy, no problem. Here's the scene. Let the fellow come out and do his thing. He'll have to come back in about a month to make his report and tell you what he has found. I'll make a point of being there so that he'll have to address all his concerns to me. Now, how does that sound?"

"Terrific."

"Or you could do what your red-neck neighbour to the east did, and they'll never ever trouble you again, I'm sure." Mr. Brittle chuckled and cracked the first smile Aubrey had ever seen from him.

"My neighbour? Who? Old Art?"

"Yes, old Art Zimmer. You go and ask him what he did. He'll tell you."

Aubrey's curiosity was aroused. Art was an old, retired CPR man. Irascible and cranky, he lived a self-contained existence in an old house, an old shack to be exact, on his quarter section. With his CPR pension and his thirty cows, he was able to live just how he wanted. Suspicious of all strangers, he had taken a liking to his new neighbour, that damn cop fellah. This liking had converted itself into a friendship when Aubrey had noticed Art's truck stuck in a mud hole in his field, and he had gone over, unasked, and hauled him out.

"Hey, what brings an ex-pig like you into the world of an old railway man, eh? You don't want to borrow money, do you?" Art greeted him at the door.

"Pig no more!" Aubrey responded lightly. "Come to have a cup of tea with you and to see how things are going".

"Tea, be damned. I'll let you have a cup of tea if you have a whisky first. Then you can drink your damn tea".

"It's a deal." Aubrey was always left a bit breathless when he entered Art's house. A two-room slap-board house insulated with shavings and paper, it was nothing but a fire hazard. Cleanliness and hygiene were obviously not a part of Art's vocabulary: a fact reflected by the layer of grime on the mug that Aubrey willed himself not to look at too closely when Art served his tea, a tea-bag in boiling water. He just hoped that the boiling water would kill whatever wildlife might have taken up residence.

"Now see here, young fellah, this is the cheapest way to make damn good whisky. You buy one of them oak barrels that they used to make whisky in. Every goldarn hardware store is selling 'em these days. You put in about five gallons of hot water, a mite less if you want a stronger brew, and then you throw that goldarn barrel in the back of your pickup. You drive around with it like that for a couple of weeks and bingo, you got yourself some damn good whisky. Them barrels have a lot of residue in them. Here, try this".

Again, Aubrey willed himself to ignore the film of grease on the glass. He was astounded. The brew was good, and definitely not too watery. A strong tang of wood smoke went along with it, but the taste was delightful.

"Say Art, I've just been told that I've got the taxman, you know, the Revenue Canada guys, coming to do an audit on me. I was told to ask you how I should deal with him".

"Huh," Art sat bolt upright. "Who told you that? Who's been blabbing off his mouth, eh?" His demeanor had changed instantly from one of generous hospitality to one of a cornered cougar.

"Oh, my accountant, Mister Brittle."

"Oh him, he's harmless," Art relaxed. "That little fart couldn't hurt a fly without having himself a nervous breakdown, could he?" he chuckled. "So the government boys are on to you, eh, and you being an ex-cop and all," he roared with laughter. "Have another whisky, my boy, have another whisky and I'll tell you".

"Don't mind if I do. This is sure better than your tea, let me tell you. This is damn good!"

"Sure it's damn good. You young fellahs don't know nuthin'."

"So how did you deal with the Revenue Canada fellow that came to see you, then?"

"Well, see, it was like this," Art smiled to himself as he recalled that day. "Them guys phoned me just like they phoned you. And I was plumb mad, them goin' after an old pensioner and all, and I told the man so. He acts as if I had just pissed on his wheels and says he's comin' out on such and such a date, I don't recall exactly when, and I'd better cooperate with him or else I'd be spendin' some leisure time in jail. So I says to myself, 'I'll learn them guys not to fool around with us old-timers'. Hell, we built this country, not them little farts in their suits and ties squatting behind a desk all day." A pause was called for, and another dram all round.

"So then I didn't shave or nothing up to the day the fellow was to come. Place was a mess, just like it is now come to think of it. Maybe a bit worse. So I'm sitting here waiting, and there's this knock at the door. I yell out, 'Come in if your feet are clean'. Well that must have scared him some already because he takes his shoes off outside. Hell, there's more crap on my floor inside than you'd ever find outside. So he picks his way in and I tell him to put his goldarn shoes back on. A bit too late mind you, his socks were already caked with all kinds of crap. Anyway, he puts them back on".

"'Are you Mister Zimmer?' he asks, a young whippersnapper he was, suit and tie and all."

"'Who the hell do you think I am?' I says. "Mahatma Ghandi or Whitney Houston? I thought you guys knew everything." Art continued his story.

"'May I sit down?' the young fellah says".

"'Sure, sit yourself down.' 'I say," Art recounted. "Just move the gun to one side will ya?"

"Gun?" said Aubrey. "Did you say gun?"

"Yeah, I said gun. I had my .38 handgun sitting on the table."

"'What's the gun for?' the kid says. Poor little bugger was pissing himself", continued Art. "'For mice', says I. 'I got mice in here like you wouldn't believe. And for pesky tax collectors who might piss me off'. Little fellow was now as white as a sheet".

"So then I offer him a whisky. 'Nobody leaves this house without having a whisky', says I and pour him a good one".

"'I'm not allowed to drink on the job' says he. Man, was he ever uncomfortable".

"'And who the hell is gonna be around to see you?' I ask".

"So he takes a nip and darn near gags. 'I'm not used to strong liquor', he says." Art is bent over with laughter, tears rolling down his cheek. A further top-up is called for as soon as he can continue.

"So then he says, 'Where are your papers Mister Zimmer?' as if he thinks I have everything in some fancy filing cabinet like they do down at the bank."

"'In that there box', says I. 'And in that one there, and maybe some in that one with the whisky bottles in it'. Well, the little man is mighty unhappy. That's when I picked up the gun and fired at a pretend mouse. 'Damn, I missed the little bugger', says I. Well, the man, he almost up and died. His face was whiter'n my ass".

"'What, what are you doin'?' he asks."

"Shootin' at that darn mouse. You know, that little bugger has more lives than a cat, but I'll get him yet, you be darn sure I will.'"

"'Mister Zimmer,' the man says still standing up, 'Mister Zimmer, I've decided not to disturb you any further,' he says. 'I'll let my superiors know that your books are in perfect order. See you.'"

"Well, he couldn't get outa here quick enough. Never heard from 'em again, either. Have another, cop-man".

"I don't mind if I do," replied Aubrey, feeling no pain.

When it came time, Aubrey decided to walk the half-mile home, and even then he barely made it. Putting one foot in front of the other presented an intellectual challenge as great as any he had ever faced.

"Where on earth have you been?" Sabine confronted him, recoiling from the reek of wood smoke and whisky.

"Talking to my tax consultant," Aubrey remembered saying before passing out on the chesterfield.

Chapter Thirteen

BUBBLES

$\mathcal{S}$ale day!

Sale day: a day to anticipate, a day to dread, a day of reckoning that creeps its stealthy way upon you, whether you sell through a private deal or through the sale ring at the local auction. Most of Aubrey's neighbours chose the latter, convinced that buyers would be falling over themselves to buy their superior calves. "No doubt about it," they said. "You would get the best that the market could offer."

Sale day is the day when, as a beef producer, you get your annual paycheck, the one paycheck that is surely going to reflect all of your efforts of the past year and the hours that you spent nursing babies back from death's door because of frostbite, pneumonia, scours, you name it. It is time for the payback for all those dollars that you spent on a C-section, a vaccination program, and the hay you had to buy last year. Wrong, Mister Hanlon! These don't even factor into the equation; they are unrecognized, not acknowledged in the slightest. Aubrey's quaint idea that he and Sabine might be rewarded on merit was just that, quaint. If a buyer can twist and turn to bring the price down, that indicates he is good at his job, that he is a master of his game. It is not as if he has any ulterior motive; if he can get your year's work for nothing, he will be quite at ease doing so. Sale day is business in the raw, and there is hardly a seller who does not feel half naked on sale day.

Aubrey's take was slightly different in another aspect as well. Some people would jump on a plane and go all the way to Las Vegas, he reasoned, or head down to the nearest bar with a slot machine. Here he was, a small-time cow-calf operator, hauling his calves into the auction, all the while trying to convince himself that it was something other than a gigantic game of chance. He'd made his effort to study market trends, had he not? He had read all the stats in the sale reports from the region's various marts in the local paper three weeks in a row, hadn't he? He had talked to Fred Bloodworthy the cattle buyer from Camrose who insisted that the calf market was about to peak. Then he had spoken to that insufferable Brent Wigsby, the field man from Sampson Brothers whose advice was to hold on for a month because "the market's gonna surge like a tsunami." And finally he talked to Art Zimmer who pronounced that "It don't matter sweet tootin', you'll be screwed by 'em all whatever day you sell." Coupled with all of this were the tales of somebody who got this astronomical price or took that severe beating, of somebody else who did so well he might have to pay income tax this year and he's never paid income tax in his life!

Pete was the catalyst who precipitated the Hanlon's first ever calf sale date. "When are you ever going to wean them calves of yours?" he asked Aubrey. "You shouldn't leave 'em on the cows much longer, not if you want your cows to calve without too many problems next spring." The decision to sell the following week was made right then and there.

"Bring 'em on in," said Clayton Cole when Aubrey phoned him up to figure out the logistics. "Bring 'em in next Saturday. We've got a good bunch coming in, and there should be plenty of buyers on hand because we're now into the big runs. Say, how many have you got? I'll even advertise them in the paper."

"Forty-five."

"What kind?" asked Clayton.

"What kind? Just steers and heifers. What other kind is there?" Aubrey mumbled.

"No, no, I mean what kind? What bulls have you been using?"

"Oh, oh, pardon me. Red Angus."

And there it was, in black and white in The Mountaineer the following week.

> COLE'S AUCTION MART,
> Highway 11 West, Rocky Mountain House,
> Regular sale every Saturday. Partial listing.
> Saturday November 3, all breed cattle and calf sale.
>
> Sam Brown, Eckville, 80 Charolais calves.
> Bill Davidson, Dovercourt, 100 Gelbvieh X Red Angus calves.
> Audrey and Sabeen Hanson, Rocky, 45 Red Angus X calves.
> Clem and Sue Duckworth, Alder Flats, 156 Exotic calves.

Damn, why hadn't he spelled out their names out to Clayton?

"Honey, why on earth did you not spell out our names to Clayton? You knew he hadn't quite figured it out. Now nobody will know that these are our calves, will they?"

Aubrey just shrugged his shoulders. With no chance of victory, there was no point in getting into a pointless argument and suffering defeat. Even if the names had been spelled correctly, would it have guaranteed them a better price, he wondered discreetly to himself?

"The best way to handle it is to wean the calf straight off the cow and on to the truck," said Pete. "If you like, I'll even come over and give you a hand, but the night before, shut 'em in that field next to your corral. That way, they'll be much easier to get in when we're ready to load. Throw 'em a bale of hay and they'll be quite happy, then all we have to do is just sort 'em out in the morning."

Just sort 'em out in the morning. It all sounded so simple! But Pete had not yet made the acquaintance of Nellie. The thing about Nellie was that she had a very long memory for a cow, and she had suffered through this weaning business a number of times before. The moment that Pete, Aubrey, and Sabine made their way through the gate into the field, her head went up, and that of the calf with her. Two seconds later, she was leading her troops down to the bottom corner of the pasture, right where it bordered on a twenty acre patch of muskeg and willow. And there they waited in obvious defiance, watching every move by the trio of humans at the top end of the field.

"Oh shoot, that's the one section of fence on this farm that is in dire need of repair," said Aubrey. "There are three or four rotten posts down there." It was a sort of pre-confession for what was about to happen.

"Well, we'd best be careful not to spook them, then," said Pete stating the obvious. "Why don't you make your way into the muskeg, and come out behind them so they move away from the fence?" he went on. "Then your lovely wife and I will drive them into the corral."

"Good thinking," said Aubrey as he moved off. Nellie watched him climb through the wire, watched him as he disappeared among the willows. Nellie knew this game and knew it well, although to her, it was no game that her baby was about to be taken from her, even if he was an earless and tailless seven hundred pound monster. Despite all of Aubrey's heroic efforts in the spring, both the calf's ears and tail had dropped away because of the frostbite. Sabine had christened him Bubbles, and truth be told, he did bear a strong resemblance to one of those hot-air balloons floating over Calgary on many a weekend. But Nellie had no intention of parting with him just yet, even if it did mean an end to all that bunting of her nethers, all that butting of her udder by a calf with an insatiable appetite. As if on cue, she smashed through the fence, flattening the rotten posts as she did so. Her companions were only too happy to follow her through.

Aubrey, hearing the others shouting excitedly, knew exactly what had just happened. Had he and Sabine been conducting the operation on their own, he would have abandoned it right then and there. But because he had his kindliest neighbour helping out, he felt under some obligation to keep going, so he started running through the muskeg to head them off. God never intended man to walk in muskeg; if he had, he would have given man splayed feet like a moose. God certainly never intended man to run in muskeg either, any more than He intended man to fly, so the outcome was unfortunately entirely predictable. It was not just a small tumble; it was a headlong catastrophe into a puddle of freezing water cradled between the irregular tussocks of muskeg. Aubrey never did see Nellie, although he could hear her and her cohorts charging off through the bush. Well, apparently Nellie had made the decision for all of them. He slowly picked himself up out of the water and brushed off all the debris as best he could. Having twisted his ankle in the fall, he could only hobble painfully back to the others.

"Next week," Pete announced as soon as he saw him.

"Next week," reaffirmed Aubrey, panting like a carthorse.

"But you'd best phone up Clayton and tell him that you're not bringing in your critters for this week's sale. That way, he can put 'em back in the paper again."

"And change the spelling of our name," Sabine piped in. "Honey, are you all right?"

"Got myself a twisted ankle, courtesy of that bloody Nellie."

"Maybe you should load her on to the truck and dump her. Sell her as a bred cow. I always make a point of selling any hell-raisers in my herd before they contaminate the rest," said Pete.

"Oh no, sell Nellie?" exploded a horrified Sabine. "We could never do that, could we honey? We love her way too much to just dump her, don't we Aub?"

"On rare occasions," growled Aubrey, "and this isn't one of them." He would have been quite happy to skin her alive at this precise moment.

Nellie and her friends did not come out of the bush for a full three days, not until hunger and the memory of that bale in the front pasture got the best of them. They found that Aubrey had repaired their getaway hole, but that, in the corner, he had installed a gate that he had left open for their convenience. Full of suspicion and mistrust, Nellie was ready to bolt in a second. But Aubrey played a mean hand of "Cow Chase Poker". He got up before sun-up the day after they had come back in, and he slunk his way through the muskeg to shut the new gate, and then he wired it shut. In the meantime, he had phoned up the auction mart to make his apologies.

"No problem," Clayton had said jovially. "Bring 'em in next week. We've got a dandy of a sale coming up." Aubrey went so far as to spell out their names too. "Oh, I'm really sorry," said Clayton. "It'll be right this week, you see."

The ad duly appeared in Wednesday's paper.

Audrey and Sabine Hanlon, Rocky, 45 Red Angus X calves.

"What the hell? It was still AuDrey! Did everybody around here think he wore women's underwear?" Aubrey thought bitterly.

God bless Nellie! Although the Hanlons never did make it to what was supposed to be their first official sale day, Aubrey's ankle had been too painful for that, they sure heard about it. To Aubrey's way of thinking, the prices ranged from near awful to virtual disaster. In actuality, they were bad, but they served as a reality check in that they convinced him that he should not expect his calves to go as if they were triple-A steaks on the hoof. He had to accept that they were just run-of-the-mill calves and that there were thousands of them out there. But it also transpired during the week that three of the major buyers had been seduced away to a "Salute to the Cowboy" rodeo and concert up at Ponoka. "The chance to leer at Shania Twain may have had something to do with it," Pete said. But it all made for an incredibly tense week for Aubrey and Sabine. Would they too take a terrible beating? There wasn't another rodeo, concert, calf-buyers' congress, cowboy poetry convention, country wheezing jamboree scheduled for this Saturday, was there? Would Sabine have to think about getting a job? Heck, would Aubrey himself have to take a job? Could he get on as a county cop and do what he hated doing, harassing ordinary country folk because they were too fast, too slow, too overloaded, too insecure? Aha, but Nellie and her gods were about to smile upon them; so much so that Nellie was to become a sacred cow on the Hanlon spread.

Friday came around surprisingly quickly, Friday being the day they were to truck the calves in for Saturday's sale. Of course, Nellie checked out the bottom corner and then seemed to resign herself to the inevitable; she led her troops straight into the corral. The calves were quickly split from their mothers and loaded on to the Flying Zube's truck. Two loads and they were gone. Aubrey accompanied his calves on the second run to make sure he got all the paperwork right and The Zube dropped him off on the way to his next consignment. Where the hell was Sabine? She wasn't in the house. She wasn't in the garden. Maybe up at the corral, but what on earth would she be doing up there?

He decided that he had better take a look. There she was, propped up against the fence, she bawling her eyes out on the one side, the cows bawling their lungs out on the other. Aubrey gently pulled her away, explaining that solidarity with the cows was okay but suggesting that this was taking it a little far. Sniffling heavily and stressing how sad she felt, Sabine agreed, and allowed her husband to escort her back down to the house where she could reconstitute both her serenity and her looks. The bawling of the cows continued unabated all through the night. Much to Aubrey's chagrin, the moment Sabine stepped out of the house the next morning and heard the cows still protesting, her angst was instantly rekindled. Aubrey took her back inside, sat her down and urged her to be strong because he wanted her at his side during the sale. It was his smartest move of the week as it turned out!

Sale day!

When you enter the auction mart on your sale day, you do so with great trepidation, and your perceptions are altogether different from a regular visit. It's as if you find yourself in a state of elevated consciousness.

Why are there so few people today?

"Honey, where are all the people?" Sabine asked her husband almost frantically. "There's not another rodeo on somewhere is there?"

How many of these people were buyers?

"Honey, none of these people look like buyers to me. Do you think the buyers have turned up today?" Sabine was almost out of her mind with apprehension. "That fellow with the tan cowboy hat, do you think he could be a buyer? He sure looks like a buyer."

Were there any farmers who were in the market today?

"There's old Fred and Mabel Courtwright. I wonder if they're in to buy. No, they come in every week, don't they? It's their day out on the town."

Sabine did not stop, could not stop, the spate of questions betraying her extreme state of anxiety. Aubrey would have asked the same questions of her, but her volubility forced him to keep his questions inside, his only contribution being an occasional "maybe".

They went out to the pens to check on their calves one last time before going to look for a seat in the sale barn. The calves had looked so good and so big yesterday, why did they look kind of stunted today? Maybe it was the monster calves in the next-door pen that made them look so puny. Sheesh, if they were that puny, what could they expect realistically, a conjecturing that Aubrey wisely kept to himself.

As they walked into the sale hall, their hearts began to pound. Where should they sit? Up at the top where they might stand a chance of seeing who was bidding? Down towards the bottom where they could hear better? How about in the middle where Clayton would be sure to see Aubrey's signal if he wanted to pass on any particular group, something they agreed they would do if prices were at the level of the previous week? The decision was made for them. The crowd already seated forced them to find a spot high up, in the left-hand corner.

Enduring the "miscellaneous livestock" portion of the sale—the seventeen ewes and one ram, the thirty or so pigs, the dispersal sale of thirty-some Boer goats—was nothing short of excruciating. But the real torture came when the first of the calves were ushered in. Prices seemed to flip-flop all over the place: some good, some fair, some almost brilliant, some rock bottom. Soon, however, there was an even flow going through the ring, but after the first hundred or so, Sabine's refrain began again.

"Honey, where the hell are ours?" she hissed, careful not to have her question trapped in one of those silent pauses that are a regular feature of any auction, a pause that had caught her off guard once before.

"Dunno. They'll come, don't worry," said Aubrey, beginning to wonder himself why it was taking so long for theirs to come through.

"What if the buyers run out of money?" persisted Sabine.

"Then either we'll go home a lot poorer than we had hoped, or we'll be taking our calves back home," said Aubrey in resignation.

Both of them did not realize how often they were both surreptitiously surveying the crowd to spot who might be a potential buyer.

"Quite a few of the local boys are in the market right now," Clayton had said. "So your chances should be pretty good."

There was "the walrus", so christened by Sabine because of his big droopy moustache, his gray leather coat, and his black leather ball cap. He would have been quite at home in the Vancouver Aquarium with a red ball balanced on the end of his nose, Sabine decided. Then there were the two or three obvious buyers, suave cowboy-hatted types, each one armed with the requisite cell phone, pocket calculator, and generous beer belly, ready to do battle with each other and to pounce on any stray bargain. Full of their own importance, they could not sit still in one place, preferring to strut their stuff where they could be seen and heard. Then there was row on banked row of local farmers. Who among them had money? Who among them would hazard a bid?

"Now here's a dandy bunch of calves from Audrey, 'er that's Aubrey Hanlon. The Hanlon's place is just south of here. Red Angus-cross. You won't find a better set of calves anywhere, let me tell you."

Sabine's heart stopped for a second then raced madly with pride at the auctioneer's flattering comments as the first batch of six steers was brought in. They looked so uniform, so red, so, well, good.

"Are you sure those are ours?" she fired off at her mate.

"Yes, they're ours all right. Bill Hockenhammer sure does a good job sorting them out, doesn't he?"

The price started out modestly, way too modestly for Aubrey, but gradually Clayton massaged it upward with a mixture of cajoling, coaxing, haranguing, and using every trick in the auctioneer's book, so that it had soon climbed beyond what Aubrey would gladly have settled for. And still it went up; so much so that Sabine started hissing a spirited "yes!" as each counter-bid raised it further. Finally, the bids stalled at $1.32 a pound, the highest price of the sale so far. Ah, but they were only six out of forty-five, so their ship was still some way out to sea. Still, the average weight had come in at six hundred and eighty-five pounds so they had done very well. So far!

The next batch was ushered in, Newt using his cane a little too freely. Sabine caught his eye and shook her head vigorously. Nobody would take on Sabine in full combat mode despite her china-doll looks. Nellie's calf, Bubbles of curio cabinet fame, was among them, his lack of accessories making him stand out like a sore thumb.

"One out," yelled a buyer before the bidding could begin.

"One out," agreed Clayton.

"What does that mean?" whispered a terrified Sabine to her husband.

"It means that any bidder is free to remove one animal out of the package and it will be sold separately. He's going to take out 'Bubbles', you will see."

This batch too was heavy, coming in at an incredible seven hundred and one pounds. Up and up climbed the price, eventually leveling out at $1.26 a pound. That was when one of Sabine's "suave boys" stepped up to the front.

"I don't want that thing with no ears and no tail," he directed Newt the ring-man. Bubbles was separated from his peers who were then run out of the ring. Sabine did her admirable best to hold her tongue, incensed that her Bubbles had been referred to as "that thing".

"Who'll start me on this one?" Clayton began again. "Dollar ten, dollar and ten, dollar and five, dollar five, dollar two, dollar two, dollar even."

Silence.

"All right, you guys start me any place you want."

"Thirty cents," came a muttering from somewhere in the middle of the crowd.

Aubrey gasped. "That's bloody thievery," he said between gritted teeth. "The calf weighs seven hundred and thirteen pounds, for Pete's sake. It's not as if anyone eats the ears and tail!"

Slowly, painfully, the bids crept up to a paltry forty-five cents a pound with one of the cool dude buyers holding the edge. There it stopped as if in embarrassment. Everybody in the hall knew that this was a steal of a deal in spite of all the stories of frozen-eared calves supposedly doing poorly in the feedlot.

"Going once, going twice."

"Stop! Stop right now!" To Aubrey's utter consternation, Sabine was up on her feet yelling at the auctioneer. "Don't even think it! Don't you dare sell my 'Bubbles' to that, that, that man for that price. I'll, I'll damn well take him home if I have to. Nobody, but nobody is going to take advantage of all our hard work for a price like that! Not least some buyer who thinks that a cell phone is a ticket to heaven."

There was a strained silence. The buyer sat down right where he was, totally dumbfounded.

"Right on, lady," yelled an older woman down towards the front.

"You heard the lady," Clayton resumed, anxious to regain control before anyone else decided to get in on the act. "You heard the lady. So let's do it one more time. If there's nobody interested, we'll pass him out just like the lady said. Now, who'll give me eighty cents?" He asked on a whim. At least five hands shot up as Aubrey hauled his wife back down next to him. Bidding was brisk, taking the price all the way up to $1.15 in the space of a minute. When the final bid was taken, a spontaneous round of applause broke out.

"Well done, lady! Strike one for the little people," the older lady interjected again to a second round of applause.

Aubrey was so proud of his wife he was speechless, but not so the auctioneer.

"Good eye, Jack," he said to the purchaser. "There ain't nothing wrong with that calf, just missing a few of his extremities, that's all."

The atmosphere in the mart was now almost overwhelming. Aubrey and Sabine's calves went on to top the sale, but that in itself was not the point. What mattered was that the Hanlons had made their mark in the wider community, and all because of Bubbles.

Chapter Fourteen
CAN'T STOP NOW!

Sabine was one of those people who was continually on the lookout for the latest deal; Aubrey labeled her "an advertiser's dream". She could be manipulated into buying anything, he said, particularly if some sort of freebie came with it. Why, the very first time they bought themselves a bull, Sabine urged her mate to buy from a particular Angus breeder because he was offering a free fleece-lined jacket with the purchase, and she liked both the colour and the styling—of the jacket that is, not the bull. She would not miss trade fairs and any type of agricultural or craft show for anything. Their dates were always clearly highlighted on the calendar on the fridge. They would always come away with a sack full of free pens, promotional knick-knacks, and free samples of everything from emu oil to buffalo sausage. Yet it wasn't all this that drove Aubrey to distraction so much as her absolute insistence that she enter every free draw she could find, and almost every booth had one.

"But we don't need a collapsible garage," Aubrey would say.

"Honey, if we get it for free, we need it," she would snap back, the accompanying glare warning him to respect her territory and back off from his annual refrain.

It wouldn't be so bad if I didn't have to tag along inconspicuously behind, Aubrey would muse wisely to himself while he rested her already three bags of loot on the floor as she entered yet another draw—this one for a free pig, of all things. At this rate, it would take them three full hours to get out of the place!

"Are you looking for a little extra support my friend?" It was the annual Rocky trade fair, and Pete and his wife had drifted out of the crowd.

"Uh? Well, as a matter of fact, oh, oh I guess it kind of looks that way, doesn't it?" Aubrey blushed and moved a flyer advertising the new breed of 24 hour bra for busy ladies into a less visible spot in his collection. "I was wondering if they made something along the same lines for fine gentlemen with a beer belly," he finished lamely.

Pete's cackle of laughter brought Sabine into the play and a neighbourly visit ensued.

"Make sure you take a visit to a little booth called "Fix-N-Fence", said Pete. "It's over on the next aisle, at the very end. They've got the darndest tool you ever saw for fixing a broken wire on a fence. Go take a look."

That parting advice at least gave Aubrey some focus, even though Sabine felt compelled to enter a draw for a $2000 shopping spree at the local grocery, a free furnace cleaning, a free shampooing for their imaginary dog, and a free holiday given away by some outfit offering timed-shared holiday condos in all of those exotic hot spots that Canadians so craved. When finally they made it to the "Fix-N-Fence" booth, the man lost Sabine's interest by the second sentence, she being lured away to the draw for a free hot tub at the display next door. Aubrey duly purchased a fencing tool and then decided it was time to hustle his wife home, even though hustling Sabine was something of a contradiction in terms: it was something like hustling Nellie somewhere that she had no inclination to go.

It was two weeks later when the call came. It was after supper, actually; Sabine was soaking in the bathtub, and Aubrey was reading the local paper.

"I'm looking to talk to a ... er ... an Aurberry, I think that's how I say the name, an Aurberry or a....a Sabine Hanlon," said the female voice on the phone.

"This is Aubrey."

"Ah, Mister Hanlon. Congratulations! You've won yourself a pig, probably many pigs."

"Who is this?" said Aubrey. "Who is this?" Somebody was obviously having him on, but he was having a hard time placing the voice.

"Oh, I am so sorry. This is Mrs. Sally Sorenson representing the Pork Producers of Alberta. Congratulations, Mister Hanlon, you have won yourself a pig."

"A pig, you say. Who the hell is this? Who is having me on?" Aubrey was frantically racking his brains trying to figure out who might be playing a big joke on him.

"Sir, this is Mrs. Sally Sorenson of the Pork Producers of Alberta. You do have a wife by the name of ... of ...Sabine, don't you?" Clearly she was having as much difficulty with the name Sabine as she had with the name Aubrey.

"Well, yes I do," Aubrey confirmed.

"Well, your wife entered our draw at the Rocky trade fair recently, and I'm pleased to tell you that she won the first prize, a pig. As I said, probably a whole lot of pigs within a few days or so."

"What do you mean 'a whole lot of pigs within a few days or so'? I don't think I understand." It was becoming horribly clear to Aubrey that maybe, just maybe, this caller was genuine.

"Well, the grand prize in our draw was for Miss Piggy, a very pregnant sow, may I say. She is due to farrow in about ten days. I'm calling because I would like you to come and pick her up."

Silence.

"Are you there Auberry,...er.....Mister Hanlon? Are you still there?"

"Yes. Yes, I'm still here."

"I'm so sorry that this seems to have come as a bit of a shock. Did you know that your wife had entered our draw? I mean to say, surely she would not have entered it if you people had no way to deal with a pregnant pig, or would she? I mean, we assumed that only farmers would enter such a draw."

"Well,...er...we are farmers and I'm sure...er...er...we can find something," said Aubrey very uncertainly.

"Well, we have sold our farm, so we need you to come out and pick her up. Miss Piggy has always been quite a pet to us so we were hoping that she would be going to a good home. You do want her, Mister Hanlon, don't you? I mean, we could try looking for somebody else to take her."

"No, no. We'll take her," Aubrey responded almost involuntarily. "We've raised a freezer pig before, but we have never had one have babies. I just need to talk it over with Sabine. Besides, we have to figure out how and where we are going to house a pregnant pig."

"All you need is a roof of some sort over her head and plenty of straw for bedding. We can help you with straw if you don't have any."

"No, no. We've got straw. It's just that I never figured that we would be going into pigs. May I call you back tomorrow evening at this time? Sabine is not available right now ... and thank you very much for calling."

Eventually Sabine appeared from the bathroom. "Did I hear you on the phone just now?" she asked innocently.

"As a matter of fact you did," said Aubrey somewhat coldly. "It would appear that we, or rather you, have won a pig."

"A pig? Oh my God, a pig? Oh my Lord, we won that draw at the trade fair. You remember, don't you? First prize was a real live pig. And we won it. That's great, really great."

"That's the good news," sighed Aubrey.

"Okay, so what's the bad news, then?"

"The bad news is that the pig is heavily pregnant."

"Pregnant? Did you say pregnant?"

"Yes, but not simply pregnant—heavily pregnant."

"Oh fantastic, that's absolutely fantastic! Why, she'll have six or seven babies and we'll have lots of baby piggies running all around the place. Now we'll really be able to call ourselves mixed farmers. The couple of freezer pigs we raised didn't really count, did they? And heaven knows, I always thought of you as being a bit of a swineherd." Her enthusiasm knew no bounds.

"Well, I suppose all the wise men are forever talking about diversification," said Aubrey dubiously. "I guess that's what we are doing, even if neither one of us knows the first thing about raising a pig."

"No worries," said Sabine. "We'll just have to buy ourselves a couple of books and read up on it. They're bound to have something on pigs at the local library. It can't be that difficult, can it? I mean peasants the world over seem to raise pigs without too much difficulty, why should we be any different? So when are they delivering this pig?"

"They? Delivering? No, no, no. We have to go and fetch the pig ourselves. You and I. These people have sold their farm. They need her gone, like right now."

"Oh, but this is so neat!" bubbled Sabine" We'll have to call her Miss Piggy, after the Muppet Show."

"Actually, that is her name. The lady says that she was some kind of family pet, if you can believe that. Apparently, she is very gentle and very friendly."

"Well, you'd better talk to your trucker friend, no? We don't exactly own a truck that we can go and get her with, do we?"

"Truck? Why do we need a truck? We'll bring her home in the station wagon. After all, just how big can a pregnant sow be? Maybe a hundred and fifty, maybe two hundred pounds, max. We only have to go about eight miles north. It's not as if the old station wagon is our luxury limo or anything, is it? I mean it is our version of the farm runabout is it not?"

Sabine thought it wise to bow to superior wisdom if she wanted to claim her prize. But then again, maybe it would be better to sell the pig. After all, if the lady was a big wig among the pork producers, she would have the right contacts for sure. Why could she not have won a hat or a garden umbrella instead, anything but a live, very pregnant pig?

"Two innocents abroad" was how Sally Sorenson summed up the Hanlons when they arrived to pick up Miss Piggy. It was a great story that was to get richer with every telling. "They come cruising into the yard in one of those huge station-wagons, you remember those gas-guzzling aquariums of the seventies? There was this great bear of a fellow and his china doll of a wife, both of them absolutely clueless about raising a pig. So we had to sit them down to coffee and do an instant crash course in pork production. Lovely people they were, but absolutely clueless."

When the Hanlons actually laid eyes on Miss Piggy for the very first time, they were aghast.

"How.....er....how much does she weigh?" Aubrey tried his best to keep the consternation out of his voice.

"Oh, she's one big girl for sure," chuckled Harry Sorenson. "I'd say she would come in at about four seventy to five hundred. Somewhere around that, anyway."

"Four seventy?" Aubrey exploded. "Four seventy? You mean four hundred and seventy pounds? How the hell are we going to get four hundred and seventy pounds of live porker into our station wagon?"

"With some difficulty, but it could be done," said Harry cheerily. "You'll need to fold your seats down, and then back up to that chute over there. As soon as we get her in, she'll be fine as long as you get going right away. She'll be too busy keeping her balance to do any exploring, at least that's the theory anyway. Actually, she'll probably lie down because it will be far more comfortable for her."

Miss Piggy was indeed a gentle soul. She ambled her way up the chute and into the back of the vehicle with virtually no prompting. The old car on the other hand seemed to let out a wistful sigh as the full weight of the animal came aboard. To complicate matters further, Mrs. Sorenson now found time to burst into a flood of tears as she saw her beloved Miss Piggy going forever. Or maybe it was because she was the last animal to leave the place.

"Look after her, won't you," she sobbed at Sabine who was, herself, now torn between leaping into the car or consoling this poor distraught woman.

"Go! Go! Go!" yelled Henry Sorenson, desperate to wash his hands of this tragi-comedy before Miss Piggy made any decision that might indicate that her temporary accommodation or her new owners were not to her liking. Sabine jumped in, Aubrey let out the clutch with panache, and promptly stalled. Miss Piggy was not perturbed in the slightest, she just grunted contentedly as she stared out of the rear window, maybe already assured she was in good, loving hands. Aubrey gave his engine more power this time. The car lurched forward and Miss Piggy toppled over with a mighty crash as she lost her balance. Both Mr. And Mrs. Hanlon thought they would have one very angry pig on their hands, but no! Miss Piggy just lay there grunting contentedly.

The real entertainment occurred when they made it from the mile long driveway and on to the main highway.

"Eight miles of pure hell," Sabine was to describe the journey home later. The problems began when Miss Piggy decided that she would prefer to be on her feet. As she got up, she voided her bowels, great aromatic pig turds dropping over the bench seat to land innocuously between Aubrey and Sabine. The latter, almost gagging now, pressed herself up against the door and began yelling "Stop, Aubrey, stop!"

Aubrey, always the pragmatist of the duo, realized that to stop now would be to court disaster. He simply hunched himself up and increased his speed. "We can't stop now, honey, no way. We can't stop now," he yelled back. Evidently Miss Piggy felt much better, grunting happily as she gazed out of the back window at all the scenery flashing by. Then suddenly and without warning, she arched her back and let loose a copious stream of bright yellow urine, buckets of it, much of it splashing down Sabine's neck. The split second's delay as Sabine struggled to grasp what was going on did not help much either. By the time she was able to release the catch on her seat belt, she was apoplectic. Screaming blue murder, she rolled herself up into a ball and flung herself on to the floor into the space below the glove compartment.

"Stop, Aubrey! Please stop," she beseeched her husband. But Aubrey was not about to stop for anything: not for her, not for Miss Piggy, not for the queen of England.

"Stop you bastard! Stop this second, damn you!" shrieked Sabine, as the flow of yellow slowed down to a trickle that splashed idly over her vacated seat. Aubrey was intentionally oblivious, at least until Miss Piggy decided to get a better, more direct look at life in the raw. Grunting serenely, she stuck her nose straight through the back window, glass shattering both inside and outside of the car. She liked this, the air circulating freely around her snout. Aubrey braked hard, and for the second time on her journey to her new home, Miss Piggy went down like a ton of bricks. Sabine, just deigning to uncurl herself from her fetal position on the floor, was propelled back into the recesses beneath the dashboard. Aubrey's anger had taken over. He leapt out of the car with absolutely no idea as to what he intended to do. Miss Piggy grunted a happy greeting at him from her berth in the back, but showing no real inclination to get up and deal with a chauffeur who seemed every bit as disgruntled as a slighted New York cabbie.

"Shit!" he yelled. "Shit, and more shit!" He climbed back into the car. Deliberately ignoring the bleating of his beleaguered mate still crouched down somewhere beneath the dash, he made for home, determined to end this nightmare without more ado. Sabine stayed where she was, partly in terror from the ride, partly in fear of her now unhinged husband.

They screeched into the yard. Well, they would have screeched into the yard had the old station wagon been up to the part. But they did enter the yard with a sense of urgency. Their arrival seemed to prompt a rekindling of some interest on the part of Sabine, none on the part of Miss Piggy.

"Hang on, honey. I'll back up to the granary. She'll probably just get up and walk in by herself." When they got as close as they could get, Aubrey opened the rear door. Miss Piggy opened one eye, grunted contentedly at her new owners, stirred only enough to defecate one more time from the prone position, and then went to sleep.

"C'mon now, Miss Piggy. C'mon now. You haven't got a piano tied to your butt." Sabine had all but forgotten her wet tee-shirt look as she tried her darnedest to coax their new pet out of the vehicle. Miss Piggy remained studiously unimpressed.

"I'll go and get a bucket of chop, that'll get her out for sure," said a now much calmer, more contrite Aubrey. When he returned, Miss Piggy made it clear to him that she was not the least bit hungry. That was when Aubrey discovered that a 475 pound pig constitutes an immovable object if it decides that it is not going anywhere. For nearly an hour they struggled without success.

"The bloody thing can stay here all night for all I care!" Aubrey admitted his defeat as he climbed out of the back of the station wagon for the last time. "She'll have to come out by herself when she's good and ready. Typical female of any species."

Uncharacteristically, Sabine did not bother to respond. "Yes, let's just leave her be," she said. "We don't want to make her hostile to us if we don't have to. Oh dear, I smell horrible."

The next morning, just at sun-up, Aubrey went out to check on the pig. She was gone; or at least there was no sign of her, and the vehicle was empty. He peered into the granary. Nothing, no trace of any pig, let alone a monster one. Where on earth could she have got to? Where on earth could she have possibly gone? He trekked all around the yard, up into the corrals, and around what passed for his workshop. Miss Piggy had vanished, totally vamoosed. He decided to take one last look in the granary before hopping into his car and taking a drive around the general area. From the doorway, the straw bedding looked undisturbed, exactly as he had left it when he had forked it in. He took one step forward, then another and another. Who got the worst fright will never be known. Miss Piggy's vast bulk suddenly materialized from the straw beneath him and lifted him clean off his feet. Aubrey was later convinced it was this particular incident that made them kindred spirits, although it was not evident at the time. Psychologists will probably have some obscure term like crisis-bonding to describe the phenomenon.

Miss Piggy's first instinct was to head for sunlight, Aubrey astride her back. As she charged through the door, Aubrey caught his head on the doorframe and was knocked clean off his unwonted perch and into the straw. He was out cold.

When he came to about a minute later, something gigantic was standing over him, nudging him, trying to urge him to his feet. As his eyes duly came into focus, there was this mother of all pigs, grunting gently and nosing him first in the ribs, then at the torso, trying to coax life into his inert form.

"S'all right, Miss Piggy," he mumbled. "S'all right. I'm gonna make it, I'm sure." The pig's grunt in response indicated perhaps delight, perhaps relief, or perhaps just plain satisfaction. At any rate, she gave him one last giant nudge that rolled him right over before she retreated and went back to bed—well, not quite bed in the human sense. As Aubrey stood up, she was busy reworking the straw with her snout. Then, within minutes, she had once again rendered herself virtually invisible.

"Sorry about that, old girl," said Aubrey as he departed, a large bump beginning to form on his head. "We're going to be good friends, you and I."

Within two days, Miss Piggy had completely endeared herself to her new foster family. Sabine's idea of bringing in an occasional carrot, fresh from the garden, and scraps from the table made her an instant hit with Miss Piggy. "We both speak the same language," she told her husband who was wise enough not to comment further. Miss Piggy seemed to grow even larger, more voluminous, with her underbelly almost scraping the ground and her nipples turning a flushed purple as the milk came in. Reluctant to stray far from the granary that she had claimed as her new home, it was very evident to Sabine that Miss Piggy was about ready for the big day. Meanwhile, Aubrey told himself that his wife was getting as maternal as the pig, judging by the spate of house cleaning that was going on.

Despite their very best intentions, neither Aubrey nor Sabine witnessed the great event, or at least the major part of it. Aubrey went out to do his six-in-the-morning check, and there they were: a fighting, fussing, furious mound of baby pink all squabbling over the two rows of engorged nipples on offer to them. Aubrey himself was so excited that his first thought was not to do the logical thing and make sure all was well, but to rouse his wife out of bed. Sabine was beyond simple excitement; she was in a sort of maternal ecstasy. It was lucky that it was high summer because she ran out dressed only in her baby doll nightie to visit the new mother. She was totally unprepared for the sight that greeted her: a version of absolute anarchy the like of which she could never have imagined.

As her eyes adjusted, she took in the great wallow of afterbirth at Miss Piggy's tail end, a tiny creature marooned in the center of it as if in a vast lake of jelly. She reached down and gently added it into the general melee. And melee it was. Crawling all about Miss Piggy's belly was a horde of babies. It wasn't that mother was oblivious; you could tell that she wasn't from all the maternal grunting. It was simply that the newborns had to find their place in the pecking order, or more specifically the sucking order, that had to be established. Once a baby had staked its claim to a particular nipple, it would fight all comers. One big fellow had his mouth firmly glued to a front nipple, his eyes firmly shut until one of his siblings pushed his luck and endeavored to take his prize. Two others were fighting furiously over a top nipple when there was a vacant one below. The rest were all milling about, stumbling over each other, stumbling over the mother's legs and belly, all with the mission to find their place at the food counter, so to speak. One hardy little fellow made it all the way up to mama's snout. Sabine watched in fascination as Miss Piggy opened one big eye to grunt a greeting at her little one. At that same moment, she gave one last involuntary heave and a tiny new piglet was propelled into the world from the womb, landing with no ceremony on top of the pile of afterbirth. When it showed no sign of life, Sabine reached down frantically and grabbed it, dunking the comatose baby into Miss Piggy's water bowl as she had read she should do. The sudden shock of the cold water brought the tiny creature's heart into instant circulation. Sabine was so proud that she just stood there for a good minute cradling the little mite to her bosom.

That was how Aubrey found his wife when he reappeared with a bucket of chop for the new mother. There was his wife, happily engrossed in the world of motherhood that he could never ever join, clad only in her baby doll nightie— a garment that any spokesperson for the pork industry would suggest offered "both impractical and inadequate coverage for a professional livestock technician." Sabine could have cared less as she bent over to place the tiny animal on to a currently vacant nipple. The baby knew exactly what to do and was sucking away greedily within seconds. Sabine had just finished counting fifteen babies when she spotted the dead one as mother pig moved her back leg forward. With an anguished cry, Sabine grabbed on to the minute cadaver only to find that the life had been squashed out of it some time ago.

Death is very much a part of life when you raise livestock, but Sabine did not relish being brought up to it so close and personal. Aubrey had always dealt with it when a calf had died, so when it came to their cattle, death had always been somewhat remote for her. True, she had seen a couple of her chickens die, but for them death had been a release from evident suffering, so she had been almost glad of their demise. But this poor little creature's life had been snuffed out right at the start, even before its first meal, and that was not fair!

"I want you to bury this tiny creature," she said to Aubrey.

Aubrey knew his wife well enough not to argue. Yes, he would bury it, as long as he got away without having to conduct a funeral with full military honours, he thought to himself.

"But I think you could be dressed a little more appropriately."

Only then did Sabine look down and realize what a sight she must have presented. The mysteries of her peek-a-boo nightie were hardly mysterious any more now that copious globs of birthing fluid had rendered most of the front of the garment readily transparent.

"Oh dear, now what would a real live pig man have to say?" she sighed.

"A real live pig man would probably say that you must be the sexiest swineherd ever to set foot in a pigsty," responded Aubrey. "Run along, now, and change before one of your traveling brush salesmen comes along and sees you in your entirety." That new reality jolted Sabine into making a move, not that she was gone that long, mind you. She just could not stay away from "my new babies" as she called them.

All that night she did not sleep well, fretting the hours away worrying about how many babies Miss Piggy would roll on in the darkness. Sure, the light from the heat lamp that they had rigged up would help, but she was not sure if she could handle six or seven dead piglets in the morning. But she had underestimated Miss Piggy; mama pig may have been around five hundred pounds, but she was the essence of gentleness. Sabine was up at first light, not in her baby doll nightie this time; she no longer felt "agriculturally sporting" she told her husband. Surprise, surprise, her babies were all there, vigorously "mewling and puking" as a good Shakespearean might say. But there was cause for concern. Every so often, and for no apparent reason, Miss Piggy's head would jerk upwards and her legs would give a kick when the babies were feeding. Was she responding to pain? Was she having spasms? Did pigs get milk fever like cows? Had she been hurt internally? Maybe she could not handle such an unruly mob of little ones? Then minutes later, all would be still as the engorged piglets dropped off into deep sleep, most of them lying up against the warm expanse of mother's belly. Sabine went off to read up on the section titled "Diseases of the Sow", fearing that certain calamity was about to strike.

Later that day, John Upham showed up. As soon as he had got out of his truck, Sabine had to show her favourite neighbour and sometime co-conspirator her litter of newborns.

"I raised pigs one time," John said. "Yep, had 'em for years. A lot of work for not much money, if you ask me."

"So John, can you tell me why the mother pig seems to experience spasms of pain when her babies are feeding?"

"Have you ever been bitten on the nipple?"

"Pardon me!" Sabine retorted in some shock.

"Have you ever been bitten on the nipple?" he repeated.

"I....I....don't think I understand......"

"You haven't cut their teeth and tails, have you?"

"Now you really have lost me. Cut their teeth and tails? You're joking, of course, aren't you?"

John said nothing. He reached down and picked up one of the babies. "Here. Feel that." He opened the piglet's mouth and pointed to the needle sharp eyeteeth. "Now, you tell me, would you like one of them little critters biting you on the nipple?" Crudely put maybe, but the message was blunt. "And if you ever see a mob of pigs get into the habit of tail-biting when they get bigger, you won't ever forget to cut tails again. No sir! They can make hamburger out of each other."

"Well.....er.....er, how do you cut them? I mean, do we have to get the vet? Does he have to anaesthetize them, you know, put them out?"

John laughed heartily. "You got a pair of nail clippers?" he asked.

"Well yes," said Sabine dubiously. "Aubrey uses a pair that looks like a set of bolt cutters."

"Perfect. They'll be perfect. Bring 'em on out, and we'll do these critters right now if you like. The earlier, the better." He grinned that toothy trademark grin of his.

Somewhat against her will, Sabine went off to the house to fetch the nail clippers. She wished that Aubrey had not gone off to town; he would have known better how to handle John, who seemed, well, a little too enthusiastic. She could not face the idea of hurting her little babies.

"Aha, they'll do the job just fine," John observed when she returned. "You grab a piglet and hand it over to me. I'll do the first four or five and you can see how to do it. Then you can do the rest. How's that?"

Fully expecting Miss Piggy to go ballistic, Sabine reached over and grabbed the biggest piglet from the front tit. Miss Piggy did not bat an eyelid despite all the squealing.

"See here," said John. "Put your index finger in the mouth so. Snip, snip. Off come the teeth. One, two, three, four. Then a quick turnaround and off with the tail." Obviously John had done this many times before. He passed the little squealer back to his helper who passed him the next one. He did not see the pallor in her cheeks, he did not see the tears begin to flow, he could not hear the muffled sniffles with his hearing aid turned down as it was. He processed another two then turned to her.

"It's your turn," he announced grandly.

Just as she toppled over, he saw the tears and realized the utter distress that she was experiencing. But he was not quick enough to catch her, and down she went like a limp sack lying stretched out the full length of Miss Piggy's back. The latter's only reaction was an extra grunt of welcome. John, always the pragmatic farmer first, finished up the chore of the tails and teeth before turning his attention back to Sabine. She, poor girl, came to life to find herself stretched out next to a huge pig, a bearded gremlin staring down at her and talking.

"You'll be all right, my dear. You're all right. C'mon, get yourself up, lady. You owe me a cup of tea."

Sabine sat up, looked about her, spotted the tailless piglets and burst the dam again. That was how Aubrey found them when he arrived back from town, his wife standing unsteadily on her feet, old John trying desperately to comfort her, very hesitant about how he should hold her to prevent her collapsing once more. As for the pigs, mama went right on grunting, the babies went right on sucking, the world of humanity completely irrelevant to what they were bound to do.

— Chapter Fifteen —
LOOSE TALK

*L*isten to a gaggle of farmers talking and soon you discover that farming has its own vernacular, its own language, so to speak. And each specialty in farming has its own distinctive vocabulary and context which means that an exclusive tiller of the soil could conceivably have little or no idea about the agricultural aspects regarding the discussion of a couple of pig farmers. Now if such conversations should ever be taken or heard out of context, there is potential for great amusement, sometimes extreme embarrassment, or even downright disaster. As Aubrey himself became steeped in the ways of cow and crop, so too would he talk glibly of this and that without first necessarily checking his surroundings. It had to be said that one of the things he enjoyed about having retired from the police force was not having to be on his guard all of the time; not having to project a public persona that tended to all but imprison the humor and the happy-go-lucky nature of his private persona. But then again, he was to find that agriculture was not always a benign subject either.

The first major incident began innocently enough one Monday morning in February. The calving season, only three weeks old, had already proved challenging to say the least. There had been two prolonged spells of bitter cold, and on this particular day, Aubrey was exhausted after spending a fruitless hour trying to persuade what had to be the dumbest calf in the world to latch on to his mother's tit. The mother had raised a huge calf the year before, but unfortunately she had one of those udders that if the calf did not find sustenance right away, the tits would swell up into four bulbous monstrosities that any calf would not then recognize as the grocery store. To vent his utter frustration, Aubrey decided to drive into the local RCMP detachment and have a visit with his old friend Bud Perkins, whom he knew was on duty.

"C'mon in and have yourself a coffee," said the ever hospitable Bud. "You look as though you could do with one, maybe even two," he laughed.

"So how's it all going?" he asked, once they were seated in the detachment staff room. There were only the two of them in the room at the time; not that it mattered that much because in such surroundings, it was always open season on anyone's conversation.

"How's this farming thing compared to a life on the side of law and order? Don't you miss a life fighting for truth and justice?" Bud always liked to razz his friend about his foray into agriculture. A farm boy himself, "from way back" he liked to say, he had gone into policing "because it offered a hell of a lot more excitement than watching grain grow and chasing some dumb cow around a half section south of Didsbury." Now many years later, and close to retirement himself, he had decided to return to his roots and had bought a small farm just north of Rocky where he raised a small purebred herd of Black Angus cows with his wife Angie.

"Well, I tell you, on some days I wonder what the hell I got myself into. Like today for instance, I just about reached the end of my rope."

"Oh, and why might that be, my friend?" Bud was always the attentive listener, and a fount of knowledge of the most obscure kind, particularly when it came to cattle.

"Well you know how it is when you have a calf that is too dumb to suck, too bloody stupid to figure out where he is supposed to get his groceries? The one I'm fighting with is worse than interrogating the dumbest prisoner that I ever had to face, let me tell you."

Neither man paid much attention when a young woman constable, evidently just new to the detachment, walked in and headed for the coffee pot. Even in a uniform that did its best to downplay the glamorous, she had the sort of profile that any male eye would take note of as she passed by, an effect that she was very well aware of and enjoyed, not that she had any options otherwise.

"Yeah, I know what you mean," Bud resumed the conversation.

"Problem is, his mother has great big fat tits that you can hardly get your hands around. You know the type, all bulbous and flabby."

"Yeah, I know what you mean," said Bud. "They're the worst type. Them and the ones I call sausage tits. You know, them ones that hang so low that they are dragging just above the ground."

The crash of the coffee pot startled both men just about out of their wits. Both of them looked up to see the young policewoman staring at them aghast, her eyes blazing red hot fury, hot coffee splattered on her perfectly creased pants. Just at that precise moment, the moment she was about to fire from the hip, in walked Juliana the ever-jovial receptionist.

"You boys discussing those damn cows again, I'll bet," she said good-naturedly, smiling at the two men. Then her eyes took in the hapless constable in the corner. "Oh dear, are you all right, Constable Petrie? What on earth happened? Are you okay?" She rushed over to lend a helping hand. "What happened? You dropped the pot?"

The poor bewildered rookie was still too busy digesting what she had just heard to hazard any kind of reply. Truth be known, she was now even angrier, although now the anger had been redirected against herself. Damn it, they had been talking cows—cows, not people. Oh my God, and she had been quite ready to hurl the coffee pot at those two male chauvinist pigs who she thought had been discussing, it did not bear thinking about.

"Here, let me help you." Juliana was one of those types who automatically took charge in a crisis situation. "Luckily, we have a spare pot in the cupboard, so don't feel bad. Here, take this paper towel. You go and clean yourself up and let me deal with this mess." The poor woman just nodded numbly and left.

"Now what were you two boys talking about that got your new colleague so upset, eh?" grinned Juliana. "Tell me that."

"We were just sitting here and talking about… Oh no! Oh shoot! She must have misunderstood completely, picked up the wrong end of the stick! Oh no! I'm sure going to have to apologize to that young lady," said Bud, now all flustered and hot under the collar.

"I'm sure glad it's not me who's got to work alongside of her," added Aubrey, much ashamed of the grief they had caused so inadvertently by their loose talk.

"Let me smooth it over for you two boys," offered the veteran receptionist after she had finished chuckling at the story; she had worked with too many policemen over the years not to know precisely how to patch up an embarrassing situation such as this, and in a way that nothing but good humor would come of it.

When the young rookie returned, Juliana soon had her laughing with "the boys" by admonishing them for their "idle chatter" and then turning to her and asking, "Doesn't everybody know that peasant farmer types masquerading as cops have great difficulty keeping their minds from dunking in and out of the manure pile? I thought everybody knew that. Of course, you weren't to know that these two were dumb farmers either." The ensuing laughter could only bring genuine rapprochement, and a palpable relief that a nasty situation had been averted.

Aubrey should have learned from this incident; after all, the embarrassment had burned itself far enough into his mind. But when you are at ease in comfortable surroundings, the coffee is good, and your companion has sprung for a delicious chunk of Black Forest cake in one of Red Deer's trendy little bistro-cum-coffee houses, your brain does not always tune into your surroundings. Quite apart from the other customers, a smattering of earnest business types and garrulous shoppers taking a break from the great consumer drive, there was a group of four elderly ladies seated at the next table sipping tea.

"So when did you get your boy home?" asked Frank. His neighbours had christened him "Frank the friendly foghorn" because his affable voice tended to carry to every corner of any room. Frank had graciously agreed to accompany Aubrey to a nearby farm some five days previously to pick out a new bull, a purebred Red Angus. Aubrey now knew enough to admit to his inexperience, so Frank, widely recognized for his "cattle smarts", had come along as "counselor, mentor, adviser, and sometime psychologist."

"He may be loud, but he sure knows his cattle," Aubrey's neighbour Pete had insisted. Indeed, it was Frank who had recommended the breeder that they had visited. And Frank did not fail him. It turned out that the breeder had not had the time to do the requisite measuring and testing that any seasoned bull buyer would request automatically. So they had picked out "a real winner", according to Frank, and Aubrey was to take him to his own vet in Rocky "to do the honours", the sale being contingent on a satisfactory outcome. More to the point, the breeder had discounted the price generously because of the inconvenience to Aubrey.

"So did you get your boy home?" The question came from somewhere out of a mouthful of Black Forest decadence.

"Actually, I got him home yesterday."

"Well you be damn sure and get down to the clinic and measure his scrotum. Remember, if it's under thirty-six, it ain't gonna be no good." Aubrey was facing the four elderly women at the adjoining table. He saw their conversation falter as they took in what Frank was saying.

"And you be damn sure to get his semen tested too, you hear me. Can't have your boy gallivanting around the countryside shooting off blanks, now can we? Damn good cake, eh?" Frank was oblivious to the fact that practically the entire room was in on the conversation.

Aubrey watched as the obvious matriarch of the group almost choked on her bran muffin, crumbs scattering outwards from her mouth as great indignity blasted them over the tablecloth.

Her companions, not yet certain that they should be indignant as well, had also heard Frank's pronouncement and now they were staring at him with apprehensive eyes. But Aubrey's attention was monopolized by the no-nonsense power broker of the group. Her brow deeply furrowed as she pushed the remnants of the bran muffin out of the way, her eyes blazed a zealot's glory as she pushed her chair away from the table with all the drama of an impending execution. Strikingly tall, her blue rinse bouffant giving her the look of a medieval man-o-war in full sail, she strode over to Aubrey's table. Towering over them as if assessing the range, she suddenly let them have it with a broadside like no other.

"How dare you! How dare you talk of someone's precious child like that! For it shall be made known unto thee," she paused momentarily to make sure that all cannons were fully loaded. "For it shall be made known unto thee that the sins of the fathers..."

"Shall be visited," Frank interjected in a vain attempt to halt the barrage, if not to slow it up.

"Shall be visited upon the sons. Mend your ways, oh ye of so little faith." Seemingly she had a thing about repetition as the sonorous voice repeated itself. "Mend your ways, oh ye of so little faith, for with that kind of talk both of you should be consigned to hell in a hand-basket."

Aubrey was utterly speechless, but not Foghorn Frank. First, he responded by saying, "Madam, you have a piece of bran muffin stuck to your chin, and it sure makes you look as weird as you sound." With that, he promptly cracked up, his booming laughter reverberating around the room.

The woman, now suddenly becalmed as she sought to wipe the offending morsel away, struck back like a rattlesnake. One hand shot out to scoop up the half-eaten portion of Black Forest cake on Frank's plate and then to grind it into his mirth-filled face. The force was so great, he flipped over backwards in his chair to land in an ungainly heap on the floor. The self-appointed keeper of public morality sailed over to stand over him, her sides heaving with the fury of the righteous and the blessed. The sound of Frank's continued amusement emanating from where he lay on the carpet served to confirm his continued existence, though not necessarily survival. That was when she suddenly wheeled in the wind ready to beat a dignified retreat away from such wickedness.

"Let's go girls!" she commanded. "We cannot, nor will not, continue in such a den of iniquity. Gladys, you pay the bill. We'll wait for you outside." Again a pause as the full fury of her glare settled back to Aubrey, still seated meekly in his place. "And you sir," she drew herself up to her full height, "and you sir, wash thine hands of such filth and seek the Lord. C'mon gals, we shall not spend another minute in this viper's nest."

As they moved off in flotilla formation, the whole place erupted. Gales of laughter cascaded around the room as the diminutive gremlin of a manager seemed to metamorphose out of the furniture. He reached down and did his tiny best to haul Frank back on to his feet, solicitously wiping gobs of cream and cake from his face with a napkin as he did so.

"Oh thank you, thank you," he gushed. "Thank you so very, very much."

"Thank you? Did I hear you say thank you?" Frank's voice boomed back at him. "Why thank you? We just about started a riot in your café."

"Oh yes, and thank you, thank you very much." The little man was bursting with gratitude, his bow tie exhibiting a life all of its own as it bobbed up and down with the man's enthusiasm. "You see, for over a year now, I have been trying to get those ladies to go and take their tea somewhere else. Twice a week they come in here, take up a table for a minimum of three hours, and all they buy is one pot of tea between them and one bran muffin each. And this is not the first time they have interfered with my customers, no sir. But this time," he paused to rub his hands with glee, "I don't think they will come back. In fact, I am sure they won't."

"What it means to be misunderstood, eh Aubrey, old fart? Ah well, bring on another coffee, and better throw in another chunk of that cake, the first piece didn't get to where it was meant to. I'll go and clean up."

"It's on the house sir," said the manager. "It's all on the house. I shall be happy to give you the whole bloody cake. Thank you. Thank you so much."

Chapter Sixteen
AN UNNECESSARY
AND USELESS EXTRAVAGANCE

That damned auctioneer!

But then again, Aubrey and Sabine began a long and happy holiday tradition because of him. Moreover, Aubrey had always longed for a boat, always. He had been around boats as a kid, and for the rest of his life had hankered after one of his own. Sabine would have none of it.

"If the good Lord had intended us to be creatures of the water, he would have given us fins and big googley eyes," she said. "Besides, when would we ever use a boat? It would sit out there in some shed eleven and a half months of the year just rotting away. We've got far better things to spend our money on than a boat." That was it, an inescapable puritanical logic that said if you bought a toy and had too much fun with it, you might become hopelessly addicted to pleasure, and that would be somehow too decadent.

"An unnecessary and useless extravagance" was her final pronouncement on the subject.

For the longest time, Aubrey was forced to admit to himself that she was right, but only because he could not think of some unnecessary and useless extravagance that she might crave: something that he could buy for her to engender a sense of guilt on her part. But she made it clear that she had become a woman of simple pleasures; her garden, a glorious sunset, baby animals of any sort—these were the things that enriched her life. As she had adapted to farm life, her appetite for the expensive trappings of modern life just seemed to fade away. In turn, this meant he had to suppress his own maritime ambitions until that fateful day.

It has to be said, here, that in the agricultural sector, most males of the human species have trotted off to an auction and come back with some extraordinarily wonderful purchase that made their spouse's jaw simply drop. If they haven't, it has been suggested on good psychological authority, it should be said, that this is an indication they are too hen-pecked or too strictly policed to even take the risk. Of course, when it came to Aubrey and Sabine, it tended to cut both ways, her having become a devoted aficionado of the auction herself. For instance, she announced to him one Saturday that she had bought "a swing seat to put on the deck."

"How much did you pay for it?" Aubrey asked over an earthy auction coffee.

"I think it was two hundred."

"Two hundred? Two hundred dollars? Are you nuts? You bought a swing set for two hundred dollars?" Aubrey was incredulous.

"Well, it's my money as much as it is yours," she said petulantly. "Anyway, it looked so good from where I was standing. Besides, I was bidding against that Agnes woman, you know, the wife of the dentist you don't like."

"It looked so good from where you were standing. Humph. What you're telling me is that when you saw it close up, it wasn't so good, was it?"

"Well, yes. But once you've done a little welding on it here and there, I can repaint the frame and re-cover the cushions. But I do wish now that Agnes had got it."

"Humph!"

Close up, it was hideous; it was outstandingly vulgar, according to Aubrey. The frame was cracked in three of the most strategic places, the cushions were liberally stained with the flavor of the day, and worst of all, they reeked of stale cigarette smoke. Initially, Aubrey was so mad that he was going to leave it there, but then he decided that in the great game of spousal chess, this two hundred dollar fiasco should leave him in a position to checkmate further down the road. "Leverage" is what he liked to call it, "spousal leverage". The monstrosity was consigned to the back of the garage without even a whimper from Sabine.

The problem was, he succeeded in engineering a major imbalance in the equation because after going to his own auction and spending not two but seventeen hundred dollars, it was less of a checkmate and more of a clearing of the board.

What happened was that on the spur of the moment, he went off to an estate auction near Eckville. Sabine did not feel like going because the deceased had been an old bachelor so she decided that the household items would probably amount to a bunch of burnt pans, a couple of girlie calendars, and a prehistoric TV set. It turned out that she was right on that score. But the farmer had owned an old rake like Aubrey's, so Aubrey was hoping to pick it up cheap for parts. He had not noticed in the flyer that the man had owned a boat—a twenty-foot cabin cruiser with a sixty horse Johnson outboard. There was not much listed, so Aubrey had made a point of arriving early, too early in retrospect. In fact, he wondered initially if he had found the right place as there were so few people in attendance. But then it was that time of year when many farmers were in their fields doing their seeding. Aubrey drifted along with the small crowd and soon realized that some incredible bargains were to be had this day. He got the rake. In complete working order and in much better shape than his rake, it was a steal at a hundred bucks. He had stumbled across the boat early on, and had resolved to stick around and see how much it went for. It had obviously been meticulously cared for, but it was now covered in a thick layer of dust, having sat in a back shed for the last five years. The motor looked sound, but then anything mechanical always looked so horribly inscrutable to Aubrey.

"Ten thousand dollars worth," he overheard one grizzled old veteran say to another. "Old Hank sure loved that baby." Obviously one of the neighbours, thought Aubrey.

"You know, he went and rebuilt that motor from the bottom up the year he died, and be damned if he didn't get to use it," responded the other.

When finally it came to the boat, "Lucy Goosie" she was called, Clayton started out appropriately at ten thousand. But this was one of those auctions that had lost its head of steam. Try as he might, he could not get a meaningful bid.

"She's gotta go, boys, she's gotta go. Who'll start me off?"

Silence.

"C'mon now guys, there's still many a day's fishing in this baby yet. She's just a little dusted up, that's all. C'mon Joe, make me an offer, any offer. This is an estate sale; the boat has got to go. Hey Orbrey, you need a boat, don't you? A man of your style? Here's your chance."

To cut a long story short, somebody started the bidding at a paltry twelve hundred, with two more tentative bids popping up before Aubrey got his boat for seventeen hundred on the nose.

"Going once, going twice. You got yourself a boat, Orb. She's all yours. Pick up the operator's manual, the keys, and the bungs for the hull from the ladies at the office. Don't forget to put them bungs in, will you, otherwise you're gonna find yourself in deep water. Ha! Ha!"

Aubrey decided that tactically it would be wise to take the boat home first. That way he could get the civil war over with right away.

"Whose boat is that?" Sabine asked innocently when she saw him pull into the yard. She was absolutely certain in her own mind that she had demarcated her territory so clearly that the boat simply had to belong to somebody else. Aubrey was always doing favors for various friends, usually retired cops like himself; maybe he was going to store the boat for a buddy, they had done that before.

"It's ours," came the deadpan response.

"Ours? What do you mean it's ours?" She paused as the information sank in. "You mean, what you mean is that it's yours, don't you? You went out and bought a boat behind my back. Isn't that what you are saying?" She studied what she could see of the boat through the kitchen window.

"Well, it went very cheap at the auction." This statement was naturally followed by a stream of justification mixed with liberal doses of appeasement. "There was hardly a soul there. I got one hell of a deal. By the way, I got a fabulous deal on the rake, too. I got it for a hundred bucks, and it's in better shape than ours."

"What did you pay? For the boat, I mean. What did you pay for the boat?" she said staring stonily out of the window. "What did you pay, Mister Hanlon?" He knew that he was in deep water when he heard that "Mister Hanlon" bit.

"Seventeen hundred."

"Whaaat? Did you say seventeen hundred dollars?" Her attention was now focused strictly on her husband, her wide eyes fixed firmly on his for the inevitable confirmation. "You know that's a cow and a calf, don't you?" she added evenly.

When cornered in spousal warfare, the male can often do worse than to arouse his mate's curiosity.

"Come and take a look," he said disarmingly. Sure enough, despite something of an extended pause, her curiosity got the better of her; she was out the door before he was.

"Lucy Goosie" she cried as she came up to it. "That'll have to go. Oh, that'll have to go for sure!"

"Hold your horses, honey. I'll go and get the step ladder so you can climb up and see inside." Aubrey was calculating that if he gave her a couple of minutes to digest this new reality, she would be more likely to digest it rather than spitting it out with a whole lot of bitterness. Then, almost too chivalrously, he helped her over the side and into the boat.

"These seats are genuine leather," she pronounced. "Genuine leather. Wow! It sure is nice inside, even if it is full of dust. Did we get the downriggers and the rod holders with it?"

Aubrey did not miss the "we".

"Yes, we got everything you see, including the trailer she's sitting on."

"Oh Aub, now we can go salmon fishing on Vancouver Island. We can go boating on the lake. Oh Aub, we can have so much fun with this." Then came the moment when she had to make a pause to accommodate her more puritan dimension. "But seventeen hundred dollars? Maybe we should turn round and sell it. Oh honey, how are we ever going to pay for it?"

"With money," Aubrey said flippantly. "With dollars. We have enough, don't you worry. The point is, you don't get a deal like this every day. This is the deal of a lifetime. The thing is worth around ten thousand dollars, or so they tell me."

"You realize what this means?" Clearly she was not interested in anything he had to say about value. "This means that you've got to take me on holiday to Vancouver Island." She had that impish smile he so loved on her face when she said it, and she followed that up with an impulsive hug.

"It's a deal," he said thinking that had he known he would get an automatic holiday thrown in, he would have dared her wrath a lot earlier. "We can go to the coast before we get into haying this year. That's in a little over a month, so it'll give us a couple of weeks away. How does that sound?"

"That sounds wonderful," she gushed.

"Here's what I'll do," Aubrey continued. "I'll have Walt down at the small engine place check the boat over. There are a couple of disconnected cables, that sort of thing. We'll get all the oils changed and have him tune up the motor. After all, the old girl has been stuffed away in a back shed for the past five years. That way, we know she'll work for us even before we put her in the water."

"Do it," said Sabine enthusiastically. "I'll make some new curtains for the cabin."

The boat signaled a veritable bonanza for Aubrey. Sabine decided, with appropriate commentary from her husband of course, that the old station wagon was just not up to towing a boat all the way to Vancouver Island, so they were forced to invest in the pickup truck that Aubrey had always coveted. To Sabine's chagrin however, they decided that they probably had to leave the boat's name as "Lucy Goosie" because she had been officially registered that way.

Finally the big day arrived. They were to mosey their gentle way down to Mara Lake at Sicamous, camp there for the night at one of the commercial campgrounds, and then head down to French Creek at Parksville on Vancouver Island. Surely their two weeks would give them enough time to catch a salmon or two?

They made it to Mara Lake in very good time, arriving there by three in the afternoon on a scorcher of a day. The sight of all that water beckoning him to cool off prompted Aubrey's suggestion.

"Honey, how about we give our new girl a whirl on the lake?"

"Should we?" asked Sabine apprehensively. "I mean, won't it take a long time to set it all up?"

"Nah! All we have to do is back down the ramp, slide the boat off into the water, and off we go!"

"Well, if you really think so." Sabine was reluctant to put a damper on her mate's enthusiasm.

Down at the boat launch, they encountered a "Me-Tarzan, She-Jane" couple, those fount of all youth (fountain of youth?) types, artificially bronzed and bulging in only the right places. Strategically placed at the dock nearest to the launch ramp, they were properly positioned so that everybody could admire both them and their boat: a shiny, chromed monstrosity with a motor every bit as big as the man's ego.

As soon as they arrived on the scene, Aubrey proceeded to steal the spotlight. First he managed to jack knife the trailer backing down towards the ramp. Sabine was already given the very distinct impression that Tarzan figured they were lowering the tone of the neighbourhood. She wished Aubrey had not worn his haying hat, a cowboy hat stained with evidence of an illustrious career in farming.

"Look at them Alberta hicks," she overheard Tarzan sneering to his beach bunny. "Someone should tell 'em to go back and try their boat out on the pond in the back forty." Sabine bit her tongue; this was not a good time to start a ruckus, not with Aubrey now jack knifing in the other direction.

Finally he got it right and backed the trailer and the boat well into the water. He stopped and hopped out of the truck. Seeing Tarzan flexing his various assets on the dock, he asked. "Say. I've never done this before. Am I far enough in?"

Tarzan, feeling even grander now that somebody was paying some attention to him, and better yet, according him the status of expert, jumped into the water. "No," he said. "You need to come back a bit more. I'll signal to you." Jane stayed put on the dock, the better to be noticed in all her busty glory. Aubrey backed in further until signaled to stop.

"Thank you," he said warmly to Tarzan as he got out and began releasing the tie-downs securing the boat to the trailer. Tarzan elected to stay put in the water, assuredly as a last line of defense between this country cowboy and his technicolour speedboat emblazoned with the name "Strike Force 1".

"Honey," Aubrey shouted to Sabine. "I'll slide the boat off, and you pull forward with the truck when I tell you."

Much as she had no desire to contribute further to this saga of ineptitude, she could not let her husband down. With great misgivings, she

162 Unnecessary And Useless Extravagance

162 *An Unnecessary And Useless Extravagance*

jumped into the truck. Just as she was supposed to, "Lucy Goosie" gently slid off the trailer and floated. Aubrey could not help it; he was filled with the same sort of pride a young lad feels when he gets his first bike. There she was, his very own baby riding high in the water. Wait a second! High on the water? Well not exactly, she seemed to be sort of settling down, and getting lower with each passing second.

"She seems a bit low to me, does she seem low to you?" he asked Tarzan.

That was when Tarzan spotted the telltale bubbles. "You haven't put your bungs in the hull," he said inscrutably. "Your boat is about to sink."

Aubrey glanced inside the boat. Sure enough, water was streaming in through the drain holes in the transom.

"Back! Come back!" he yelled furiously at Sabine. Oblivious to the high drama going on behind her, she only had an ear for what she had been told to do. She let out the clutch, the truck jolted forward like a stuck pig, and stalled on the ramp.

"No! No! Come back!" This time, Aubrey's scream penetrated her consciousness. She restarted the truck, rammed the gearshift into reverse, and surged backwards. Just in the nick of time. Even though she went much further back in the water than she should have, she happened to hit the boat right on before she stalled again. The boat teetered precariously on the rollers, nose up, stern decidedly down, while Aubrey struggled mightily to push both it, and the ton or so of water it contained inside, further on to the trailer. Ah, but Tarzan was not about to stand idly by, not when presented with a genuine opportunity to strut his strength. He came charging in and put all his weight behind the other side at the back and together they managed to get the boat fully on to the rollers. The two bungholes now spewed the water back out.

"Another minute and you'd have drowned her, country boy," said Tarzan dismissively.

"Yes, but thanks to you we got her back." Aubrey was truly grateful. "Thank you again."

Tarzan moved his physique back to the dock, his herding instinct now urging him not to leave his escort unattended.

Sabine, a very chastened Sabine, located the offending bungs in the glove compartment of the truck. Once inserted, the boat responded with zest, now floating without reservation high and proud on the water. Sabine pulled the truck and trailer away to one side and came back to help where she was needed. She took the rope from the boat and pulled Aubrey up alongside the dock. Tarzan and Jane stood morosely at the deep end of the thirty-yard long structure, suspicious of every move Aubrey might make.

"Come on board, honey," shouted Aubrey.

"No way! You go and check her out first. I'll wait here in case you need help," unsure as to what assistance she could ever render from the shore.

"Okay then. Cross your fingers and say a prayer. Here goes." Squeeze the primer. Switch on. Gear lever in neutral. He pressed the switch... nothing, not a thing. He looked over at the battery. Damn, one of the leads was off. He rectified that. Press switch. The motor fired once, then died. Press switch a second time. Deep rumble as the motor caught. He throttled back and the motor settled into a gentle purring. For Aubrey, the thrill was indescribable; his whole body tingled with excitement as he sat there reveling in the noise of the engine, his engine, his boat!

Okay! Okay! Enough of this romantic self-fulfillment kind of nonsense, it was time to move. Put the gearshift into forward and throttle up.

Whenever it comes to forward and backward motion, if you end up going in the opposite direction to the one you anticipated, it always comes as a rude shock. Naturally, Aubrey had faced the boat towards the open water of the lake and was completely focused on where he intended to go. All the adrenalin, all the anticipation called for going forward, so when the boat roared off backwards, his brain got hung up for a split second or so. The resultant time lag saw "Lucy Goosie" charging around backwards in a half circle threatening a whole flotilla of small craft moored nearby, including of course "Strike Force 1". Finally his brain reconnected. He shoved the gear lever back into what should have been reverse. The boat came to an abrupt stop, hesitated a second as though in great surprise, and then surged forwards like a porpoise on steroids. Aubrey, his heart pounding, nosed out into the open lake and gave "Lucy" full throttle, urgently seeking to put a credible distance between his self and any shoreline angst. Ah well, he hadn't hit anything, yet, but such carryings-on were not good for his ego.

Back at the dock, Sabine was mortified to hear Tarzan take no pains to mute his colourful commentary. "Let's get the hell outa here, babe. These frikkin' lasso jumpers make me bloody nervous. They're gonna be a downright hazard to anything that comes within fifty feet of them!"

Maybe he was right, Sabine conceded to herself as their boat pulled away in a huge wash of righteous indignation. And for good measure, Tarzan gunned his motor as he passed Aubrey circling his way in. The wake from "Strike Force 1" threatened to swamp an inexperienced boater, but not Aubrey. He had grown up around boats; he knew enough to face into the waves.

"Come out for a quick spin, honey," Aubrey grinned as he pulled alongside the dock. "Then I guess we'd better shake a leg and put up the tent."

"What, what happened when you left?" asked a still breathless Sabine. "I mean, why did you suddenly shoot off in reverse?" She hoped that her reticence to climb aboard did not show too much.

"Oh that! That damn Walt must have reconnected the gear cables the wrong way round. It's pretty tough to tell when you're bench-testing a motor. We'll sort it out when we get to the coast. Are you coming, or what?"

The spin was great, casting away all of Sabine's apprehensions to wind and water. The lake was alive with craft of all shapes and sizes zooming around the water like over-zealous water fleas.

The erection of the tent proved to be the other end of the nightmare for Aubrey; for Sabine, it came as a second round of questioning about her husband's abilities.

It was one of those Canadian Tire specials, "so simple to put up" proclaimed the label on the box. But Aubrey immediately discovered that he had left the instructions back home on the kitchen table where he had been taking a sneak preview. The picture on the box showing a sanitized little boy helping an equally sanitized suburban daddy was no help at all.

"Oh well," he sighed in resignation, "just how hard can it be anyway? Look honey, all the poles are colour-coded. Just a wee bit of fancy footwork and we'll be set, don't you worry."

Sabine hated it whenever Aubrey made that last statement; it was tantamount to a signal for her to get out her book and retreat somewhere remote because now it was almost inevitable that putting up this tent was going to be an ordeal.

The three sets of poles with their identifying colours defied his every attempt—first at logic, then at artistic creation—to set up the tent. Nothing, no combination, showed any inclination to fit the tent. Sabine finally got so embarrassed that she went off for a quiet walk, praying the whole time that Aubrey would have a sudden inspiration and that all of his cursing and swearing would evaporate into a delightfully mellow evening. She was not going to take any responsibility for the damn tent. After all, she had not had a sneak preview of the instructions, and she had not stupidly left the instructions on the kitchen table. She had just made it around the corner of their particular avenue of tents when she spotted two young women, in the skimpiest of bikinis, setting up their barbecue.

"Thank God they're this far around the corner from us," she thought to herself, because Aubrey would assuredly succumb to TES, "Twitching

Eye Syndrome", and would start bumping into things. "Still, they sure have some nerve, hanging out like that." Then she gave a start. Wouldn't you know it; the women's tent was exactly the same model as their own. It looked simple enough, if only she could describe it to Aubrey. On second thought, she'd send him down to take a look at it himself, knowing full well that he would have difficulty selecting which channel to watch. But then again, surely he had figured it all out by now.

The two boat paddles propping up a drooping tent shell told a different story. "Honey, there's a couple of young women just around the corner with the same model of tent that we have. Why don't you take a walk on by and take a look? Maybe you'll see enough to inspire you, or to remind you about something you read in the instructions."

"Some damn thing is missing, I tell you," Aubrey growled. "Okay, okay, I'll go take a look. Where did you say it was?"

"Go down to the end of our line and turn right. You won't miss it," she finished enigmatically.

She was right. He didn't miss it, couldn't miss it, and couldn't miss them either, which presented a problem all of its own. How did he study the tent without attracting the wrong kind of attention, he being an ex-policeman and all? As he ambled on by for the first pass, he caught the eye of the bigger woman, which was fine except that she was so magnificently proportioned, the tent got very little of his attention. Flipping her burgers on the barbecue, she smiled at him as he sauntered on by. Down to the end of the line he went before turning round and wandering his way back. There was no doubt about it now; this was some kind of diabolical conspiracy. The other woman was busy chopping wood with an eye-catching wobble.

"Waa! Waa! Mommy, mommy. Waa! Waa!" The howling stopped him dead in his tracks. He had not noticed the little boy playing in the dust and had stepped on him. Now of course, every eye in the neighbourhood was diverted to this new commotion. A female wrestler, surely the feminine version of Hulk Hogan, appeared from nowhere.

"Why in hell don't you look where the hell you're going, Mister?" she snarled. "C'mon now, Jimmy. Let's go back to grandpa."

Aubrey was so acutely embarrassed, he could barely think up an apology. "I'm real sorry little fellah," he said lamely to the child.

"Yeah, you watch your big feet!" the little boy shouted at him, now secure in the custody of Godzilla.

"That's right! You keep your roving eye on the road ahead in future," added Godzilla for good measure. "Forget about what's on the side of the road. At your age, too! Men!"

He saw the maidens giggle, reveling in the extra attention. He felt the crimson spread to his ears, his neck, his cheeks, even his feet, damn it!

"Did you solve your problem?" Sabine asked brightly when he got back to their site.

Should he mention the incident? Should he tell her that he got badly distracted, or did she already know that? Or should he just play dumb? After all, he seemed to be doing that well enough already. Nah. What the eye had not seen, the heart would not grieve. He squatted down to have another go at the tent, but within minutes, he was even more frustrated than he had been before.

"Go on down and take another look," suggested Sabine.

He seemed curiously reluctant at first, but continued frustration forced his hand. This time though, he made a point of walking further into the roadway between the sites. Both women were now at the barbecue. Both giggled at him as he went on by; he would have far preferred a smile, he thought morosely to himself. A giggle was too evocative of, well, stupidity. Then back he came again, making a final supreme effort to study the tent. His extreme concentration served only to give him a more sinister air, so this time the women did not giggle nor even smile as he passed by.

Aubrey was by now quite ready to rig up a "handyman special". He could use the paddles and the rope from the boat anchor and make some form of passable shelter. What the hell did he care what any passers-by might think? But Sabine was not to be denied.

"Go on down and take one more look," she said gently. "Please, just for me, and before your frustration gets to ruin our holiday."

"Oh, all right," snapped Aubrey, shuffling off dejectedly. This time the women saw him coming. Despite the intense heat, the smaller one reached instinctively for a wrap. The larger one was much more brazen, she accosted him directly.

"Say old man, are you looking for an autograph, or a photo, or a swift kick in the butt from a pair of young ladies who are getting decidedly pissed off at you staring at them?"

"Ex-cop in Voyeurism Scandal", screamed the headlines in Aubrey's panicked mind.

"Actually, if you must know, I'm trying to get a good look at your tent."

"Our tent? What's so bloody fascinating about our tent?" the woman shot back, apparently unconvinced.

"Well, my wife and I have the same model, but I went and left the instructions behind, and we've been trying to figure out for the past hour and a half how to put it up. I am really sorry if I scared you. I just cannot figure out how the poles are meant to fit together."

It took a couple of seconds, either for the message to sink in, or maybe it was for the distrust to melt away.

"Oh, oh, then we're sorry too, aren't we Jen. We were starting to think that you were some dirty old man or something. You know what, we'll just finish up our supper and then we'll come round and give you a hand." Gone was the aggression, gone was the hostility, all replaced with sweetness and light. "Tell you what, if you haven't got it up in five minutes, come on back and we'll put it up for you."

"It's a deal." When Aubrey realized what it was that had set off Jen's dirty laugh, once again he felt the crimson spread to his ears, his neck, his cheeks.

It goes without saying that Aubrey kicked himself when he saw how easy it was. The bonus was that the two young women, more appropriately dressed for the task at hand, hit it off with Sabine who insisted that they share a couple of bottles of wine for their pains.

After that, the holiday took a more sedate turn, with "Lucy Goosie" being nothing short of a triumphant success.

Chapter Seventeen
LET US BE THE CONTRARIANS!

*A*ubrey often used to think of his little farm as a microcosm of the wider agricultural world of the prairies. All across the Canadian landscape, unassuming men and women tilled the landscape and tended to their stock—all to keep that elusive consumer nourished and fed. Some would say overfed. There was no deep resentment of that fact, at least not initially. We all have a job to do, a contribution to make, thought Aubrey, and surely the provision of good, healthful food was the most vital. But gradually it began to irk him that this "consumer" was so protected, so pampered even, so shielded from those evil market forces that increasingly threatened to engulf the family farm. Moreover, "the consumer", this fictitious character that Aubrey came to love and hate, seemed so fickle. Less than ten per cent of his or her income went toward food, whereas nigh on thirty per cent of it was fizzled up in entertainment, or so the economists said, anyway. This was a reality that he realized he had no choice but to accept, though for many years he could not quite decide why. What grated on him the most, however, was the characterization of the Canadian farmer as a perpetual whiner, the flip side of the corporate bum who, even dead, would have to be buried with a hand up seeking the next subsidy or rescue package. Could society at large not comprehend that this simply denoted a structural problem in the economic underpinnings of the country? Was there truly this much of a disconnect between the consumer world and his world—the world of the primary producer of food?

As the years went on and the returns for their labour dwindled downward rather than expanded upward, Aubrey and Sabine became first bitter, and then downright cynical. They watched, often almost writhing in pain, as input costs rose unfettered by any sort of government control or inbuilt structural constraints. They would listen in puzzlement as the parts-man at the machinery dealer justified his case for the ten per cent surcharge for shipping and handling on a part because it had been ordered and shipped on a weekend, not a regular business day. They would have to listen stoically as the man at the fertilizer depot attributed the twenty-something per cent hike in cost for product to the soaring price of natural gas. The irony was not lost on either of them that natural gas was one of Alberta's most plentiful resources, but this still did not prevent Canadians from having to pay world market price. They recoiled as the so-called "think tanks" and other watchdogs of the tax burden on the average consumer lamented that "tax freedom day", that day when the tax portion of a person's annual income was fully met, occurred sometime in June. Did they not know that "food freedom day", the day when the food portion of that same taxpayer's income was fully paid, fell sometime in early February? Was it not time that the consumer knew that the farmer's portion of what he or she ate was paid for in just eight days?

Farming became akin to riding on a roller coaster as new and globalized economic forces took hold. The corporate squeeze began to make itself felt as the Monsantos of the world set out to monopolize the biology and the chemistry of seed and herbicide, deliberately setting out to patent knowledge itself, as though the common person was not entitled to knowledge any more unless he or she paid for it. The gradual concentration of corporate power saw farmers raise their heads in alarm as the big players like Cargill and Tyson Foods set their sights on independent feedlots and auction marts, marginalizing the smaller producers into expendable bit players and reducing them to the level of medieval serfs in the much-touted "New Economy".

Sure, there was always the usual cycle of crises: the mini-tornado that dumped John Upham's barn roof into a slough a mile away from the homestead, major rainstorms, crazy snowstorms, that kind of thing. There was the flood of '84 that dealt Aubrey and Sabine a bum hand. A period of incessant rain not only flooded their basement, it also caused their sewer system to back up in spite. Sabine was devastated by "the unmitigated mess downstairs", made even worse by the reek of soggy, decomposing carpet. Never the kind of person one would associate with any kind of unsavory smell, it was a real trial for her to be so brutally reminded that every human being has a biological aspect: that they too can be fecal creatures with a vengeance. However, she did brighten up considerably when the insurance company agreed to cover the damage, especially when she was informed that she could throw her hand into choosing the colour and texture of the new carpet and wallpaper, within the specified budget of course. Aubrey, on the other hand, was not so lucky; the problem of dealing with the sewage backup fell to him.

First he convinced himself that the line to the lagoon was somehow blocked, but how to find the outflow pipe? That was it; he needed a pair of waders. The sort that avid fisherman poured their lower half into before they had someone significant take a picture of them casting a fly on pristine waters. But where could he get a pair? No great fisherman himself, he certainly had no wish to buy a pair. He was in the local Tim Horton's coffee stop, having a lonesome coffee, when "the force" arrived for the morning donut: first two police officers, then four, then two more. Since his friend Bud was in the first pair, the table expanded outward from where he was seated.

"Say, would any of you fellows know where I can get my hands on a pair of waders?"

"Waders? What the hell are waders?" asked the one fellow whose known world did not extend much beyond writing tickets for the usual range of minor offences, every one of which he seemed to take as an affront to his own dignity.

"Waders? Waders are ducks, eh," said one comedian.

"Fishing boots," growled his partner, ever stoic in the education of his junior.

"Actually, I think I might have a pair," said a very gregarious constable. "They're hanging on the wall on my garage; that is, if the wife hasn't thrown them out."

"What do you need them for?" asked a more worldly officer.

"Well," said Aubrey, "I have this problem with my sewage lagoon. I need to wade into it to see if I can find the outflow pipe."

"Come to think of it, my waders had a great big hole in the crotch," said the friendly one, a little too quickly. "Sorry about that."

The upshot of Aubrey's honesty was that nobody volunteered any waders. Okay, he and Sabine would have to do it some other way. They could use the tractor and the loader, although he would have his work cut out trying to sweet-talk his mate into it because running the loader, never mind the tractor, was still not her cup of tea.

"Here's what I want you to do," explained Aubrey. "I am going to tie a thick piece of rope that will hang down from the loader bucket. I'll be hanging on to it and you will drive forward and lower me down when I signal. I'll do a quick look around for the overflow pipe and we're done. Got it?"

"I think so," said Sabine hesitantly, wishing that there had been somebody else around to do it—Ernie or Dick Conley or somebody. But, as she told her husband later, she did not know the half of it. She had not reckoned on her husband stripping off. Now she was really uncomfortable. What if somebody happened to drive into the yard while he was dangling stark naked off a rope on the end of the tractor? It did not even bear thinking about.

"What did you expect me to do?" he had asked. "Work in a sewer field fully clothed? Can you imagine how bad my clothes would have smelled? Once that stuff gets into clothing, it permeates every fiber in the cloth. I would have to throw everything away." Aubrey never threw anything away; his wardrobe attested to that.

Sabine climbed into the tractor and started it. She checked out which levers she would have to push and pull in order to raise and lower the bucket. That was when Aubrey removed his clothing and beckoned her over to the edge of the sewage field, an area still heavily flooded with all the excess rain and the gray water pumped out by the sewer pump. She lowered the bucket, he stepped in, and then he signaled her to raise it and move forward. As soon as he was over where he thought the outflow pipe might be, he motioned for her to stop. Carefully, he worked his way out of the bucket and started sliding his way down the rope. Sabine was sitting there waiting for the next signal and thinking mischievously that her husband with all that body hair was closer to the apes than she had ever surmised. Maybe it was because she had never seen him hanging from a rope like this?

No doubt about it, the bumblebee was on a mission: a mission of sabotage, of guerilla warfare behind the lines. And Sabine's relationship with bumble bees, with any insect for that matter, had never been very cozy. She was terrified of anything that flew, crawled, slid, or buzzed. When the insect flew straight into the tractor cab through the open door, she immediately went into panic mode. The bee did a couple of circuits around the unyielding glass of the widows with Sabine swatting madly at it with her floppy hat. Assuredly, the manual on "Strategy and Tactics for the Modern Bumblebee" prescribes offense as being the best form of defense. In accordance with this accepted wisdom, the bee flew directly down her blouse, a move that instantly shifted her focus away from her dangling husband.

"Saaaaabine!"

To begin with, Sabine was oblivious. She had problems of her own to contend with for the bee was apparently highly mobile inside her blouse.

"Saaabiine! Sabine, what the hell are you doing?"

This time she heard the Sabine part all right, but she was still very busy on another front, so to speak. So while her one hand was actively undoing buttons to allow an exit for the bee, her other hand flew out to push the joystick controlling the up and down motion of the bucket. Aubrey had a premonition that something like this might be coming given the distraction of his partner, but that did not make him any readier for it. Not only did the loader drop him without ceremony into the gray slop, the bucket itself sought to make sure that he was properly immersed, even tamped in. Meanwhile Sabine, having released the bee and much of herself with it, was able to refocus fully on the job in hand, although her current lack of modesty bothered her because now both of them were somewhat on show. What if someone drove into the yard now; it just did not bear thinking about. She yanked back on the joystick. Up jerked the bucket with a sordidly discoloured Aubrey still clutching on to his rope for dear life. Momentum being the essence here, he had to let go as the bucket sped on upwards without him. He dropped a perfect belly flop, it has to be said, straight back into the slop. When he resurfaced for the second time, he was not very happy, especially as the outflow pipe that he had landed on quite by accident showed no sign of any blockage. So he still had his problem and he had got himself covered with, what should he call it, with "effluent", and all for naught. He looked up to see Sabine emerge from the tractor in an inexplicable state of undress. Being the male animal that he was, the baser instincts kicked in, the effluent was forgotten. Never one to pass up a conjugal invitation whatever the circumstances, he lumbered after his wife who suddenly found a fleetness of foot she never knew she had. She, for one, was not about to be embraced by any ghoul from the lagoon, any monster from the slough.

Actually, Sabine would not venture near her mate for over a week; he was "downright odiferous," she said. Damn, if somehow he could have unzipped his skin and thrown it into the washing machine, he would have done so with alacrity. The mud and water had seeped their ugly stench so deep into his pores, he did not even dare to go and have coffee with his policemen buddies at Tim Horton's, not when he had asked to borrow somebody's waders in the first place.

After the flood came droughts and hailstorms, deep freezes, and scorching ovens. They all made acquaintance with El Nino and La Nina and probably half of the rest of the family as well. But nothing could compare to the drought of 2002; even the old-timers had never seen the likes of it. For the first time in his life, Aubrey had to think, really think about their very survival. Unlike a flood, which is more or less instant, the drought was more deceiving, more conniving. Like a thief in the night, it crept up with a stealth that allowed so many to retain a false optimism. "It'll rain," they said, but it didn't. Making an ally of time, it snuck up in the back forty and the front sixty. Its initial friendly warmth gradually transformed itself into a malicious searing heat. The smaller plants curled themselves up like onion sets, trees and bushes literally panted for moisture. Promising hay and grain crops wilted away in a slow agony, and the hopes of the year faded with them in parched surrender to Mother Nature. Talk turned from the usual comfortable anticipation of winter to an urgent and desperate discussion about basic survival. Aubrey, never having been here before, was a bit slow off the mark. Only when he had finished baling his hay did he grasp the extent of his misfortune. Woefully short of hay to carry his beloved girls through winter, he began to cast around for bales that he could buy. There were none, at least none at a price that he could remotely afford. And he had to almost physically stop himself from being drawn into the bitterness and the recrimination that began to rip apart many rural communities as neighbours tried desperately to procure hay from neighbours.

"I'm bloody well entitled to ask whatever the market will bear," some said defensively. "Isn't that what we are all in business for anyway?"

"GOUGING! Farmers are happily into gouging each other," screamed the media, reveling in the sights and sounds of the agricultural world pitted against itself.

The stories began too: tall tales, short tales, tales of incredible generosity and sacrifice, of avarice and downright theft. Ah yes, there was Joe Muncey, down the road, who was told by his wealthy neighbour to quit whining and sell his cows if he could not afford to feed them. And dear old Stewart Wells who claimed he had to rake five lines of hay together before he could get enough of a swath to bale. There were farmers who had put up fifty bales on the one day, only to find them all gone the next when they came to pick them up and transport them home. The major impact of such talk was to fuel the general panic and to prompt the talkers in their columns and chat shows to lament the demise of good old rural togetherness.

But truly, what were Aubrey and Sabine to do?

"Dump all of your older cows," counseled Pete. "Keep only the best. Anything with the slightest thing wrong with her, get rid of. Get rid of your bull too, if you have to, and buy another one in the spring. He's only an extra mouth for you to feed."

What was he saying? Get rid of Nellie? Get rid of Snowflake, and Petunia, and maybe Lulu? Yes, that was precisely what he was saying, and it was highly unpalatable.

"You can't feed hundred dollar hay to five hundred dollar cows and come out on top, not if you budget the normal six bales per cow over winter." Mrs. Banker, too, was blasé with her economic logic.

"Be careful that you don't sell off the factory," advised the accountant, Mr. Brittle. "If you do that, what will you have to sell next year?"

They were all so maddeningly, dismissively wise, even to the point of smugness and flippancy. But you could not afford to be smug and flippant if your livelihood was in such a direct line of fire. But then again, what if next year produced its own drought, what then? What then indeed? The so-called experts would be scuttling back to their boltholes, hucking their useless advice to the winds as they ran.

For the first time ever, Aubrey decided to make himself a "hay budget". How much hay did he need for minimum survival, although he conceded that his idea of minimum survival might mean substantially more than the starvation diet others were already using. God, but how he hated the sheer brutality of numbers, hated the bald, flat-faced message that told him he needed at least two hundred more bales. Usually anywhere from thirty to thirty-five dollars in this neck of the woods, they were now up around the hundred to one hundred and twenty mark. He knew that craggy old Percy Bishop down the road would have some, had to have some, for he had just thrown up his hands and sold off his entire herd. But twenty grand? Twenty grand that Nellie and her cohorts would chew through unthinkingly to give him only a seven hundred dollar calf the next year if he was lucky? This was crazy! Aubrey bit the bullet and hurried on down to see Percy.

"Hundred bucks. Certified check or cash. Take it or leave it," Percy rattled off in his staccato style. "Either that or sell your cows. Sell 'em all like I did. I'm too dang tired. Sold 'em all, every last one of 'em."

"You can't come down, even a little bit?" said Aubrey getting his begging skills into gear. "Even for a neighbour?"

Percy would have none of it. "Neighbour. Neighbour. Everybody and his dog are telling me I'm their neighbour. Hell, I got bills to pay same as everybody else. Lots of 'em. So let's cut this neighbour crap. Hundred bucks takes 'em. First one in the yard with the cold hard cash. Better hurry, though, if you want 'em, my phone is ringing off the hook." Percy turned on his heel and stumped off back into his house.

Aubrey now faced the harshest financial moment in his life. Did he halve his little herd of sixty? Did he sell off Petunia and Snowflake and, God forbid, Nellie? Not that they would bring that much, it was not as if they were highly photogenic. Or did he sigh, grit his teeth, and reach into his savings as so many other farm families were doing, burrowing a tunnel under their equity and hoping that the roof would not collapse? He would head back home and talk it out with Sabine, dear Sabine, who thus far had seemed so blithely detached from it all.

When he got in the door, she was having a quiet cup of coffee. "Come and join me, honey," she said sprightly. "Rest those weary legs of yours."

"Honey, we have a problem, a big problem," he blurted out. He knew his voice was unsteady, and he knew he would not be able to hide it, not from her. "Yeah, babe, I'm afraid we have ourselves one big problem. We are going to have to get rid of some of our girls, maybe all of them." He looked away as he said it, dreading that she might instantly agree.

"Depends," she said. "Depends on how badly we want to keep all of this," she gestured at everything around them.

"Well," he said heavily," we need about two hundred bales to be sure of getting all our girls through winter; that's two hundred on top of what we already have. That's twenty thousand smackeroos if we were to buy locally, let's say from someone like Percy Bishop. That means a loan, if the bank will even give us one, or a mighty big hole in our savings." Why was she so … so unperturbed?

"So what do you think we should do?" she countered, betraying no hint of what she was thinking.

"Oh shoot, I dunno." His voice cracked with raw emotion. "We've worked so damn hard for everything we've got." He paused. "You know, honey, I love those old girls so much; they have become a part of me, a part of what I am." He paused again, hoping vainly that Sabine would interject, but still she hung back. "No. I need you to decide. I'm too biased, too caught up. I'm so choked about it all, I just can't think it through any more. I'll go along with anything you suggest, I promise." He stared blankly at his coffee, not daring to catch her eye.

"My decision has already been made," she said quietly. "My decision is made."

Aubrey looked up in astonishment. They had always been extremely close but this was a new first in their relationship.

"Yes, she said. "We stay put. We are who we are, and we need to stay that way. We don't need accountants and bankers and country sages to tell us who we are and what to do. We know what to do."

"We do?" said Aubrey uncertainly.

"Yes, we do. We stay and fight," she said. "For once in our lives, let us be the contrairians. Let all of the others sell their cows at fire sale prices. Let all the others join the panic. We hang on. Cows will be worth something again next year or the year after, you'll see."

Aubrey was still trying to digest what he had just heard, trying to get to grips with this new dimension that he had never seen in his wife. She seemed so serene, so sanguine. Had she really thought about the dollars and cents, or was she still in the poetry section?

"I talked to Jim and Helen this afternoon. They have agreed to sell us up to 150 bales at eighty dollars. Jim reckons that is a fair price in today's market, that the others are just being greedy."

"So you're still 50 bales short," said Aubrey.

"Yes. So I called some fellow who is advertising range pellets in the paper. We can supplement with pellets and a bit of grain, and that will carry us through. They're a lot cheaper than bales."

Aubrey was tongue-tied, utterly incredulous. This was Sabine after all, his own "Serene Sabine"; she who had spent most of her life somewhere between whimsy and fantasy, or so he had always thought. "I don't want you doing this just for me," he said eventually.

"Don't be so silly," she retorted. "It's for both of us, you and me. Besides, what on earth would we do if we were to sell this place? Although ... although we could start a flower shop or a lingerie boutique."

Aubrey remained in shock for two days, somewhat ashamed that his level of emotion had blocked his ability to think rationally. He felt guilty that he had worked himself up into such an emotional lather that it was his whimsical wife who had come to his rescue, and with so little fanfare.

"The government has to come through with some sort of program," she had said confidently. "They have to realize how deeply this is cutting into rural communities. Yes, we'll be okay, just as long as we have a half decent year next year."

Of course, all of this did not preclude Sabine's return to the poetry section. "I've got this idea for a mobile pellet dispenser that I want you to try building. It's kind of like a mobile wine glass on wheels." Aubrey was so full of gratitude to his mate that he decided he had to honour her idea as best he could, so together they constructed a plywood contraption on wheels, a sort of giant ... well, wine glass. It had a trap door in the bottom that you could activate by yanking on a rope from the seat of the tractor.

The concept was fine, even ingenious. The design was okay, once they had got the spring-loaded door to cooperate and not just jam open. The material used in the construction, plywood and wooden studs, should have been adequate, but neither Aubrey nor Sabine had been thinking enough like a cow. The cows, ably captained by Nellie, loved the pellets, and frantically came to life the moment Aubrey started the tractor. To them, the contraption was the equivalent of a mobile ice cream parlour that they could chase after with wild abandon. In the beginning, Aubrey could drop a good sized pile of pellets just as he got into the field, and all the cows would congregate there, butting and shoving each other so as to get their share. This would give him the additional time needed to drop more piles further in the field. But the cows soon wizened up to this ploy, and many decided that it was more fun to gallop after the machine. A game developed among some of them where the goal seemed to be to get the first taste from each pile before moving to the next one. Then the challenge came to be to see how much any one of them could lick from out of the contraption itself, this achieved by leaning over the top and putting extreme pressure on the plywood sides. All of this forced Aubrey to go faster and faster to keep one step ahead of them, which the girls found to be great sport. This worked fine until the day he blew a radiator hose on the tractor. The abrupt stop saw Nellie and Petunia come charging full bore straight into the "wine glass". Like any wine glass that has been directly assaulted, it disintegrated, this one into a pile of splintered wood and pellets. Not that either Nellie or Petunia cared that much; they now had total access to what remained of the contents. For the first time ever in a crisis of this magnitude, Aubrey did not give in to cussing and swearing. He sat down and laughed hysterically. Sabine, too.

They went on to survive another winter, made it through to another new year so full of promise. But Aubrey fretted mightily. For the life of him, he could see no place for "the little people" in the much-vaunted agribusiness scheme of things. He could see that the industrialization of agriculture was going to make them indentured slaves to the major corporations and the multinationals, to "the suits with no hearts", to the countless faceless shareholders of the money pie. He recognized this as a force that, like a tidal wave, would overwhelm them all. The challenge was, what were they to do about it? Little did they know that the question itself was about to become academic.

May 20, 2003, was a date set in infamy as far as any Canadian rancher was concerned.

It was early morning when the phone rang. Aubrey answered it to hear Dick Conley on the line. "Have you heard the news yet?" he said with no attempt at the usual "How's it going?" kind of greeting.

"What news?" asked Aubrey, never certain that he would get a straight answer from his friend.

"They've shut the border. Locked 'er down tight, old son. I'm sorry."

"What border? Who's locked 'er down? What the hell are you ranting on about now?" No sense of alarm yet, just a wary circling of the issue.

"They've found a mad cow in Alberta," Dick came back.

"So? I've got a mad cow right here on the farm. Her name is Nellie, and she's particularly mad with a guy by the name of Conley, Dick Conley."

"No, no. You don't understand. Mad Cow as in British style Mad Cow—as in Bovine Spongi-whats-it Disease. As in your whole beef industry is suddenly mired in deep excreta, my friend."

"Okay," said Aubrey dubiously, his mind still pondering whether to throw in another joke about Dick's love-hate affair with Nellie. "So what's the story?"

"The story, my lad, is that this year's calf crop is going to be worth next to nothing. The story is that the value of your cow herd has just dropped through the floor. And our friendly neighbours to the south are talking of keeping the border shut for seven years."

Only now did Aubrey's stomach knot. Only now did all the colour drain from his face, the face itself suddenly haggard as if in some final surrender.

"So where do we go from here?" The question was addressed more to himself than to Dick, who remained sympathetically silent. "Thank you Dick, thank you for letting us know," Aubrey managed finally.

"My advice to you is to switch on the radio, and hang in there, lad. Always remember, you've got a ton of meat-eating friends out there who will never give up on their steak, Mad Cow or no Mad Cow. Keep that chin up, my friend, love to the wife. Cheers for now," and he hung up.

Sabine's entry in her journal two years later said it all.

B.S.E IS SOMETHING ELSE!
We thought two droughts were bad,
But they were Mother Nature.
We thought the grasshoppers were bad,
They were Mother Nature too.
Then we stumbled into B.S.E.
And that was Man, all Man,
His science, his politics, his hysteria.
As farmers, we live with Mother Nature,
Work around her as best we can,
We understand her, love her ways,
But Man, vindictive, unpredictable Man
Is so utterly incomprehensible!

Even if they had wanted, Aubrey and Sabine could not have made it out of farming, not with their dignity intact. They were in siege mode, and they knew it. They were at the mercy of their fellow man in a way they had never been before: at the mercy of the movers and the shakers and policy makers, and the packages and programs they devised. It was hard to keep perspective when so many neighbours were giving in to depression, to penury, to hopelessness even. As a couple, they learned to hold each other up. Aubrey and Sabine, their marriage now far stronger than a mere social convention, were now a true fusion of two spirits. Stoic, they soldiered on. What else could they do? Like farmers the world over, they could only look forward to another season's promise. The stark reality though, and the essence of their siege mentality, was reflected in Sabine's poem inscribed in her journal as she looked down the road into 2005.

THE END OF THE LINE?

Like mites on a cow,
          They crouch upon our backs
Sucking up our life blood,
          And talking, always talking
As if, as if they knew
          All of the answers, and more
For us, our problems, our lives
          And sucking, positively guzzling,
At our vitality, our beleaguered souls.
          Lawyers, bankers, accountants,
All of them must have
          A piece of us, have to have
For their own survival
          Their claims enshrined in law,
Doctors, dentists, caregivers all,
          They take their due, entitled
Decreed by man not nature,
          Mining the frailties of our bodies
And even, even of our minds
          To keep them and theirs in comfort.
See how quickly they lose interest
          If we cannot pay, or dare to question.
And those smiling politicians,
          Primary producers of babble
And photo opportunities,
          They coat us with sugar
And their stale hot air
          To keep us supportive
Of their feeding frenzy
          Upon the bounty we provide them,
Smacking their lips obscenely,
          And all of the so many others,
The salesmen, the middlemen
          The packers, and those at the end
All pleading a case or a cause,

Their standard of living depends on it
As if, as if ours even matters.
Ah! But they're all right, Jack,
Because if we stop, or rather when,
Like a flea, they will jump, unhesitatingly,
To the next accommodating host.
They will have to,
They won't have left anything of us!

Author Biography

Colin and Felicity Manuel were both born and raised on farms in Kenya, East Africa. Married in 1974, they took a giant leap into the unknown and decided to immigrate to Canada. Colin joined the teaching profession and Felicity worked in a bank, but the couple's yearning for the rustic lifestyle led them to Caroline and Rocky Mountain House, Alberta. In 1983, they purchased their farm in the area and named it "Shambani", Swahili for "home farm", and as they say, the rest is history....

Be forewarned! The Hanlon adventures in agriculture are far from complete. This book is the first in a planned trilogy. The next book in the series is "Fancy Free in the Back Thirty!" and will be available in the near future!